CROSSING PATHS

SUSAN LEWALLEN

KONSTELLATION
PRESS

Published by Konstellation Press, San Diego

www.konstellationpress.com

ISBN: 978-0-9991989-6-4

Cover design: Scarlet Willette

Cover photographs, front and back: Paul Courtright

Editor: Lisa Wolff

Dedicated to the staff of the Kilimanjaro Centre for Community Ophthalmology who embody many of the best aspects of Tanzanian society.

CONTENTS

THE CORTEGE, 2006

The small procession moved slowly down the hard-packed mud road. A tightly bunched group of men and women supported a couple with two children as they followed the tiny coffin, carried respectfully by several men, although one could easily have hoisted it on his shoulders. The long rains were just ending, so the maize, haphazard in cramped plots, stood tall and green. Even the small patches of earth that had escaped planting were a riot of green and yellow grasses. Far across a large field, a tall, thin figure with a long stick stood out against the sky as a dozen cattle ambled past him.

On this morning, unlike most, the snow-covered peak of Kilimanjaro was visible above the clouds, stark white against the blue sky. But the beauty of the mountain was lost to the shuffling procession; it was just part of a landscape they saw every day.

Men and women in the procession were dressed neatly, their clothes old and threadbare but freshly washed and ironed, with patches carefully applied. Their singing ebbed and flowed in a melancholy harmony, the women's voices rising in counterpoint to the deep bass voices of the men before the sound died down. The couple and two children followed the minister in his black suit, but they did not join in the singing. The husband occasionally glanced anxiously at his wife's stony face. The tiny grave, less than a meter long, dug in the rich volcanic soil as the sun rose early that morning, steamed after the light morning rain. A few meters away, several white molded plastic chairs stood at the side of the hole. The desolate couple took chairs and the two children stood beside them, holding hands and watching silently.

The minister spoke for some time, frequently invoking God's will and human beings' general difficulty with accepting it, particularly when it twisted their lives in ways they didn't like. The mourners stood with their heads hanging low, all except for the woman in the chair, who trained her stony face on the minister. He finally stopped speaking. As the mourners threw the first handfuls of earth onto the wooden coffin, the woman gave way. She fell forward and sank to the ground as her ululation rose above the field.

From across an empty field, another couple slowly approached. They stood out because they were *wazungu* — white people. They reached the gathering and stopped, standing respectfully at the back of the crowd as earth was heaped on the grave. Then, without speaking, each added a handful of the rich earth and followed the mourning family and friends back across the field. At a crossroad they turned away from the group and went their separate way.

The bunched mourners headed back down the hard-packed road they'd come from earlier that morning. They were less organized than they'd been earlier and quiet conversations broke out in small groups. A sorrowful old man, trudging slowly along, shook his head and whispered to his companion, "I've heard some bad things about how this happened. I don't know what's going on in this country." The bereaved couple clung together and walked, bowed in pain but surrounded by supporters. The massive base of Kilimanjaro dominated the land, but its snow-capped peak was no longer visible through the clouds.

NEEMA, 1965

Neema Moyo loved the sultry Sunday afternoons at the family house in Bagamoyo, north of Dar-es-Salaam. The veranda was cool, thanks to ocean breezes and slowly revolving fans. If she looked out across the white sand and surf into the Zanzibar Channel, she could watch naked children shouting, jumping, and splashing. Farther out in the channel, men on dhows cast their nets into the blue ocean in fluid movements and hauled them in hand over hand.

When she tired of watching the children and fishermen, she squinted her eyes and spun around fast until the colorful shirts of the men on the veranda, the multicolored patterned cushions on the chairs, and the orange, white, and magenta bougainvillea surrounding the veranda all blended into one fantastic vibrant vision.

She liked the coming and going of visitors on the veranda and she could count on at least one of them to have a small sweetie for her. Aunts, uncles, and family friends lounged in wicker furniture and rehashed the stories around Independence and the rise of the new President, *Mwalimu* Julius Nyerere. She liked to watch her father, Godfrey, who was usually on the veranda with the guests. He was powerfully built and he towered over most of them. Neema's young heart overflowed to see the awe he inspired and to know that he was *her* father.

Only a few years before, she'd often performed in the garden off the veranda, hoping for his attention by progressing from somersaults to cartwheels. "Watch, *Baba*!" When Godfrey ignored her, she'd run up onto the veranda and try to wiggle into his lap. But this rarely got her what she wanted.

"Neema, I need to talk to these men," Godfrey would say, giving her a half-hearted pat and shrugging her off as he continued his conversation with the men around him. Then Neema would turn to her beautiful mother, Imani, who'd open her arms to Neema to soothe away her father's rebuffs.

Neema looked for other ways to get her father's attention.

She often stretched out on a chair on the veranda and just listened, until the sounds of the waves, the gulls, the fans, and the murmuring of the visitors lulled her to sleep. But on the afternoon of her mother's great anger, the ten-year-old girl was eavesdropping from behind the curtain hanging over a big window that opened from the living room onto the veranda. This was her favorite place to watch her parents while they talked with guests.

The voices on the veranda rose in excitement. The grown-ups were talking about the recent merger of Tanganyika with Zanzibar to form the new country of Tanzania. Neema stared as her mother's eyes grew large over the steamy cup of tea she cradled against her chest. Abruptly, Imani put the cup down on a table, sloshing tea as she did.

"Oh, really?" she challenged Fat Uncle.

"Well, sure. Nkundwe Ntabaye would make a good leader for the new Ministry of Education," said the tubby man.

Imani shot a glance at her husband as he cleared his throat before speaking.

"Ntabaye's been a loyal worker. We know him and we trust him," Godfrey said, looking pointedly away from his wife's annoyed face. The four other men on the veranda nodded their agreement.

"Or we could consider John Ochiengo," suggested someone. "He's young, but I like his strong spirit." Murmurs of assent filled the air. The men proposed three other candidates as Imani's face grew stony. Neema couldn't take her eyes off her mother. What was making her so angry? For a few minutes the only sound on the veranda was the slow breaking of waves as they rolled in from the Indian Ocean. Then Imani spoke.

"I've also been a loyal worker — trusted by the party," she said in a steady voice. "And I have experience in education. In fact, considerably more experience than any of the men you're suggesting."

No one said anything, but several men raised their eyebrows as she spoke, and Godfrey looked down. Fat Uncle cleared his throat and spoke in a low voice.

"*Bibi* Imani," he purred, "you know how much we value your work and sacrifices towards Independence." Heads nodded around the room. "We just don't think you should have to do more."

Imani was not actually a *bibi* — a grandmother — but Neema knew the title was used to show special respect for the work her mother had done towards Independence. Neema watched her mother's eyes narrow and her nostrils flare as the men's nods grew more vigorous. Imani drew her head back and squared her shoulders. "I see," she said, and Neema had to strain to hear this because her lips barely moved. Imani turned her head slowly, looking at each of the men in turn. She rose abruptly and her knees hit the low table that held her sloshed tea, jarring the cup and spilling more into the saucer. She walked into the house.

Neema let out her breath. She was disturbed — and a little afraid. What was going on? Only one thing was clear — the men, her father included, had agreed on something that angered her mother.

She kept watching the men as several shifted in their seats and one cleared his throat. Fat Uncle put his hand briefly on Godfrey's shoulder. The conversation started up again, more talk about appointments in the new government of Tanzania.

After her mother had stormed inside, Neema stood up and wandered towards the kitchen at the back of the house, thinking maybe she could get Juma to give her a biscuit. He and his wife, Dorothe, cooked and kept house at Bagamoyo and Neema could usually count on them for small treats, such as plain biscuits, as long as she asked nicely. The couple was together in the kitchen and they didn't disappoint her. She held the small, round brown wafer carefully so it wouldn't crumble, taking little nips out of it until the last bit dissolved on her tongue. Then she wandered back to her place by the window. She jumped, but made no sound as three geckos fell out of the curtain and darted away; she was used to the little creatures. She settled down again to watch the action on the veranda.

The guests had all gone and Imani came back outside. She took a seat across from Godfrey, who sat with a newspaper open on his lap.

"Godfrey, I want to talk about who'll be the Minister of Education."

Godfrey looked at her across the paper, giving it a shake to straighten it out. "Imani, you can't possibly have thought you'd be a minister in the new government."

Imani looked straight into his eyes as she responded. "Yes," she said. "I can." Her voice was firm and determined. "Not only have I proven my loyalty and willingness to work hard, but I'm the only one of us who has the necessary experience for the post. I know about education in this country. I know its problems. I have exactly what this position needs." Godfrey folded the paper but still said nothing. Imani continued, her voice sharpening. "Ntabaye has no experience at all in education. He just happens to be the cousin of one of your friends. You know what I've given to this cause. You know how hard I've worked — how hard we've both worked — to see this country free of the British without bloodshed."

Neema's eyes widened as her mother raised her voice and made angry hand gestures at her father. She'd never seen her parents argue before.

Imani switched into a lower voice to reason. "What does Ntabaye know about education? Has he developed curricula? Does he know who we need to work with to achieve the dream of free primary education?" Godfrey was still silent and Imani kept going. "You have the ear of *Mwalimu* Nyerere. Can't you say something to him?"

Neema's father shook his head slowly and firmly. "No, Imani. It doesn't work like that. *Mwalimu* Nyerere is the President. He's busy. He doesn't want to hear a man argue that his wife should be put into a post. To head a ministry we need someone the people can believe in, someone with real strength. Only a man, an older man, a real *mzee*, will be powerful enough."

Imani glared at her husband for a long time. "Godfrey, being a good minister isn't about power. It's about *leadership*." She clenched her fists in her lap and tears overflowed onto her cheeks. She stood abruptly and left the veranda without further words. Godfrey sat motionless for several minutes before he also got up and left the veranda. Neema sat behind the curtain, watching and shaken; she'd never before seen her tall, strong mother cry.

The image of her mother crying on the afternoon of the great anger lodged firmly in Neema's head. She didn't understand it, but she carried with her a vague sense that somehow her father had done something wrong. And that her mother couldn't have what she wanted because she wasn't a man.

A few months later, the appointments in the new cabinet were announced. Godfrey was appointed as the Minister of Labor. He would move from Bagamoyo to take up his post in Dar-es-Salaam, where he was assigned one of the houses provided by the government for ministers. As he packed up to move to Dar, the heaviness between her parents weighed on Neema's shoulders.

Imani was offered a post in the Ministry of Education, based in Bagamoyo — at the regional and not the national level. She would stay in the family home with Neema. A week after the appointments were announced, they both watched from the veranda as an official ministry vehicle picked up her father and took him away.

Even among educated people like her parents, it was uncommon to have only one child. Neema was fascinated by the babies of the neighbors and the servants. "Mama, why can't I have a little brother or sister?" she'd begged a number of times. But her mother always turned away silently at this question and Neema eventually sensed that she should quit asking. Having lots of children was not just a sign of power for men, but for women too. In Swahili, the polite title for all females over a certain age was "mama."

When Neema was a very young child, Imani often took her to her own childhood village of Ndungu, nearly two days away from Bagamoyo. There, her grandmother gave her treats and caresses, and the rough-and-tumble play with her cousins was fun. She felt like part of a real family in the village.

The throng of children provided examples for all ages in taking care of those younger and getting along with those older. Infants slept peacefully against their mothers' backs, tied on securely by the women's brightly colored *kangas*. Babies who were old enough sat or crawled around on the ground, crusts around their noses, conveniently naked from the waist down, watched over mostly by older siblings, with a mother or aunt or grandmother nearby. Toddlers wobbled through the dust, sitting down hard every now and again and laughing when an older child pulled them up. Past the toddling stage, both boys and girls, old enough to be more or less fully clothed, ran screaming and chasing after each other. "Yeeiii!" sounded the continual shrieks and laughter of children. Woven into this were the occasional shouts of a woman to an errant child. "Popo! You come back here!" or "Taba, stop that right *now*!" And Popo and Taba obeyed, since children knew there were consequences if they didn't.

Slightly older children, those of five or six years, segregated themselves by sex, and the little girls watched the babies and toddlers. The boys spent their time building small toy push cars from scraps of wire and tin and kicking balls made of bundled rags, ropes, and old bits of tire. Older girls took on more household and childcare duties with each year they gained, while the boys continued to run and play until adolescence, yelling and laughing as they pushed and shoved each other through the village.

This rural scene gave Neema a taste of what privilege meant. Not only was she, the oldest of the children, free to play all day, but she was the best dressed. "I'll be the mama," she insisted when she played with the village children, "and you'll be my children who love me and obey." The ragged, dirty youngsters mostly gazed at her in awe and followed her orders.

One day, when she was six years old, a boy had balked. Neema was, after all, only another child. She pushed the boy hard, partly just to see what would happen but also because his refusal outraged her. He fell onto a patch of rocks, cutting his knee. She rushed to see what she'd done, but her shame, seeing the wound, was less than her fear of being caught and punished.

"Shhh," she begged, wrapping him in her arms and trying to soothe him as he started to wail. "It was just an accident. You be the *baba* now and I'll do what *you* say." To her surprise, he stopped crying, took one long, shuddering breath, then assumed the *baba*'s role. She played on for a while until she got bored by her inferior position and found a reason to leave. When she thought about the incident a few months later, she realized that it hadn't been difficult to get away with mistreating the boy — she'd been able to make him do what she wanted.

3

NEEMA, 1965–1975

Neema spent most of her time in the town of Bagamoyo and she accepted her comfortable life there as normal. The family driver collected her each morning, in a freshly washed and pressed uniform, and deposited her outside the private school she attended a few miles from home. Before Neema started school, Imani had argued strongly with her husband that any children they had should go to the government schools they hoped to start. He'd never really supported the idea, though, so Neema was enrolled with other advantaged children in one of the private primary schools that had always existed for those who could pay for them. When the time came for secondary school she was enrolled in an academy in Dar and a servant drove her the hour each way daily.

Neema worked diligently at school most of the time. She thought she was smart and the prizes and awards she won at the end of term reinforced her belief. There were potential distractions for a girl with her family's financial resources, but she didn't have a lot of friends. A sense of the importance of her family — her parents' contribution to Independence and her father's position as Minister of Labor — was always present in her mind. Coming from a prominent family opened doors to parties given by her schoolmates, but once there she often ended up on the sidelines, observing their fun. Aloofness provided a convenient shield and saved her from having to figure out what to say.

"Oh, come on," cajoled Foshi, a classmate. "You study too much. Do it later. Let's get my driver to take us to look at jewelry at one of the new shops." When Neema hesitated, Foshi encouraged her. "You're lucky to be so tall. The yellow earrings I saw last week would show off your neck — especially if you had your hair up." She looked sideways at Neema and added, "You can wear them to my party next month. My uncle owns the shop and he'll give you a good price." So Neema went with her and she bought the yellow earrings, but she was tense the whole afternoon with the effort of trying to figure out what to say to Foshi. And then she didn't even receive an invitation to the celebration.

"What happened to that party you bought the earrings for?" asked her mother several weeks later.

"Oh, *that*. I decided I didn't want to go," Neema muttered, turning away from her mother and leaving the room before she could ask another question.

Six months after the shopping incident, Neema *was* invited to a party, along with her entire class. It was Helen's fourteenth birthday and everyone would celebrate it at one of the big hotel pools in Dar. Neema was determined to wear a two-piece swimsuit that made her look at least eighteen years old.

"I don't know, Neema," said Imani. "It's such a mixed group. You've got Muslim, Sikh, and Hindu children in there. Their mothers aren't going to let *them* wear two-piece swimsuits."

"Mama, it's never been a problem before," pleaded

Neema, who never thought about the fact that she went to school every day with children from varied cultures and religions. "And we're not children."

"I know, Neema," said Imani. "That's the problem." She sighed. "But I guess it's okay. Let's be sure you have a decent dress to cover the suit when you're not in the pool."

The party was every bit as impressive as promised. Colorful banners and streamers rippled in the breeze. Water from the fountain in the middle of the pool sparkled in the sun, and the boys emptied the bowls of snacks and tables of soft drinks as quickly as they were refilled. A small band played popular music.

"Neema, I love your dress!" said someone to Neema as she stood near the pool observing her classmates and wondering if anyone would talk to her. Several other girls gathered to admire it and Neema warmed to the feeling of belonging to a group.

Later she went for a swim. "Wow!" she heard a boy exclaim as she launched herself in a smooth dive from the board at the deep end of the pool. Many of the kids weren't even getting wet. Most of the girls were just dangling their feet at the edge, talking to each other or to those boys who weren't yelling and chasing each other around. In the cool blue pool, Neema wondered if they were afraid of the water.

Neema loved to swim. At the party, for the first time, she felt grateful to her mother for the hours she'd spent in the ocean, where Imani methodically showed her first how to float, then to use her arms to crawl and, finally, to kick, until she learned to cut through the waves like a fish.

After a few lazy laps in the pool, she pulled herself up onto the concrete edge and toweled off. She pulled on her dress so she could enter the hotel to use the ladies' room.

"Wait, Neema. We're coming too!" shouted two girls who'd been watching her from the side of the pool.

They entered the restaurant together and stopped, all

temporarily blinded after the bright sun. But once Neema's eyes adjusted to the light, she recoiled in shock. At a table, only a few meters away from her, sat her father — and he wasn't alone. He was leaning in to talk to an attractive woman whose hand he was holding across the table. The woman was smiling and looking down. "Neema, isn't that your fa . . .?" one of the girls started to ask, just as Godfrey lifted the woman's hand to kiss her fingers. Neema's stomach lurched as the betrayal knifed through her. She abandoned the girls and barely made it to the ladies' room before she was sick.

At thirteen, Neema had started menstruating. She'd been looking forward to this sign of womanhood, but within two years she'd come to dread the monthly bout.

"Mama, the hot water bottles don't help. I need more of those tablets."

"It's not getting any better, is it, Neema?" Imani asked, stroking her daughter's head. "I'm going to make an appointment with Uncle Doctor."

Uncle Doctor was a family friend. He worked for the government most of the day, as all doctors in Tanzania did. But in the late afternoon and evening, in spite of a ban at that time on "for profit" medical practices in Tanzania, he, like many of his colleagues, ran a private clinic in his home. The office was only one small room with a curtain separating the desk from the examination table, but it was clean and neat. He'd imported the minimal shiny stainless-steel equipment from overseas. He booked appointments himself and there was no secretary or nurse, only a girl who cleaned and made tea on request.

"Well, *Bibi* Imani," he said, standing up from the desk to greet her mother as they entered. "How are you? Good to see you. I thought I glimpsed you and your daughter last Sunday at the church, but you got away before I could greet you." He took his seat and leaned back, picked up his cigarette and inhaled, then set it in a small ashtray and blew the smoke out slowly. "What's the problem?" he asked, still addressing Imani. Neema glanced over at her mother, who nodded for her to go ahead.

"Well, uhh, Uncle Doctor, uhm," Neema began, her face heating with embarrassment to be discussing this woman's matter with a man, especially one she'd known since she was a little girl. Her hesitation gave the doctor the space he needed to speak.

"Why don't we let your mother tell me?" he interrupted.

Imani shrugged at her daughter, then spoke. "Well, Neema has terrible pain every month when she bleeds. We've tried hot water bottles and aspirin, but they don't help."

"Where is the pain, exactly?"

"Neema, can you show him?"

Neema glowered at the doctor. "It's not just here," she said, gesturing towards her groin. "I have pain all across here," she said, running her hand across the front of her dress. She moved her hand to her lower back. "When I have my monthly time it goes clear into my back. And it lasts for days after the bleeding stops."

"Oh, well," he said dismissively. "Pain with your monthlies is to be expected."

"Well, it does seem to be especially severe," said Imani. "I've suffered this way for years, but Neema seems worse."

"Oh?" he said, raising his eyebrows and then turning to face Neema. "Well now, you don't want to overdo it during your monthly time. That might be the reason for your pain." He paused and seemed to be considering something, so he couldn't have seen the look of annoyance that crossed Imani's face. He drew in again on his cigarette, exhaled, and then stood up. "Lie down on the table so I can examine you."

Neema hesitated a moment. "Just like this?" she asked, looking down at her clothes, surprised but relieved that he didn't seem to expect her to undress.

"Yes," he said briskly. He watched as she stepped up on the stool and climbed onto the examining table. She lay on her back and he began to push on her abdomen with one hand, through her skirt, blouse, and jumper. He placed his stethoscope on her abdomen, again through the layers of her clothes. "Mmm." He stopped for a moment and went back to feel once more in one particular area. "Mmm," he intoned again after a few moments. "You can get up now."

Neema, thankful for the brevity of the examination, raised herself from the table and took a seat again next to her mother. The doctor took his place behind the big desk, where his cigarette still smoldered.

He looked at her solemnly over his glasses. "Many women have pain like yours," he said. "You see, it's God's way of preparing you for the pain of childbirth. Giving birth to children is what women were put on earth for. You need to grow up and accept it. It's time to face your womanhood now." He scribbled something on a small pad, ripped the sheet off, and handed it to Imani. "Here's something that may help," he said, standing up and ushering the women out the door. "Hope to see you next Sunday at the church."

Outside, Neema looked at her mother with a frown.

"I guess that wasn't much help, was it?"

"No," Neema said, choking back tears. "No it wasn't. I don't like him and I don't want to see him again."

～

Godfrey and Imani had grown farther apart over the years since he'd been appointed a minister and he no longer lived at home. He came out to Bagamoyo only once every few months. Neema wished he'd visit more often. One afternoon, she made a suggestion. "Mama, maybe I could move to Dar and live with *Baba*."

Imani looked up from the flowers she was arranging in a large vase. "Why would you want to do that?" she asked, tilting her head to one side to view the arrangement.

"I spend nearly two hours in the car getting back and forth to school each day. It's boring. *Baba*'s house in Dar is near my school and if I lived there, I'd have a lot more time. Maybe I could even do more things with friends," she added. That might help convince her mother.

"Well, I guess it might make sense," said Imani. "I'm glad you're getting interested in more social activities. Why don't we ask him when he's here next time."

Two months passed before Godfrey made his next visit to Bagamoyo. Neema was waiting on the veranda when his driver brought him up the driveway, eager to show him her latest marks from school.

"*Baba!*" she cried, hurrying to meet him with open arms. She got a perfunctory hug before he turned to greet Imani.

"Hello, Godfrey," Imani welcomed him coolly. "I hope you had a good trip." She turned to smile at Neema. "I think our daughter has something to show you."

"Well, let me see it later," he said, massaging his neck. "It's been a long day and the road out to Bagamoyo needs work. The potholes double in size each time I come out here. I need a shower and a drink." He disappeared into the house, leaving Neema and Imani standing in the driveway.

He was sitting on the veranda, showered, reading a newspaper and sipping a drink when Neema approached again later. Plopping into a chair across from him, she thrust out a school report. "I wanted you to see my recent marks," she said. "I came top of the class last term."

"Hmm," murmured Godfrey from behind the paper. He twitched it out of the way long enough to glance over the top and smile at her. "That's very good, Neema," he said, without looking at her report. He shook the paper to straighten the sheets before he disappeared behind them again and resumed reading.

"*Baba*, I'd like to talk to you about something," Neema tried again, putting the report of her marks to the side as Imani came out to join them. "*Baba*, I've been thinking that it would be very nice if I could move to your house in Dar. You know yourself what a long drive it is in from Bagamoyo — and how bad the road is," she added, pleased with herself for thinking to remind him of that. "But your house is only a short walk from my school." Godfrey made no response. "I'd have a lot more time to study if I lived with you. I spend so much time each day now in the car."

Godfrey shifted in the wicker armchair, let out a short, sharp exhalation, and shook the newspaper but still stayed behind it and said nothing. Neema forged ahead. "I could come to your house each Monday after school. I'd stay the week, then return to Bagamoyo on Friday and have the week-ends here. There's room at your house and it wouldn't be any trouble at all for you. Please, *Baba*?"

Godfrey's exhalation this time was deep and loud. He put down the paper and looked from Neema to Imani. "Was this your idea?" he asked Imani, scowling over his reading glasses.

"No, Godfrey. Neema asked me about this a few weeks ago. I think she has a good point."

"Well I don't think it's a good idea. I really can't have a young girl living there with me." He frowned and shook his head. "I wouldn't have any time to spend with her anyway because I have meetings almost every night." Godfrey folded the paper and rolled it up in his right hand, then used it to strike the open palm of his left. "No, Neema. This isn't a good idea. You need to stay here at Bagamoyo while you finish secondary school. When the time comes for you to start university, of course you'll have to move to Dar and you can live in the house then. But I see no need for you to come any sooner."

Neema rose and walked with slumped shoulders into the house, wondering if her father still kept company with the woman he'd been with at the hotel. She paused behind the curtain near her old hiding place, stooping so she wouldn't be seen as she listened to her parents.

"You really don't have to send her into my house to keep an eye on me."

"Godfrey, this was Neema's idea. I'd think you might be pleased to have an opportunity to spend more time with your daughter."

But Godfrey was already getting up to leave the veranda.

≈

"Neema, we need to go to Dar to shop for fabric for your graduation dress," Imani reminded her daughter over breakfast several months before she finished secondary school. "Would you like to ask one of your friends to go with us?"

"No, Mama. I wouldn't. And do we really have to go this weekend? Can't we wait until next week?"

Imani frowned. "Neema, I'm surprised at your lack of enthusiasm. Graduation from secondary school is a milestone most people celebrate. And aren't you even a little bit excited about the opportunity to go on to university?"

"Hmm. I guess I always knew I'd go to university," said Neema flatly.

"Well then, have you thought about what you'd like to study once you go?"

"I really don't know." She gave an impatient jerky motion with one hand, then sighed. "I haven't found anything that really interests me. But I *would* like to end up somewhere where I'd be in charge. I mean, that's what I've always imagined."

Imani's eyes widened at this naked admission of ambition. "Neema, authority and responsibility have to be earned. I hope you'll keep that in mind as you consider your future career."

～

The following week they went to look for fabric. As they wandered up and down the aisles at a large shop run by one of the many Indian merchants in Dar, Imani brought up the subject of Neema's future again.

"Have you thought of doing medicine?" she asked, walking slowly between aisles of textiles, letting her hand pass lightly over each bolt to feel the textures. "We still don't have enough doctors in Tanzania and almost no women. But I believe that will change."

"Oh, Mama. I don't know. I'm not sure I want to be a doctor," said Neema, following behind her in the aisle.

"But, just imagine if you could have gone to a woman physician instead of Uncle Doctor! Don't you think a woman would have treated you better?" Imani pulled a bolt off the shelf. "Look at this one. Isn't the blue background pretty?"

"Ugh," said Neema, close behind her. "It looks like something the house girl would wear."

"Mmm. Well it would depend on how it was made up. Perhaps as a skirt?" Imani put it back on the shelf and returned to the subject of medicine. "As a doctor you'd have a real chance to do good for lots of people in our country. Our friend Dr. Shao went to Russia for medical training and he says there are as many women as men in medicine there."

"Sure. But he also said that doctors there don't get much respect."

"True. But it's different here," said Imani, taking another bolt down and starting to unwind it. "Oh, this one drapes so nicely!"

Neema stepped over and felt the fabric. "Okay. Let's take it. If the tailor can do it right, it'll look good."

The shopkeeper cut and wrapped their fabric, and mother and daughter stepped out onto the street to hail their driver. Imani still wasn't finished with her efforts to interest Neema in medicine. "I know you're not interested in a career in education, Neema, and I won't push you in that direction. But do think about medicine. We need to do so much to develop our health systems in this country."

"Of course I want to do something that helps the country. But I also want something that gives me an important position at the national level. I don't want to be passed over and end up at some regional-level post." They were climbing into the car and Neema barely noticed the flicker of pain that crossed Imani's face.

"Actually, Neema," said Imani once they were settled in the car and headed home, "I've been pleasantly surprised at the satisfaction I've felt working these past years at the regional office in the Ministry of Education. I've been able to help a lot of promising young people to understand the problems we face. I think we've made some real improvements in our region." She smiled. "And it's been very satisfying to see these younger people move up. Many have become good friends — you've met them at the house."

Annoyance flickered in Neema. Indeed, she'd met them on the veranda, where it sometimes seemed like they got more attention than she did. As for a career in medicine, though, she did turn over the idea in her head as they wove through the traffic to get back to Bagamoyo. She was not especially enthusiastic about some of the realities of medicine in her country. She'd seen patients, many of them not very clean, lined up for public hospital clinic visits. All hospitals in Tanzania were public and she could just imagine how they must smell. Still, her mother was right. She could probably do a lot of good for the country as a doctor.

But she didn't say any of these things to her mother, who smiled at her as they got out of the car back at Bagamoyo. "Think about it, Neema. There'd be many ways you could do good with a medical degree."

Weeks later, when Godfrey visited again, Imani broached the subject of Neema's future career as they ate dinner together. He wasn't enthusiastic about medical school. "Why not do nursing? It'd be a lot easier and it's a nice career for a woman. If you're any good, you could become a nurse tutor at the hospital." Hurt washed over Neema for a second before anger distorted her face. She glared at him, but her anger was wasted as he disappeared behind the paper.

4

JOY, 1976–1987

J oy Mollel was born on a cool day in the middle of the rainy season with help from a traditional birth attendant who served her parents' village. Joy's father was delighted at the news of the birth of his first child, but he didn't see the baby until the next day. When his wife recovered enough, she wrapped the baby in a clean scrap of blanket and placed her in his arms. He smiled all day.

Joy's family lived near Moshi town on the east side of Tanzania's majestic Mount Kilimanjaro. Once, Moshi was a refueling station for airlines flying from Cairo to Cape Town, but when that was no longer necessary, it sunk into small-town oblivion in the shadow of the great mountain. As more and more people left their villages on the steep slopes of the massive elevation, new villages, made up of squatters, sprang up haphazardly around Moshi. The hardscrabble groups of one-room huts sat on pieces of land just big enough to put up a shack, keep a few chickens, and grow a few beans and stalks of maize.

Joy's father was one of the transplants from the higher elevations. His family's land on the east side of Mount Kilimanjaro had been subdivided many times. There was no piece left for him, the youngest of the family, to farm the maize, tomatoes, or abundant bananas that grew on the slopes. He had to move away to find another way to make a living. He settled with a wife in one of the new villages.

The uneven walls of the house where Joy was born were mud brick. There was a hinged door with a hasp that could accommodate a padlock, but the door was tied with a piece of string since the family had no lock. In the scraggly thatched roof, lizards, rodents, and occasional snakes rustled, especially at dusk. The windows were covered by plastic sheets scavenged from various places, and these highly valued scraps helped keep the rain out. The family pulled them back during the day to let in light.

Joy had no memory of her mother, who died before she was two. Her father, her *baba*, loved Joy, his only child with his beloved first wife, and it was a source of sorrow to him that they had no other child. After her death, he wanted to keep Joy with him rather than send her to an aunt up on the slopes of the mountain as most fathers would have done. Joy stayed and became part of his new family when he remarried a woman from his home village a few months later — a man had to have a wife. This one came with a one-year-old daughter, so Joy suddenly had a new sister and a new mother.

Within eighteen months there was also a baby brother, Heri, and four-year-old Joy was kept busy watching, carrying, and washing her young siblings. At five she was in charge of gathering the eggs and trying to keep the raucous old rooster off the hens long enough to let their feathers grow. Her jobs also included carrying water from the village standpipe to the big old yellow bucket in the house. She was proud as she took her place in line with older girls and women early in the morning, filling her own small bucket. "Ooo, what a good girl!" her mother's friends chuckled, watching her balance the load carefully on her head to carry home. By the time Joy got there she could hear the *pop pop* of the day's *ugali*, bubbling in a pot on the fire. Later she'd smell the frying onions and garlic that would go into a sauce to flavor the thick maize staple.

Even before Joy started school, she dreamed of becoming a teacher. Every morning she heard the radio broadcast blaring from the neighbor's house. A deep, resounding male voice pushed parents to send their children to the new schools and encouraged young people to become teachers. She envisioned herself grown up, standing before a group of students and confidently explaining to them how to read and write and use numbers. She imagined the pride she and her parents and family would take in her work. But first, she'd have to complete six years of school, and this was not easy for a rural child, especially a girl.

Joy was lucky. Her new mother loved her like the babies she gave birth to, and Joy quickly accepted her as mama. She was also lucky that the occasional manual labor jobs her father found enabled him to scratch together money so when she turned seven, she could start Primary One. And he paid for this willingly. *"Elimu haitekeki,"* he said to Joy as he sent her to school the first day — education cannot be stolen.

Joy went off giddy with excitement, skipping down the dirt road under a green canopy formed by the acacia and jacaranda trees.

"Oh, Mama, I learned some letters!" or "Oh, Mama, I wrote my name!" she sang out on her return many days. She loved the special care her mother took to make sure that her uniform was mended and clean every Monday morning. She understood why many children's uniforms were washed out and pale from the fading of the sun's rays, but she was surprised that mothers would let their children go to school in uniforms that were dirty or torn.

As December came around and the jacaranda trees dropped their brilliant purple flowers, she kicked them off the road as she made her way to school. Once there, she tried to be careful as she sat in the schoolyard with the other two dozen children under the umbrella of the old mango tree. She practiced hard to copy the squiggles her teacher demonstrated in the sand. When the young teacher admonished her friend for her poor copying, Joy gave her friend's hand a surreptitious squeeze. "I'll help you later," she whispered. When the teacher looked at her own work and nodded a curt "*Nzuri sana*" — very good — Joy smiled with pride. She couldn't wait until she was older and would get to move into the schoolhouse, with its wooden tables and benches and a real blackboard at the front. She'd get to use a slate and chalk then.

Her favorite lessons were about the history of her young nation, which was just a decade or so older than she was. The stories of the wisdom and selflessness of the father of the country, Julius Nyerere, always referred to as *Mwalimu* Nyerere — teacher Nyerere — left her spellbound. Her teacher told the students that this man, from the small Zanaki tribe on Lake Victoria, had been a schoolteacher too. Through devoted service and integrity, he led Tanzania to independence without war. Joy's father, who remembered very well the day in 1964 when *Mwalimu* Nyerere became the first President of Tanzania, loved to repeat the stories of Nyerere's accomplishments.

"It's my duty to send you to school," intoned her *baba*, as Joy sat on the dirt floor of the one room that made up their home while Mama cooked the *ugali* over a wood fire. "It's my responsibility. And *Mwalimu* Nyerere says the country has the same responsibility to provide schools and teachers."

Joy's schooling placed a burden on her mama, who had to spend more time taking care of the younger children and fetching water. During the dry season, when the standpipe was dry, this meant a trip to the stream, a kilometer away. But Joy's father was determined that she would learn to read and write, and her mother didn't complain about taking on Joy's household tasks while the girl was at school. Joy made it a habit to hurry home right after school ended and to work hard to help. She got up early every morning to pitch in before she left the house. Her younger sister, who had no interest in school, walked with her each day to fetch water, balancing her own little bucket, and she eagerly took over the collection of the eggs.

But at age eleven, Joy had a painful surprise. The maize planting season had come and the clouds building up over Kilimanjaro were heavy with rain. Her father, usually away doing manual labor in one of the flower plantations run by the Greek families, was working in the hot mid-morning sun, repairing the family's precious hoe. It was time to prepare the tiny plot for planting. He called her over.

"*Pole sana*, Joy, I'm very sorry." He set down the handle he was whittling and wiped sweat from his brow. "There just isn't enough money to send both you and your brother to school this year." He picked up the handle and examined the end of it as he continued. "This year your brother will go. You'll have to stay home." He looked so sorrowful that Joy suppressed her urge to beg him to change his mind. It was a hard fact — there was only enough money for one child to attend school. Even a father as loving as *Baba* was not going to deny his eldest son the opportunity of education in order to send a daughter.

Since Independence, there were no fees to attend primary school in Tanzania, but parents still had to have money for uniforms and supplies. And additional expenses were creeping in. Some school guards intimidated parents by suggesting they should top up the poor wages paid by the government. Late one evening, when the pounding rain less-ened for a while, Joy heard her parents talking angrily about a family in their village with a boy in secondary school. It seemed the parents had been forced to pay a teacher in order to get the passing grade that the child had earned by his hard work. She thought about this as she walked back home with a large can of water balanced on her head. Had she misunderstood? How could a teacher, a *mwalimu*, do something like that?

Joy cried in private for many days after she got the bad news that she had to quit school, and her tears made her eyes red and swollen. Her mother watched her silently but didn't talk about it. She may have been sorry for Joy, but the extra work Joy could offer at home if she quit school would help. Joy contributed far more than her brother.

Down at the stream, filling her water bucket, Joy tried to commiserate with an older friend, Blessings. She'd had to leave primary school several years before, but she had a different opinion about it. "Oh Joy, it's not all bad. Your family needs your help. And besides," she said with a meaningful glance at her younger friend, "you know it's impossible to go all month long anyway."

Joy knew what Blessings was talking about. She'd soon start having menstrual periods, and then school would be a problem for a week every month. Thinking of it caused her shame. There were only two makeshift latrines at school. Privacy was minimal, which seemed no problem for the boys but caused trouble for the girls. Joy figured that they had fewer latrines for girls because most of the teachers were men. There was no place for girls to exchange the rags they used to absorb the monthly blood, no place to keep the rags to wash later, and no water tap at the school to wash their hands. Blessings had actually bled through onto her uniform one day and been taunted by the boys, then humiliated by the head teacher for it. She didn't return to school at all after that. Most girls who were still in school just skipped the days they were bleeding. Joy knew all this, but still she argued with Blessings.

"I could have figured out a way around that problem," she insisted in a trembling voice. "Don't you see that schooling is the only way to become a person who's worth something? To become respectable? I don't want to end up like *Baba* and Mama." Blessing's eyes widened at Joy's outburst.

"Your parents are good people, Joy. Show them more respect if you want to be respectable yourself," she said as she lifted her water can to her head and turned away. Joy sat heavily beside the stream and cried again.

Only Joy and her father knew what she had witnessed when she was ten. He'd needed a birth certificate. One of his older brothers died and there was a chance that he might be able to become the official owner of some land in his ancestral village — but he'd need to be able to prove who he was in order to make the claim.

Few people of his generation had a birth certificate since registration of births and deaths had not been routine when he was born. Like most people, he was born at home with a traditional birth attendant from the village. But a few months after his birth, his mother made a trip to town with the necessary documents from the village chief so that she could register the births of all of her children. This did not mean she received official birth certificates, but it did leave open the possibility to get them in the future.

According to the story his mother told, she did this because the colonial government was introducing changes in land ownership. In a culture where everyone had been raised with the concept of communal land, this clever woman seemed to be able to imagine the perils and possibilities of private land ownership. The day might come when official proof of birth would be needed in order to claim land. She impressed upon her children that their documents were on file at the registry of births and deaths if they ever needed them.

On the day he went to Moshi to try to get the certificate, Joy begged him, "*Baba*, let me come with you." She didn't stop until he finally said yes. They left early after a quick breakfast of bananas and porridge and walked a few kilometers to get a *dalla dalla*, one of the minibuses that served the villages along the main road arching around the eastern side of Kilimanjaro. After a short ride, they got off in Moshi and walked the five minutes to the City Hall and Police Post. Even though it was still morning, there were already twenty people in the line they joined at the registry office. As they moved slowly forward, Joy watched an official in a smart white shirt and tie go about his business in a self-important fashion. She studied his face and wondered why he was so rushed and angry. When it was finally her *baba*'s turn at the counter, the official scowled at him.

"Good day, and what is your business?" the angry-looking man said, twiddling a pen impatiently. Joy shrunk at this curtness, unusual in a society where soft-spoken courtesy was the custom.

"*Tafadhali, naomba*," Joy's father said gravely, using the polite Swahili of Tanzanians when asking for something. "Please, sir, I need a certificate of my birth."

The official looked down his nose at him and then disappeared into a room behind the counter for several minutes. He came back with a form that he pushed across the counter. "Fill this out," he said. Then he used one finger to push a stub of a pencil after the form.

Joy's father stepped away from the counter with a frown. "Joy, can you help me?" he bent to whisper in her ear. They moved farther away from the counter and found two unoccupied wooden chairs they could use. Slowly and painstakingly,

Joy read the questions to him and filled in the replies as he provided them. The official glanced over at them once or twice. They finished and joined the line again. When it was their turn, the official took the form and looked at it. In a voice loud enough for all to hear, he asked Joy's father, "Is this for you or for the girl?"

Joy watched her *baba* swallow, then reply, "It's mine. That's my name on it."

"How do you know?" demanded the official. "I noticed that she filled it out," he said, gesturing towards Joy. "Can you read it? Is this letter an *a* or an *o*?"

"It's mine," answered Joy's father, his head unbowed. The official continued, pointing with his pen to a particular line on the form.

"This hasn't been completed," he barked. "See what it says?" Joy's father squinted at it. "Was your birth registered within ninety days after it happened or not?" Then, without waiting for a reply, he stated brusquely, "If you don't know, you'll have to fill out an application for late registration." He went to the back room again, where Joy and her father heard him through the thin wall, laughing with his colleagues. Joy burned with shame.

The official reappeared, this time with a very long form. "See if she can fill this one out now. And don't forget the late fee," he added as they turned to go. But Joy's father took her arm and guided her out the door. They returned home without filling out the form. He never mentioned the episode again. But Joy would always remember it. She had the feeling that her father had been diminished. She was also bewildered — why would a government official be so rude?

5

JOY, 1988–1990

Joy wished she'd had a notebook while she was going to school. Scratching letters into the ground or sharing a slate with someone else left her with nothing to study from once she had to quit. If she'd had a notebook of her own, she could have used it to remind herself of what she'd learned.

Scrubbing clothes, fetching water, stirring pots of *ugali,* sweeping the hard-packed dirt floor of the house, tending the small garden — these chores she could do with half her mind while the other half filled with thoughts of what she was missing at school. Maybe she'd get a chance to go back some-day, but probably not. There'd always be other children in the family, more each year, who'd need the few *shilingi* her father could earn. At least she could read, even if there were lots of words she still didn't know. She cringed thinking of it. She'd just have to work at sounding them out. Any father would send a son to school before a daughter, but that fact didn't lessen her longing to go. Her brother, Heri, had always looked up to her, which felt good, but since her father's deci-sion, she looked at Heri differently.

"Joy, will you help me with this word?" Heri asked, with the winsome smile that had always warmed her heart.

"Sure, Heri," she answered the first few times he asked, more out of habit than anything else. Then one afternoon, when she was especially tired from spending the entire morning in the hot sun harvesting beans and wishing she were in school, something snapped. "No," she growled. "No, I won't. I'm tired and I have too much else to do." Heri looked bewildered at this change in his beloved older sister and he turned away with a quivering lower lip. After she refused to help him several more times, he quit asking.

"Joy, why aren't you helping Heri anymore?" her mother asked as they worked together to spread wet clothes over bushes to dry.

"Oh Mama, I'm too tired when he asks," Joy whined. "And it's hard to get him to understand the letters."

Her mother studied her face for a minute or two. "Is that all, Joy? Are you sure there isn't more than that?"

"No," replied Joy, trying to hide the sullenness that welled up. She didn't want to hear a lecture, but before she could assure her mother that she'd help Heri the next time he asked, her mother had already started the sermon.

"I know you wanted to go to school like Heri does. And we're sorry we can't send you both." She drew herself up. "But if a choice must be made, then it's more important for a boy to get an education than for a girl. Everyone knows that. Boys grow up to have serious responsibilities outside the house. They must be prepared. There's no point in fighting some things. Resenting them only allows bitterness to grow in your heart."

Joy, with her head down, continued spreading her brother's shirt out in the sun. She'd heard all this before, but that didn't help her understand why it had to be this way. She was glad Heri didn't ask her again for help, because she didn't think she'd have given it to him if he'd asked.

Meanwhile, she took the opportunities she found to try to improve her reading. She worked out words on billboards and signs over shops and practiced with newspapers whenever she got the chance.

But mostly she spent the next years helping her mother at home with the endless needs of a growing family. She tried to find some time each day to teach her younger sister how to read since it didn't appear that the girl would get any chance at all for schooling.

Joy was hurrying to the queue for water one morning when she saw a knot of women gathered around an older girl balancing a bucket on her head with her back to Joy. Before Joy reached the group, to her horror, one of the women stepped out from the huddle and jostled the girl, who was forced to contort her body quickly to prevent her bucket from tumbling off her head. The women jeered and the poor girl fled, stabilizing the bucket as she went. Joy widened her eyes in disbelief. She'd never seen anything like this. Women helped each other in their tasks, and to intentionally knock something off someone's head was a cruel attack.

A week later, when Joy went down to the river with a small bundle to wash, she saw a girl alone on the bank. She looked more closely and recognized her. "Blessings!" she called. "Blessings!" The girl glanced in Joy's direction, stood up, gathered her bundle, and started to walk away quickly. With a shock, Joy realized it was Blessings who'd been taunted by the women collecting water the week before. Running, Joy caught up to her. "Blessings! What are you doing? What's wrong?" Joy asked, her brow furrowed with concern. She took a sharp breath. Blessings was crying.

"Oh, Joy. Not you too! Leave me alone. I can't stand it," wailed the girl.

"What do you mean? Blessings, what's wrong?" Joy noticed mud smudged on what was otherwise a pile of freshly washed and wrung-out clothes.

"Oh, they knocked my washing into the dirt!" cried Blessings, looking around. "You'd better be careful if they see you talking to me."

"Blessings, tell me what's wrong," begged Joy. "I'm your friend. Tell me."

But before Blessings could speak, Joy got a good look at her and understood the scorn the women had been heaping on her. The girl's thin frame made her pregnancy impossible to hide.

"Oh Blessings, I'm so sorry. I didn't know. Are you okay? What has your mother said?"

"She's going to send me away as soon as possible. At least she knows it isn't my fault. She believes me when I say I was attacked."

"But, Blessings," stammered Joy in shock. "Who did this to you?"

"A boy who wants me to marry him. He's counting on my father to force me to now."

"But Blessings, surely your father won't . . ."

"Joy, you are so naive. Your father loves you and he trusts you. If my father knows what happened . . ." She broke off. "I have to get out of the house before my father comes back next week from the mines in Zambia. He can't know about this."

Blessings turned and walked away as Joy returned to the shore and knelt to start slapping the dirty clothes on the rocks. What was worse, she wondered, to have to quit school or to fall pregnant by force? Poor Blessings — she'd suffered both.

6

JOY, 1991–1993

S crubbing stains from clothes one day down at the river, Joy listened to two women talking on the opposite bank.

"Eh, did you know about the new hotel in town? It's supposed to open next week. I heard they still need women for the laundry."

Joy pricked up her ears. She was fifteen and still living with her parents and siblings. Money was scarcer than ever. Maybe she could get a job outside her home. She tried to imagine asking someone for such a job. It would take some nerve. Still, her heart was sinking lower every day at the thought of years ahead spent washing and caring for siblings from dawn till dusk.

Joy's father nodded thoughtfully when she mentioned the idea of a job at the hotel. Then he offered a smile. "You can do it, Joy," he said, nodding more deliberately. "You're a smart girl and a hard worker and you can do it." This praise, rarely spoken so plainly, warmed Joy's heart. In the past year her brother, Heri, had disappointed the family on a couple of occasions with his poor marks from school. She wondered if her father ever regretted his decision to send his eldest son to school instead of her. She made up her mind to go to town to see about the job.

The next day Joy took out the best dress she had. She frowned to find a small stain on the shoulder. The *kanga* she usually tied on to protect the dress hadn't covered that part of it. Still, it was the best she had, so she put it on and wrapped a fresh *kanga* around it.

As she walked to town, she mulled over the strange sadness in her heart. Taking a job like this meant that she was putting her childhood dreams of education and becoming a teacher to rest for good. Her pace slowed. On the other hand, if she was lucky, she'd become the first woman in her family to be a wage-earner — and what were her options anyway? She forced herself to walk faster, overtaking a dozen or more women walking into town with trays of bananas on their heads.

Moshi town had grown since Joy first visited there with her father, but it still looked the same in many ways. The long line of people trying to get into the City Hall hadn't changed and the building still sat next to the bus station, where dilapidated vehicles belched and groaned as they pulled in and out. Patches of grass, scraggly bushes and occasional brilliant bougainvillea vines grew between cracked cement on the median that divided the big double road where traffic alternately raced or crawled by in either direction. Autos, trucks, and people with handcarts jostled for space on the potholed and unevenly patched tarmac. Vehicles were parked haphazardly along the sides of the road, often up onto the broken sidewalks. The old Indian-owned cement-block shops still needed paint, or needed it again. Any spaces between these squat buildings were filled with wooden shanties from which men offered various repair services or sold bits of hardware, household goods, fried meats and breads, or anything else they'd bought or scavenged that week. Sometimes goods spilled out onto the broken pavement and Joy had to step out into the road to get around them. She wanted to plug her ears against the shouts of handcart vendors that competed with the horns of vehicles, the groans of engines, and the explosions of unmuffled exhaust pipes. Occasionally this noise was overridden by the calls to prayer of the muezzin, amplified by electronic loudspeakers and often harsh with static as the speakers malfunctioned.

The hotel itself was just off the double road, surrounded by a high concrete wall with broken glass embedded along the top and a solid metal gate at the entrance. She stopped outside the gate and unwrapped her *kanga*, folding it and tucking it into her bag. She ran her hands quickly down her dress to smooth it, then, figuring there was nothing else to do to improve her appearance, she rapped on the gate.

"*Habari ya asubuhi?*"— how is your morning? — she greeted the young guard who answered her knock. He replied that all was well and after they finished the required exchange of greetings, she inquired about making an application for a job. He opened the gate wider, with a flourish that Joy would have found amusing if she hadn't been so nervous, and she entered the compound.

Attractive small white cottages with neatly thatched roofs dotted a green lawn at one end of the compound amid palm trees and flowering bushes. At the other end was an open-air restaurant with bright red tables and chairs. Joy could see the blue of a swimming pool beyond the tables. A low white building with a thatched roof sat at the end of a gravel path straight ahead. According to the guard, this was the site of the reception and administrative offices for the hotel.

"Go that way," he indicated, tipping his head back and pointing with his chin. Joy squared her shoulders and walked across the gravel drive to the building.

She entered an office where four girls perched on chairs,

all sitting very straight with hands folded in their laps. An attractive secretary, with fashionable extensions woven into her hair and dressed in a smart gray business suit, sat behind a desk. She looked up and, to Joy's relief, smiled and spoke as Joy entered.

"*Habari ya asubuhi*?" she said pleasantly, putting Joy at ease with the opportunity to go through the exchange of greetings once more. "May I help you?"

"Yes," said Joy with more confidence. "I'd like to apply for a job in the laundry."

"I see," said the secretary solemnly, handing her a piece of blank paper. "In that case, can you kindly write your name here? Then take a seat. Mr. Dhalla will be ready to talk to you soon."

Joy did as requested and settled on the one remaining chair. There was no talk among the girls waiting in the room. They all appeared to be around Joy's age. They studied the floor and avoided eye contact with each other. Joy glanced at them surreptitiously as she took her chair and noticed that they were wearing dresses similar to her own. There were no fancy hair extensions in this group; they had either smoothed their hair into buns or wore kerchiefs to cover their heads. How many positions could there be in the laundry?

As they waited, another girl entered the office to inquire about the job. She went through the same process with the secretary as Joy had done, but when it came time for her to write her name she hesitated. She scowled, then took the pencil. Her tongue protruded slightly through her teeth as she slowly printed her name. It took so long that several of the seated girls glanced over at her and one smirked. Joy was too embarrassed to watch.

The girls were called in to talk to Mr. Dhalla one by one, and they came out after varying lengths of time, some looking happy and some downcast. Joy's turn finally came and, trying to focus on her father's words of praise that morning, she passed through the door into Mr. Dhalla's inner office.

She was pleased when Mr. Dhalla knew her name; then she realized the secretary was showing him the papers they'd written their names on. He greeted her and asked her to sit before he got down to business.

"Joy. I see you wrote your name very neatly here. How much schooling have you had?"

A slight sweat broke out on her forehead. She hadn't expected there to be any special education requirements for this job. The memory of the day she'd gone with her father to the City Hall entered her head and her stomach turned over. But she could only tell the truth. "I . . . I only finished standard four," she stammered.

"Well, that's sufficient for this job," Mr. Dhalla said, and his smile was not unkind. "Many girls haven't gone that far. What is your previous work experience?"

"Well, sir, I've been doing laundry at home since I was a little girl. I'm the firstborn and we have five below me, so I've had to."

"Yes, I'm sure of that. But have you had a job outside your home before?"

"Uh, no, sir. I've only worked hard at home. My mama depends on me."

He asked her a few more questions, looked at her thoughtfully, and eventually spoke. "Well, Joy, you'll have to work hard here too, but we'll give you a try. Can you start right away?"

The laundry was hard work, but that wasn't anything new for Joy. She had to leave the house by six each morning to get to work by seven. She took one break at about eleven o'clock, taking advantage of the tea with sugar provided by the hotel.

She brought something from home to eat too when she had it. She knocked off work at three and walked home, where she started on the tasks always waiting there.

There were two things Joy liked about the job. The first was that there was always a radio playing within earshot of the laundry. It was tuned to the BBC's Swahili station, giving her a chance to hear what was going on in East Africa and beyond. It was interesting to hear programs comparing Tanzania and its East African neighbors. She'd grown up on legends of *ujamaa,* or familyhood, a social policy considered radical by some Western governments. Nyerere hoped the policy would unite the people of Tanzania, teaching them to put country ahead of tribe. He insisted that Swahili be the national language and the language of education, instead of using the dozens of tribal languages spoken by the people in the country. The result was a degree of unification not seen elsewhere in Africa. The socialist policies that accompanied this, the free school and medical care, and the emphasis on egalitarianism were something that Joy was taught to revere and take pride in — even if her own personal experience with school had shown that the policy didn't always work. One only had to look across the border at neighboring Kenya to see some of the bitter fruits of competition and tribalism. Joy had often heard Tanzanians disparage Kenya as a "dog-eat-dog" society. So, she was surprised one day to hear a Kenyan commentator on a BBC program agree that this might be so, but shoot back that Tanzania was a "dog-eat-nothing" society. She looked around to see if any of the other girls in the laundry were offended by this, but they weren't paying attention.

What she especially loved on the BBC, though, was the half-hour program twice a day on learning English. A few of the other girls working in the laundry were interested in this as well, so they kept down the chatter enough for Joy to hear it. It was fun, and she was delighted at how quickly she was catching on. Because there were a number of foreign tourists who visited the hotel, she had opportunities to try out her skills sometimes when she was walking across the hotel grounds. The management noticed and, pleased that she could speak some English, started asking her to deliver folded sheets and towels directly to rooms, giving her even more opportunity to improve.

The second thing Joy liked at the job, which she only noticed a year or so after she'd started, was a boy named Daniel. He didn't work for the laundry, but he was a general errand boy and laborer for the hotel. Joy noticed him occasionally on the grounds when she was making her own deliveries.

"Sure, he's a handsome one," teased one girl who noticed Joy's interest. Joy had to agree. The boy was lean and of medium height; she figured he was a little taller than her father. In the tank tops he wore for work the hard definition of his shoulder muscles was striking, especially when his beautiful, even-toned ebony skin gleamed under the sun on the hottest days. She thought his high forehead and prominent cheekbones gave him an educated look, softened by his warm brown eyes. She observed him loading and unloading boxes in large numbers from the back of a truck or flipping single cartons with ease onto the back of a bicycle he used.

One day she was carrying a load of freshly pressed sheets across the compound when she heard a ruckus. A mangy yellow dog had somehow sneaked into the compound and was slinking across the grass. Two guards were shouting, lobbing stones, and taunting the animal in an effort to get it out the gate. Suddenly, Daniel rode around the corner and took in the scene. He leaped from the bike, throwing it to the ground, and grabbed a branch from the lawn. Pushing in front of the guards, he brandished it at the dog.

"No need to kick him and throw stones!" he shouted angrily at the men, successfully herding the dog out the gate.

The guards snickered and laughed at him, but Daniel turned his back and went about his business. Joy paused and watched, then found herself smiling at this kindness toward the animal.

Gradually, from gossip in the laundry, Joy learned a bit more about Daniel. He'd worked for the hotel for nearly a year and everyone seemed to like him. He was considered reliable and hardworking. He came from Ndungu, a village a few days' travel away, and he was the first in his family to leave there. He'd moved to Moshi town with hopes of a better life.

Other girls in the laundry found him attractive too, and one of the more forward ones suggested to him that he should take tea with them when they took their break. If that girl hoped to catch his eye, though, she was disappointed, because he spent most of his time talking to Joy.

"Tell me about your family," he said. "You're lucky to have them so close. I worry about my father, who's not been well for a couple of years. I worry that I ought to be home helping my mother. But there's nothing in that village."

"Sure," Joy sympathized. "It's not so different for me. But at least we can help them with some cash — and they need that."

"You're a serious girl, Joy. I like that," he said one day when no one else was around as he finished his tea. Joy kept her face straight but smiled inside to hear this. Talking to a boy this way was new territory for her. She'd always assumed she'd grow up and marry and have children, but somehow in the long hours she'd put in to help with the family and then to get back and forth to the job, there hadn't been any time or opportunity for chatting with boys.

"So, Joy, do you go to church?" Daniel asked one day.

"Well, not often," admitted Joy. "Too busy. But sometimes my family goes to the Catholic mass." She paused, then added honestly, "I guess I think it's a little boring."

Daniel laughed. "Why don't you try the Evangelicals?" he suggested. "That's where I go. It's not that far from where you live. We could meet there next Sunday. And it's never boring," he added with a grin.

So began their relationship. Joy had to work in the laundry one Sunday a month, but that still left three on which she could join Daniel at church. He was right when he said it wasn't boring. The preacher expended a vast amount of energy shouting and gyrating, and the people responded with the same. It couldn't have been more different from the solemn, dignified Catholic mass. The congregation welcomed Joy warmly, and soon she and Daniel were viewed as an established couple.

One thing worried Joy a little. She observed Daniel several times struggling to read. At the church, the congregants often read aloud from their Bibles and Joy noticed that Daniel's lips weren't always making the right shapes for the words they were supposed to be reading. She didn't want to say anything, but in the end she didn't have to.

"I guess you can see I don't read very well," he confessed sadly one Sunday afternoon.

"Well, yes," she said gently, "I noticed that you were struggling."

He gave a deep sigh. "I had to quit school after only one and a half years. My family just didn't have enough money for expenses and I was needed to plant and hoe on the *shamba* to help feed the family. It's not that I *can't* read," he said hastily, looking up at Joy. "But it's hard for me."

"Ah, Daniel, I do understand," Joy said, reaching out to put her hand on his arm. "I also had to quit school early. And my father never learned to read at all."

"It's not going to happen to my children," Daniel said fiercely.

"Nor to mine."

∾

They'd been attending the services for several months when Daniel got bad news from his village. His father was gravely ill and his mother wanted him to come home. He didn't have to explain to Joy that he had no choice in the matter, even though he'd be gone for an indefinite, and possibly long, period. Family came first, and she knew he had to go.

It was six months before his father died and he settled matters in the village. Joy got occasional messages from him via travelers who'd passed through his village, thanks to the group of mutual friends they'd established at the church. And he managed to make it back to Moshi to visit twice, so they didn't forget each other or drift apart during his absence. Joy, newly awakened to the possibility of talking to young men, had started paying attention to a few boys in her neighborhood and at the church, but no one measured up to Daniel. His gentleness and genuine interest in her made her feel good. He was a man who could be trusted to do the right thing. She told her parents about him.

"What tribe is he from?" asked her mother. She was happy to find out he was a Chagga, like them. Her father's question was different.

"Does he treat you well, Joy? And does he realize you are a very smart girl?"

Joy smiled self-consciously. "Yes, *Baba*. Yes, I believe he does," she said, her smile broadening.

Daniel appeared unexpectedly one Sunday morning at the church, having settled matters in the village following his father's death. Joy was surprised and delighted. That afternoon they sat in the field alongside the river, talking and celebrating his return with a shared bottle of Fanta and a packet of sweet biscuits. Daniel spoke of how he'd miss his father, and Joy agreed that she'd miss her own if he were gone.

"What's the most important thing your father taught you, Joy?" he asked.

She thought for a while. "I think it is this: *Asiyeuliza, hanalo ajifunzalo*. One who does not ask a question learns nothing."

Daniel smiled. "I'd like to teach that to my children."

That was the afternoon they decided to marry.

7

NEEMA, 1976–1981

Her father's suggestion that she become a nurse stewed in Neema's mind and her determination grew to become a doctor. She'd show him what she was capable of. And her mother was right — working to improve the nation's health-care system was important. She smiled to think of the respect she'd get as a doctor. Teachers were valued too, it was true, but doctors were near the top of the status pyramid; respect was pretty much guaranteed.

She applied and was accepted into the College of Medicine in Dar-es-Salaam, where a five-year course plus an internship would result in the award of a degree that would give her the right to be called Dr. Neema Moyo. Surely this would impress her father.

Neema moved to Dar and into her father's house, which was conveniently located near the university — a collection of Soviet-style concrete buildings. She could walk to and from classes at the medical college, and it was a relief not to have to spend so much time being driven between home and school.

Neema had imagined that once she was living with her father she'd have opportunities to spend time with him, but it didn't work out that way.

"*Baba*, when will you be home tonight? Maybe we can have dinner together?" she asked after she'd been living there for a week.

Godfrey frowned at her and shook his head. "I don't know, Neema. I'd prefer that you don't count on me. I'm busy and can't say when I'll be home."

They rarely took their meals together. It took a few weeks before she realized that on many nights he didn't come home at all. Sometimes he had colleagues over, but Neema was never included in these evenings.

"I'm disappointed that I don't see him more," she confessed to Imani. "But at least I've got a lot more time now to study." That was a good thing, since medical school was challenging her far more than she'd expected.

She confidently opened the envelope with her marks at the end of the first term, and she had to look at them twice to get over her surprise. She'd done reasonably well in three courses but just scraped by in two others. In secondary school, she was used to being at the top of her class. But in medical school most people came from the top of a class somewhere, and it was much harder to stand out. Her first inclination on seeing that she'd barely passed, with scores of only 65 percent in two subjects, was to assume a mistake had been made. But, she reflected, biting at her nail, she *had* found the courses challenging. She couldn't bring herself to go to the professors to talk about the marks. Neither was she willing to discuss results with other students to see how they'd done. She'd just have to work harder.

Since medical school required so much study time, most students had little time for parties and socializing, which suited Neema well. She occasionally attended some social function, but she still found herself mostly standing on the sidelines. One afternoon in a stall in the ladies' room, she overheard a couple of her classmates talking about her.

"Yeah, that Neema Moyo, she's a cool one — or she thinks she is. Just because her father's a minister!"

"You mean a *cold* one, don't you? Brrrr." As the girls laughed, Neema's initial hurt turned into a fist-clenching anger. Who did they think they were? In ten years, she was going to be in a position where people wouldn't dare to say things like that about her! But then she sat back down and waited until they left to emerge from the stall.

～

Neema's social life improved when she developed her first real friendship. Katharine Badwel was a short, round girl with cinnamon skin, sparkling eyes, and a ready laugh. She came from Mwanza, on the shores of Lake Victoria, across the country from Dar-es-Salaam. Her father owned the large ferry service that chugged back and forth to Uganda and Kenya, providing a healthy income for the family. But, Katharine told Neema, she couldn't wait to get away from that insular existence to come to Dar.

"Oh, Neema, you have no *idea*," Katharine laughed. "You can't buy anything there. No nail polish, makeup, *nothing*!" She poked fun at her provincial upbringing first, so that no one else could. And it didn't hurt that her father made so much money. Everyone seemed to like Katharine and Neema was somewhat puzzled, although flattered, that Katharine chose her as a friend.

They sometimes went to expensive hair salons together, drinking tea and chatting the afternoon away while stylists wove extensions or intricate plaits into their hair. One afternoon, in this intimate atmosphere, Katharine confessed that neither of her parents had gone to university at all. Neema tried not to look surprised at this news.

"But then . . . well, how did your father get to be head of such a big business?"

Katharine shrugged. "Well, he had a small boat he got from my grandfather and he just worked all the time. Even my mother would be down on the shore, loading cargo."

Neema cringed on Katharine's behalf, imagining how embarrassing that must have been.

Katharine continued. "Eventually he managed to get a second boat and then a third." She compressed her lips, then she shrugged and smiled full on at Neema. "It must have been amazing to grow up as *Bibi* Imani's daughter. And your father's a *minister*!"

"Oh, sure," Neema said dismissively, although she was gratified that Katharine recognized her impressive background. But then she found herself wondering how much her parents' reputations figured into Katharine's desire to be her friend. The girl had a way of asking personal questions that made her seem genuinely interested in people, but sometimes Neema left their conversations feeling she'd revealed more information than she should have.

Still, in that first year of medical school, Katharine became Neema's closest friend. They often studied together as well as going together to the hair salon or shopping for clothes. Katharine also insisted on taking Neema out to parties. Without her, Neema would have had no social life at all.

One afternoon, in her third year of medical school, Neema hurried to get to a visiting lecturer she wanted to hear. The professor, Dr. Sanga, was the best-known gynecologic specialist in the country and the room was packed. Slipping in just before the lecture began, she spotted one of the only spaces left in the back row of the large auditorium. She took her seat and caught her breath. She felt dizzy looking at the podium, far below the rows of steeply arranged flat wooden seats hinged from wooden backs.

Dr. Sanga, a soft-spoken and dignified man, had a reputation for pushing students hard but being fair. He was one of the first doctors selected to go abroad for specialist training after Independence, and he kept abreast of new developments in his field. Neema wanted to see his demonstration of the recently available technique of ultrasound and how it could be used in the examination and diagnosis of certain gynecological conditions. Severe menstrual pain continued to plague her, and she wanted to know what was causing it.

She sat on the hard seat and listened to him describe the importance of a detailed workup for patients with menstrual pain. She thought with contempt of the cursory examination she'd received a few years back from Uncle Doctor. As the end of the lecture drew near, she determined to get this specialist to examine her.

Getting an appointment in his clinic wasn't difficult once Neema let the nurse know she was a medical student. On arrival at his clean but spartan office, she was ushered into an examination room and asked to remove her clothes and put on a light gown. Dr. Sanga entered and talked to her for several minutes, asking questions about her history and symptoms. Then he asked her to lie on the table and started a slow, methodical examination. His probing was gentle, but he went over every square inch of her abdomen. He called a nurse, who brought in a portable ultrasound, and he spent a long time pushing the instrument's probe various ways, apologizing when Neema involuntarily winced. He finished and gave Neema time to dress, and then he sat down to talk to her. She was surprised by his willingness to spend so much time with her, given his eminent status.

"Neema," he said kindly, "before we talk about your examination, may I ask how many children your mother has?"

"Well, I'm the only one," replied Neema.

"Mmm. I see," he said slowly, adding something to the

notes in her chart. He looked up at her and spoke carefully. "You've had symptoms for many years, but you said they've been getting worse over time, I believe?" She nodded.

"I think we need to consider the possibility of endometriosis. I found several things in the ultrasound that suggest this." He paused to let her take in this news.

Neema felt like she'd been punched. She barely suppressed a gasp as her open hand flew to her chest. Dr. Sanga watched her closely and didn't break eye contact. After a few seconds, he nodded and spoke slowly, giving her a chance to recover.

"I realize you know about this condition from your medical studies, but let me review it for you anyway. In endometriosis, uterine lining tissue somehow ends up in places in the abdomen where it shouldn't be. Sometimes it's a little and sometimes it's a lot; each case is unique. Every time you have a menstrual cycle the tissue responds to the hormones, thickening and then bleeding. This can cause a great deal of pain as well as scarring. Sometimes, though not always, it leads to decreased fertility."

Neema was grateful for the man's professional demeanor, which allowed her to maintain some dignity, but she was still stunned. She didn't want to hear what he was saying — didn't want it to be true. But at the same time, his words pulled her long, painful history together like the last piece of one of the wooden jigsaw puzzles she'd played with as a child. This made perfect sense. She'd *known* there was something wrong beyond the routine cramps and twinges many women felt each month. There was some relief in having an answer. But the news was also terrifying because she knew it might affect her fertility — her chances for having children.

She pulled herself together so she could continue listening to Dr. Sanga. Her voice trembled a little when she spoke. "What about treatment? Aren't there drugs that can help?"

"Yes," he said. "Of course. Birth control pills are the first thing to try." He stroked his chin thoughtfully. "The ultrasound indicates that your condition may be rather extensive. Before we talk about treatment, we need to do a biopsy to confirm the diagnosis."

"Of course," said Neema, trying to regain a sense of control and seeking to distance herself from her feelings by considering the technical details — after all, she was well on her way to becoming a doctor herself now. But that fact didn't help her deal with the curtain of fear that was descending. Hard as it was to accept, she was as vulnerable as anyone else to nature, including disease. This wasn't part of the life she'd imagined for herself. She took refuge in resentment at the unfairness of things and it helped to push the fear aside.

Neema left the office and went home after the examination. She couldn't shake off her anxiety. Several times she caught herself feeling a strange sense of unreality, and then she had to slowly relive the whole conversation with Dr. Sanga to convince herself she wasn't dreaming.

The next day, after a long study session in which she'd had trouble concentrating, she confided in Katharine, telling her about the examination and Dr. Sanga's suspicions. "Oh Neema, this is terrible. I'm so sorry. No wonder you couldn't concentrate on the pathology notes!" sympathized her friend. "What's the next step?"

"I'm scheduled for a biopsy next week," said Neema, struggling not to cry.

Katharine put her hand on Neema's arm. "I'll go with you."

A week later, with Katharine in the waiting room, Neema underwent the biopsy as planned. A week after that, Katharine insisted on going along when Neema went to hear the results.

Dr. Sanga greeted Neema kindly as she sat down in his office.

"Neema, I'm sorry. I'm sure you're not surprised to learn

that you do indeed have endometriosis, and I'm afraid it's extensive. This certainly explains your pain." Neema didn't think she could feel any worse than she already did, but as the diagnosis was confirmed, a last vestige of hope died.

Dr. Sanga was sympathetic. "Let's start birth control pills and see if they help," he suggested. "That is, assuming you're not trying to get pregnant right now?" Neema shook her head that she was not.

"It's possible that you'll have trouble conceiving a child when you're ready," he said. He paused to let her take this in, then added, "You're twenty-five now. It might be a good idea not to wait too long."

Katharine was in the waiting room as she came out. She was attentive, helping Neema into a taxi and staying with her until they arrived at her father's house. In the backseat, Neema shared Dr. Sanga's findings with Katharine, who offered occasional clucks of sympathy. Neema was glad her father was away for a few days so she didn't have to pretend not to be miserable. She felt like she needed to cry — to wail, in fact — but no tears came. Instead, she felt a deep anger and helplessness building at the injustice of her situation.

In truth, Neema hadn't given much thought to having children — but that was because she always assumed that she would have them. In the Swahili culture, the polite title for all females over a certain age was "mama." Women who couldn't have children were pitied, and there was plenty of sympathy as well for a man with a barren wife. Many people would not blame the man for looking elsewhere.

8

NEEMA, 1982–1984

L ike most medical school graduates, Neema hoped to be given an urban posting in Dar after she finished her studies. It didn't happen that way, but at least she was posted to a hospital less than an hour from Dar for her year of district service. She moved from Godfrey's house to live in hospital housing.

"Well, it could be worse," said Katharine, who *had* been posted to Dar. "They didn't send you to Mwanza! And we'll be able to get together when we have weekends off."

"I guess you're right," Neema agreed reluctantly. "And it'll be nice to be able to go home to Bagamoyo sometimes. I wish my father would come out there more often."

"Sure. I was surprised he didn't come to the graduation," Katharine said. But she cut herself off abruptly as Neema's face started to cloud up. Neema and Imani were both surprised and angry when Godfrey pled another engagement at the last minute and missed the ceremony.

District hospitals often had only one doctor, occasionally two, and many new medical graduates struggled to find the right balance between asking experienced nurses for help and establishing an identity and authority as the doctor.

"At least neither of us is in some completely isolated place. There'll be other doctors in shouting distance if we need help," Katharine said, changing the subject to something all the recent graduates were concerned about.

"True," agreed Neema. "But I think I know what I'm doing."

"Well, be sure to ask for help when you need it," advised Katharine. "It's better than making some terrible mistake."

"Sure. But *you* be sure to show who's in charge. Getting that wrong could also be a big mistake."

One of the responsibilities of the senior nurses and sometimes the doctors at the district hospital was to make supervisory visits to the small health centers dotted throughout the district. The staff at these health centers didn't have much education — a couple of years of secondary school followed by two years of training in health. Modeled on the Chinese barefoot doctors, they were supposed to serve the health-care needs for all the people in a roughly five-kilometer radius.

"It's ridiculous to expect them to provide health services with such limited training and paltry supplies," grumbled one of Neema's professors in medical school, a visiting specialist from Europe.

"Sure, but what's the alternative, when we don't have enough properly trained doctors and nurses?" argued another professor. "Those little health centers focus on maternity care and immunizations. Those affect everyone. People who need more specialty care can be referred to district or regional hospitals."

The farther along Neema went in her medical training, the better she understood the limitations of the basic health workers at medical care beyond immunizing children, handing out aspirin and malaria medicines, and providing routine maternity care. The problems usually arose when they didn't recognize their limitations or follow protocols. On the other hand, just the week before, she'd seen a poster extolling the success of the immunization service, provided at the health centers with help from UNICEF. Thanks to basic health workers, Tanzania could boast that 90 percent of children received immunizations. Deaths in children from old killers like measles had dropped off dramatically.

∼

Neema was scheduled to make a supervisory visit to Matei Health Center a few weeks after she arrived at the district hospital. She was mildly curious to see one of these rural health centers since she'd had no experience with them. As for supervision, everyone just seemed to assume she'd know how to do this — after all, she was the doctor — and she certainly wasn't going to ask anyone for help. But medical school didn't include any training in this kind of management activity and she wasn't sure what she was supposed to do.

One of the hospital drivers was assigned to take her in the district's four-wheel-drive vehicle. Once she was settled in the car, she glanced at the form she was supposed to complete. It had spaces for the date, the name of the health center, the name of the in-charge health assistant, a place to check *satisfactory* or *unsatisfactory*, and a line for her signature. That shouldn't be too hard to handle.

The short rains had just ended and the jacaranda trees that lined the road to the health center were blooming. A thin carpet of the fallen purple flowers hid some of the rubbish accumulated in spots along the roadway. The district's waste, recently including more and more plastic bottles, foil, and cellophane wrappers, was dumped along the roadside. There was no organized rubbish collection service.

Even with the recent rains, the dirt roads around Matei

District Hospital were passable, thanks to the sandy soil. Still, as the driver pulled onto the road to the health center, Neema was glad to see that it was tarred, although it was soon evident that it was badly in need of repair.

Shortly after leaving town the driver swerved over to the side where two people stood, each with an outstretched arm and a waving hand. He got out of the car to talk to them, preventing Neema from hearing their short conversation, then they all climbed into the vehicle.

"I'm just giving a lift to my cousins," said the driver. Neema yawned, pretending indifference, but she noticed that the "cousins" handed the driver some money when they clambered down from the car a few kilometers before the health center. The driver was obviously running a side business, but she'd keep the information to herself in case it was useful later.

Little market stalls beside the road reflected the main sources of income for the residents in this village. Tall jute bags of homemade charcoal stood in lumpy groups and competed for space with piles of mangoes. As they reached their destination, they pulled off the tar road and back onto sand tracks. Huge mango trees still laden with fruit dotted the landscape.

The health center was only a half kilometer off the main road. The squat cement-block building with a tin roof was about four by five meters. A large mango tree on one side of the building provided shade from the punishing sun during the dry season. The health center had been painted yellow and blue at some point but the paint was flaking, especially around the ill-fitting wooden doorjambs and the jalousie window frames. A thin strand of partly bare electrical wire drooped off a pole and snaked along the tin roof until it disappeared inside. Both Neema and the driver got out of the car and approached the weathered and stained door. It was closed and locked. Glancing around, they noticed a small boy, maybe four years old, playing in the dirt under the umbrella of the mango tree. The driver approached him.

"Where's the nurse who runs the health center?" he asked sternly.

The boy took a look at the official vehicle, jumped up, and started running down a narrow overgrown path into the bush, shouting as he ran, "Mama! Mama!"

Neema and the driver walked around the building through the surrounding low shrubs and grass. There was a narrow door in the rear, closed and locked from the inside; the building was badly neglected. As they came back around to the front, a short, heavyset woman in a health worker's uniform was puffing up the same path the boy had recently run down. She hurried up to the door, dangling a large set of keys.

"*Habari ya asubuhi?*" panted the woman, breathless but nonetheless polite. Neema responded as expected that all was fine, then inquired after her well-being. Once both agreed they were fine, the health worker continued.

"I'm sorry I wasn't here when you arrived," she said nervously, inserting a key into the padlock in the hasp on the door. Several extraneous keyholes in the wooden door suggested that keys had been lost in the past. "I had to go attend to an emergency."

"I see," said Neema, with a half-smile. "Well, I am Dr. Moyo from the District Hospital and I'm here to make an official supervisory visit. Shall we go in to talk?"

"Of course," said the health worker, pushing the creaking door open and ushering Neema in.

Inside, on the exposed rafters that supported the tin roof, the remnants of an old bird's nest clung precariously to the upper wall in one corner. The structure was divided into a large main room and two smaller rooms across the back with thin water-stained pressboard, which did not extend all the way to the roof. Neither of the smaller rooms had a door and both were filled with a jumble of old furniture, disorganized papers, bits of rope, and pieces of plastic that must have had some purpose once. A single fly-specked light bulb dangled from wires off the center rafter. Neema was taken aback by the meagerness of the big room. There was a rough wooden table on which a patient could lie down for examination and an iron chair that had been repaired with a combination of clumsy welding and rope. A smaller table with a broken leg served as a desk. Lying out on this was a dog-eared hard-backed notebook that Neema recognized as one of the patient registers that existed in every official health facility in the country. An old rusted metal cupboard with a lock on the door leaned against a wall for support and completed the furnishings. The health worker gestured towards the iron chair.

"Please have a seat," she said.

"Thank you," said Neema, sitting down with care. She pulled a paper from her handbag. "I see that you, Mrs. Tibaijuka, are in charge here, is that right?" Mrs. Tibaijuka stood straighter and nodded solemnly. "Okay," continued Neema. "And do you have an assistant?"

"Oh yes," Mrs. Tibaijuka said, nodding. "Mr. John Kabili works here with me." She edged towards the table, put her hand on the rough surface for support, and chewed her lower lip. "He isn't here today though. He's on annual leave." She moved closer to the table and crossed her chubby arms.

"I see," said Neema as she looked around at the small room more closely. She noted a second hard-backed notebook, imprinted on the front cover with *Guests*, next to the patient log book. After several moments of silence, Neema asked, "How long have you worked here?"

"Four years," replied Mrs. Tibaijuka. "We're very busy."

It didn't look that way to Neema. She picked up the guest book to write her name. The last entry in the slightly moldy book was months ago and Neema recognized the name of her predecessor. "Mmm," she murmured, not sure what to ask about next as she cast her eye around the place. "Where do you wash your hands?"

Mrs. Tibaijuka pointed to an old yellow plastic bucket with a few cups of water in it, which had been hidden under the table. Several dead insects floated on the top in the oily sheen.

"Is there a toilet?" asked Neema, trying to mask her revulsion at the hand-washing facility.

"Well, we have a latrine out in the back," said Mrs. Tibaijuka, gesturing to the rear door. She paused, then asked politely, "Would you like to use it?"

"No. Thank you." Neema shuddered, still looking around.

"Would you like some tea?" asked Mrs. Tibaijuka.

"Yes, that would be nice," said Neema. Then she considered the bucket of water and the latrine and made a hasty correction. "Well, actually I don't have time today, but thank you anyway."

"Did you bring any medicines?" asked Mrs. Tibaijuka. "I sent a message to the District Hospital to get more stock. We're without any antibiotics now for two weeks."

"No, the pharmacist at the hospital didn't issue any drugs to bring. When did you send a message?"

"I sent a letter about three weeks ago," said Mrs. Tibaijuka.

"Well, I'll be sure to let the hospital know, and the next time someone comes out here they can bring them." It was dawning on Neema that she wasn't actually sure what the system was to keep these health centers stocked — or if there was a system at all besides sending letters or mentioning it to someone when stock was exhausted, hoping the message found its mark. With a faint sense of unease, it dawned on her that this should be discussed as part of the supervisory visit. Why hadn't anyone talked to her about this? She made a note on the paper about the need for antibiotics, then folded it and put it back in her handbag. The supervisory visit had taken less than ten minutes, but she was at a loss for what else to ask about and she wanted to appear efficient.

Neema stood and offered her hand to shake. "Well," she said, briskly, "we don't have any more time today but I'll be sure you get the medicines you need." She turned and walked out through the front door with Mrs. Tibaijuka behind her. As she climbed into the vehicle, she looked back at the woman standing under the mango tree.

"Good-bye. Have a safe trip!" Mrs. Tibaijuka called out with a wave.

Settled into her seat, chagrin descended on Neema. It was likely that Mrs. Tibaijuka had more experience with district health center supervisory visits than Neema did, but she seemed content to let Neema take the lead, and Neema wasn't going to ask her what the procedure was.

Reluctantly, she turned to the driver. "How long do these visits usually take?" she asked him, as casually as she could.

"Oh, not more than ten or fifteen minutes, Doctor," he said. "The supervisors want to get back home." He paused as if in thought. "Of course, if the regional officer is along, they're often there for a half hour or more."

Neema rolled her eyes and shook her head without further comment on the visit.

As they backed up and turned to leave the small building, she asked him to stop so they could buy something to drink. He pulled off the road at a small shop, little more than a two-meter-square box with a couple of cases of empty soft drinks and beer bottles next to the doorway and some benches and tables outside. A young girl hurried out and Neema asked her for a Fanta. She sank to a bench to drink the warm soda once the girl brought it out. The driver bought a cola and retreated to the car to wait. Two older men on nearby benches noted the official vehicle and started talking about the health center in voices she couldn't help but overhear.

"My younger brother used to work over at the Matei Health Center," said one. "But he passed away over a year ago now. Wonder if he'll be replaced."

"Who knows." His friend shrugged. "The government is shrinking services, so they may leave the position empty." There was a short silence, then the man nodded slowly. "I'm sorry about your brother though. That was very sad. John Kabili was a good man."

~

"But, Katharine, I'm sure they said the man had died over a year ago," Neema said a few days later as she related the incident to her friend in Dar.

"Neema, this sounds suspicious. My aunt's a supervisor in the government schools and she told me she'd discovered at least a dozen ghost workers on the payrolls in her district." Katharine paused as she munched another crisp from the packet she and Neema were sharing. "Say a teacher dies or moves away. The head teacher at the school just arranges to have someone pick up his salary every month and this way he supplements his own income. No one at the pay office even knows what's going on." She took another crisp, sprinkled it with vinegar, and popped it into her mouth. "So what are you going to do about it?"

"I don't know," said Neema slowly. "For now, I'm going to think about it. But I'm not letting it go. We've got to root this kind of stuff out if the country is ever going to move ahead." She shook her head and frowned. "That woman shouldn't get away with this."

Neema was busy with clinics, but she continued to think about her discovery as the days grew warmer and the land started to dry out. What if Mrs. Tibaijuka had created a ghost worker? Everyone knew how low the salaries of the health workers in these centers were, so it wouldn't be a surprise if she had. And, said a small voice in her head, what difference would one small salary packet make anyway? Neema had seen directors in the Ministry of Health accept per diems of more than a health worker's weekly salary just for showing up to a one-hour meeting. On the other hand, although she hadn't seen any evidence of overwork in her brief visit, the health center might really be short-staffed due to a fraudulent scheme. Neema turned these two perspectives over in her mind, discovering she didn't feel strongly one way or the other. What really roused her anger was the thought that the woman might have lied to her — the idea that she might have seen Neema as someone who could be fooled.

Two weeks later, she stopped at the district health administration office. According to the official schedule, supervision was done quarterly. It would be three months before someone made another visit to Matei Health Center. Of course, these schedules, made annually, were not always adhered to. Visits were often cancelled at the last minute, rescheduled with a few hours' warning, or skipped altogether. It was no surprise that people at the health centers were often unprepared for the visits or that the hospitals had little idea of what was going on out there. It seemed that she had a few months to think about what she ought to do. In the meantime, she could make sure she was delegated to make the next visit.

"Mr. Ilako, please make sure that I'm scheduled for the supervisory visit to Matei Health Center next time," she directed the administrator.

"Well, okay, doctor," replied Mr. Ilako. "But it's actually Nurse Ginny's turn to go." The nurses liked making these visits, since they received a special allowance whenever their duties took them away from the hospital. "The doctor doesn't usually make more than one."

"That doesn't matter," said Neema, with annoyance. "There's something out there I need to attend to myself."

In the meantime, when she made a weekend visit to Dar, she tried to ferret out what other colleagues did on supervisory visits.

"Go in and look for things that aren't being done right," was one candid bit of advice that appealed to Neema. "The log book will almost always be incomplete. And you'll find out-of-date medicines if you look." The colleague winked at Neema. "You've got to be strict to keep them on their toes. Oh, and you might also check if basic equipment is there and if it works."

Neema began to get an idea of how she'd run things next time. She made a checklist to take with her.

Two weeks before the next visit to Matei, she asked Mr. Ilako for a list of workers stationed at health centers in the district. She hadn't received it after a week, so she went to his office again.

"Mr. Ilako, do you have the list I requested?" she asked after greetings were finished.

He looked distraught. "Oh, sorry. It's taking longer than I expected." Neema said nothing but continued to look him in the eye until he responded, "Uh, I want you to have the most up-to-date list."

Neema frowned. "Well, I'll take the most recent list you have. Have it to me by next week."

"Yes, Doctor, you will have it," he replied.

Neema left the room. The administrator sighed and pulled a poorly organized file off a shelf. The date at the top of the list of employees at the health centers was several years old. He spent a few hours over the next two days asking around to try to put together a more recent list, complaining about the time it took and the difficulty of getting current information. In the end, he essentially rewrote the old list with a new date.

When Neema got the list, she looked immediately at the health center in Matei. John Kabili was listed as an assistant to the in-charge, Mrs. Tibaijuka.

∾

The health center was in the full blaze of the dry-season heat as Neema made her second visit, and the journey seemed harder than it had the first time. The potholes the driver had avoided before were larger and the remaining patches of tarmac simply served to make the holes seem deeper. Neema recalled Katharine's comment — "You know who the drunk drivers are around here because they're the only ones going straight!"

This time Mrs. Tibaijuka was in the clinic, but she looked startled to see Neema. "I'm fine," she replied to Neema's greeting. "But I'm surprised to see you again. Usually the staff rotate visits, so it's someone new each time."

"Well, I'm doing things a bit differently," replied Neema, giving the woman a perfunctory smile. "Shall we go in?"

Once inside, Neema declined a cup of tea. "Let's have a look at inventory, shall we?"

She took out her checklist as Mrs. Tibaijuka scurried to open a cabinet. Neema peered into its depths and they established that there was one dented instrument basin, a pair of dull scissors, and two pairs of forceps, although one was so loose it was of questionable usefulness. There was one bent hemostat and a scalpel handle.

"Is this it?" asked Neema, surprised by the poor equipment. "What about medicines?"

Mrs. Tibaijuka showed her the antibiotics that had finally been delivered a month previously, a few packets of aspirin, and a few vials of essential drugs for mothers giving birth. There were no antimalarial tablets.

Neema criticized the organization of the meager supplies.

She paged through the patient log book and found the problems her colleague had assured her would be there. Then, satisfied that she'd established her authority, she proceeded to ask about John Kabili.

"I asked for an updated list of staff at health centers and I see that Mr. Kabili is still here," she said, looking directly at Mrs. Tibaijuka. "May I speak to him today?"

Mrs. Tibaijuka shifted her gaze away from Neema and looked out through one of the fly-specked jalousie windowpanes. "Oh, Dr. Moyo, what bad luck! Mr. Kabili had to go home early today to attend to a problem with his son."

"Oh, that *is* too bad," replied Neema. She acted surprised, then furrowed her brow for a moment. "He must live nearby though. Perhaps I could drop by and visit him after we leave here."

Mrs. Tibaijuka seemed to consider this. "Well, I'm sure he'd welcome a chance to talk to you," she said finally. "But your vehicle couldn't pass over the road to the place he stays. It would mean a walk of nearly an hour for you." She glanced meaningfully at Neema's lightweight shoes. "Over a very rough path."

"Does he have any other family living closer?" persisted Neema. "I'd like to ask them some questions." Mrs. Tibaijuka began to look nervous.

"Perhaps I can help," she offered. "What do you need to know?"

"Well, actually, I heard that Mr. Kabili passed away over a year ago," Neema stated flatly.

Mrs. Tibaijuka looked frightened. "Oh no, Dr. Moyo," she said, shaking her head emphatically from side to side. "That's not true. How can that be? Someone is telling a terrible lie."

Neema studied Mrs. Tibaijuka for a minute or more, while the silence thickened. Then she broke it, speaking very deliberately. "I see, Mrs. Tibaijuka. Perhaps I heard wrong. Now I need to go."

Neema got into the vehicle. As they were pulling away, she looked back. Mrs. Tibaijuka was locking the health center door. She felt a satisfying sense of power as she watched her. This woman was going to regret her deception.

It was no trouble to stop again at the little soft-drink shop as they left the village. This time after ordering a drink, Neema exchanged some pleasantries and engaged the owner in conversation.

"Is there an assistant at the Matei Health Center named Mr. John Kabili?" she asked.

"Not anymore," said the owner. "I was friends with John Kabili for, let's see, about five years." He put down a rag he'd been using to wipe a cracked cup and leaned forward onto the counter. "John worked at the health center as an assistant for at least four years, but, I'm sorry to say, he passed away over a year ago after a short illness. It was a sad situation," he said, shaking his head. "He had three young children when he passed. His widow and children left the village and moved on to live elsewhere with relatives shortly after the funeral."

Neema agreed with the man that it was indeed sad, thanked him, finished her drink, and got back in the vehicle. She had to figure out what to do next. But how was she supposed to know? Medical schools didn't teach future doctors anything about how to work with the staff they were expected to manage. Or for that matter, how to run the hospitals or health systems they'd be made heads of — often within a few years of graduation.

The next week she went to her own supervisor, Dr. Mshiki, at the Regional Health Office. The man shifted his gaze around the room as Neema told the story. "I'll definitely look into this after the first of the year," he promised as he saw her out the door.

～

By February, Neema hadn't heard anything from Dr. Mshiki, so she stopped by his office again to inquire. "Oh yes, Dr. Moyo," he replied to her question. "We looked into it. Mr. Kabili's name has been removed from the records. Mrs. Tibaijuka no longer works at the Health Center and someone else has been transferred there, along with a new assistant. So, there's nothing for you to worry about."

"But what's happening to Mrs. Tibaijuka?"

"It's been dealt with, Dr. Moyo," said Dr. Mshiki, "and she's gone. It's not your concern any longer." He stood up to end the conversation.

Neema left with a frown of dissatisfaction. That health worker needed to be punished for cheating the government. Besides, Neema didn't like feeling duped.

9

NEEMA, 1984–1985

"You've got to come to this party, Neema," said Katharine, one weekend when Neema had nearly finished her service as a district health officer. "There'll be lots of people there from university days and it'll be fun. Besides, there'll be someone you should meet."

Neema arrived before Katharine at an old colonial house on the coast just north of Dar. Getting out of the taxi, she felt a familiar stab of anxiety as she heard laughter and talk drifting from the far side of the house. She took a deep breath, threw her shoulders back, and walked in. Most of the guests were gathered on the spacious veranda in the back, overlooking the ocean. Neema walked over to the well-stocked bar and requested a drink. She stood alone with it, sipping slowly, trying to look like she was enjoying herself, and wished Katharine would come. With relief, she heard someone call her name.

"Neema! Neema, how are things going? Hey, come on over here," said a young doctor from Neema's medical school class. "We've been talking about government corruption. I don't think it's a problem in *our* ministry. Have you seen any?"

"Well, actually, I just had an interesting experience," Neema began, pleased to be asked. She warmed to the topic and told the story about the ghost worker in her district.

"But this is outrageous," fumed a woman. "This isn't what our parents worked for. How's the country supposed to develop if people are cheating it?"

"I agree," said another young man. "But I don't think it's widespread. There are lots of dedicated people working hard in the government. They want to improve our country and they don't do this kind of thing."

"Yeah, but when there's corruption at the top it spreads down. People at the bottom think it's okay if they see the leaders do it."

"I really don't know what happened in the end," said Neema. "I wonder if the supervisor at the regional office was involved. The woman was replaced, but she just disappeared and I've no idea where she ended up." She shook her head. "I hope she didn't get away with it. This kind of stuff will kill the country."

Katharine appeared at her side. "Neema! Hi!" she said, interrupting the small circle. She took Neema's arm and brushed her cheek lightly with a kiss. "Are you talking about work again?" she chided. "Enough! I brought you here to meet someone. Let's go find him. Excuse her, please," Katharine laughed, as she pulled Neema away and led her across the room.

"Ah! There he is!" she said, pointing at the back of a man in a red sweater who was deep in conversation with a petite woman with an elaborate braided hairdo. Katharine tapped his elbow. "Junior Msese, turn around! Here's someone you should meet." A tall, good-looking man turned around. A slow smile spread across his face when he saw Katharine.

"Excuse me," he said to the woman he'd been speaking to. "I need to talk to this one. Katharine! How are you? How long has it been?" he asked as he bent to kiss her cheek.

"Junior, I want you to meet my friend, Neema Moyo. Neema, this is Junior Msese, my oldest brother's best friend since day one of secondary school."

A little shiver ran up Neema's spine as she looked at the man's broad shoulders and slim hips. She liked his height — he was one of the few men half a head taller than she was. His closely cropped hair showed off a finely sculpted head and his easy, generous smile framed strong, straight teeth.

"Junior Msese," Neema said slowly, putting out her hand. "Glad to meet you."

He appraised her slowly, running his eyes down her statuesque figure and then back up to her face as his smile broadened.

Katharine threw her head back and reached out to put her hand on Junior's arm. "Neema's mother is *Bibi* Imani! And her father is the Minister of Labor."

"Well now, that's something," said Junior, obviously impressed. Then he half turned back to where the woman he'd been conversing with had stood. "Let me introduce Marvice . . ." But she'd disappeared. He shrugged and turned back to Neema.

Over the next fifteen minutes, Neema learned that Junior had finished university with a degree in engineering and then gone abroad to do post-graduate studies. He'd recently returned to Tanzania and expected to get a good job.

"I'd think your chances are very good," Neema said, "considering your overseas experience. Not many can compete with that."

Junior nodded but replied modestly. "Sure, I was lucky to get that chance. And I think I'll find something good here."

Katharine disappeared, and Junior and Neema continued to chat until Junior glanced at his watch and startled. "Look, I'm afraid I have to go, but do you think we might get together next weekend?"

"Sure," said Neema, pretending it didn't matter much.

"Let's do." She wrote her phone number on a slip of paper from her bag and handed it to him. A few minutes later, when she watched him go out the door, she was surprised to see the petite woman he'd been talking to earlier leaving with him.

~

Junior called Neema the following Thursday. "There's a good nightclub about halfway between your hostel and my family's place. Good music, dancing. Good food. How about if we meet there?"

"Hmm," Neema replied, hoping to sound indifferent. "I can do it Friday, but Saturday I'm on call, so that won't work."

"No problem. Friday it is," Junior agreed.

~

He was already seated when she arrived, and she joined him at a little table near the edge of the dimly lit nightclub. Colorful murals showing men pulling boats through the water or fishing from dhows covered the concrete-block walls. Old fishing nets, with a few seashells arranged in their webs, hung in drapes from the ceiling. Over drinks and samosas, Neema and Junior tiptoed around each other's lives.

"My mother's a nurse tutor and my dad's an engineer, so I guess they had pretty high expectations for me," Junior told Neema, leaning back on the rear legs of his chair. "I always knew I'd go to university, but I was lucky to go to Denmark for a master's degree." He took several swallows of his beer. "But what about you? Since your father's the Minister of Labor, I guess you didn't have to worry much about university either."

For just a second, Neema wanted to tell him how her father had doubted whether she'd manage to get through medical school, but the band had started and was too loud to allow much conversation. Besides, revealing her father's doubts about her was no way to impress him. Junior put his beer down and gestured towards the dance floor with raised eyebrows. Neema shrugged her assent and they swung out onto the floor to move to a fusion of Latin and African pop music.

During a short quiet break from the music, Neema nearly asked Junior about the woman with whom he'd left the party, but she stopped herself. Why let him know she'd thought about it?

At the end of the evening, he kissed her lightly as he helped her into a taxi. "Let's do this again. Are you free next weekend?" he asked.

"Sure." She smiled, inwardly elated. "Call me and we'll set it up."

～

It was only two months before they were spending every weekend together and, if their schedules permitted, they met for dinner during the week. Beyond his good looks and potential to rise in his profession, Neema liked Junior's easygoing approach to life. He didn't challenge her by asking uncomfortable personal questions. He was always ready to go to movies, nightclubs, and parties — and he understood and never complained when her schedule didn't allow them to go out as often as he wanted. And, just as expected, Junior was soon hired at a private engineering firm. With their jobs and social life, there was little time to talk about serious matters, and this suited them both. They had a growing circle of friends and acquaintances, including Katharine.

"It's great you two are getting along so well. Now, tell me exactly where this is going!" Katharine enthused one afternoon when she and Neema sat together in their favorite salon, having their hair braided. "What do you guys talk about?"

Neema bent her head back so the stylist could work on the last section of her hair. "Well, let's see . . . We talk about our jobs and chances for promotions." She pursed her lips thoughtfully. "Junior and I could do really well for ourselves. He's got potential to make a lot of money in the private sector."

"Mmm. I'm sure he does," Katharine agreed. "And you'll go high in the Ministry of Health yourself. A real power couple!" She winced as the stylist secured an extension on her scalp.

"I think so. You know, what I like about Junior is that I feel like we can just take things for granted. We don't have to dissect and analyze everything. It's nice not to be pushed to explain how I feel about every detail of my life. Let other people worry about the deep stuff — we have a good time." Neema handed the stylist a clip and then pursed her lips again for a moment. "One thing I do wonder about is the woman he was talking to when you introduced us. Do you know who she is?"

Neema couldn't turn her head to look at Katharine when she replied, but there was no mistaking the surprise in her voice. "Didn't you talk to Junior about her?"

"Well, no. He didn't bring it up and I wasn't going to ask. Who is she?"

Katharine shifted audibly in her chair. "Well . . . I think he used to see her, maybe even a lot. Maybe they were even engaged to marry, but his family didn't think she had enough education. Oh, Neema, can you hand over that jar of beeswax I set on the counter? It's a special one my mother swears by." There was a short silence and then Katharine added, "Marvice was a long time ago. You probably ought to forget her. Either that or ask Junior about her and put it to rest."

"Well, if he thinks it's important, I guess he can tell me," said Neema. Then she added, "Actually, even though we haven't talked about it specifically, I think we're both assuming we'll get married." She wasn't sure this was true, but saying it made her feel better about Marvice.

"I know the family and I think they'll be wanting to meet you soon," said Katharine.

∾

The decision by Neema and Junior to marry came about without much discussion. They had dinner with friends at a new seafood restaurant and, although Neema had to return to the hospital that night, they lingered at the table after everyone else left.

"So, Neema, when shall we plan the wedding?" Junior asked with a smile, finishing off his drink.

Her heart pounded a few beats, but she made herself relax and broke into her own smile. What a relief! Now she could let herself imagine their lives together, unfurling on schedule into the future. Their mutual friends would be pleased, and Junior would definitely impress her father. She reached across the table and took his hand, feeling no need to be coy. "How about we set it for after I've finished my district health service? That's only a few months off."

"Good," he said, squeezing her hand. "I thought we were on the same wavelength with this. Let's see what kind of fizzy drink they have for celebrating."

"Not too much, though. You've got to get back to the hospital tonight," Neema answered.

∾

Two weeks later she was invited to meet Junior's family. "Come for Sunday lunch and the afternoon. My parents insist it's past time to meet you," he told her.

The house was on the outskirts of Dar, one of many single-story dwellings built on parcels of land large enough to have good-sized gardens. High fences — the best each owner could afford — enclosed each parcel. The barriers varied from woven straw to chain link to high concrete walls with razor wire or broken glass along the top. Most were reinforced by thick bougainvillea or other thorny bushes.

The grizzled old guard's face lit up as Junior pulled his battered Lada up in front of the house. He opened the clanging metal gate, and Junior and Neema entered along the gravel driveway lined on either side by banana and papaya trees.

"Ah, Junior," said the bent gray-headed watchman with the familiarity born of having known him since he was a toddler. "*Karibu! Karibu sana!*" he welcomed them. Junior climbed out of the car and clapped the old man on the back as Neema got out on her side. Ever respectful of an elder, Junior was introducing Neema to the guard when his parents stepped out the front door.

"Welcome!" boomed his father, striding towards them. He was as tall as Junior but carried considerably more weight. He slapped Junior on the back. Then, as Junior gave his mother a kiss, his father took both of Neema's hands in his and leaned back, looking her slowly up and down. After a few seconds of scrutiny, he smiled and pulled her in for a hearty embrace. "So, this is the bride — the *beautiful* bride, I mean to say," he rumbled.

Neema found herself drawing back, vaguely uncomfortable with the greeting. She was relieved when Junior's mother gave her a more restrained pat on the back. The four made their way into the house.

Neema, still a little uncertain about the family's social position, was interested to see that the house was similar to her own family home in Bagamoyo, with three or four bedrooms, a sizable lounge, and a big veranda in the back.

Metal grills over the windows, open to take advantage of a breeze, provided protection from break-ins. The little group made their way out to the veranda to settle into wicker chairs and couches. Their view was a garden, rather than the Indian Ocean that Neema had grown up with. The kitchen, the province of servants, had been built or enlarged on the side of the house after the original construction. From there, a tall man dressed in loose white trousers and a knee-length shirt came out, carrying a tray of iced drinks.

As the eldest of four children, and a boy, Junior enjoyed the adoration of both parents and numerous aunts and uncles, a number of whom trickled in for lunch. In contrast to the intellectual hours on the veranda at Bagamoyo, this family joked and laughed the afternoon away. Or sometimes they sat in the lounge and watched movies with the new video machine an uncle had brought from the duty-free shop in Dubai.

After that first afternoon, Neema often joined the family on weekends, and soon they accepted her as one of them. Sometimes Junior's father wasn't there, but no explanation was ever offered. Walking into the lounge abruptly one Sunday, Neema realized she'd interrupted an exchange between two of Junior's brothers — but she caught enough to figure out how things were with Junior's father.

"Oh, Dad's with one of his fancy ladies till tomorrow," one brother was saying with a laugh to the other.

A wave of disgust swept over Neema. She stopped, turned around, and left the room as abruptly as she'd entered. She didn't want to hear more. This was one of those things that was better not talked about.

~

"Neema," Junior said, early on in the relationship, biting his lower lip. "Uh . . . of course I want a family, but I think we both need to be more established in our jobs before we start one." Neema caught her breath in surprise. Most young men didn't discuss this issue with their girlfriends. Furthermore, most young men were eager to show they could father children as soon as it looked like they'd found a marriageable mate, if not sooner.

Her mouth went dry. Should she tell him that she'd started birth control pills a few years ago for endometriosis? Or was it better to let him assume she'd planned ahead for a carefree sexually active life? What was the point of starting a conversation about her reproductive health? No doctor had told her she was infertile, and the issue of her ability to have children was still open. She definitely wasn't going to tell him about the endometriosis. It was a woman's problem and men didn't want to hear about that kind of thing. She plunged ahead.

"Well, I'm taking birth control pills now," she said, looking him straight in the eye.

"Wow," said Junior as his eyebrows shot up. "That's my girl! I should've known a doctor would take care about this. I'm impressed." Neema breathed a sigh of relief to have dealt with the issue. But she shifted her gaze away at Junior's next words. "You can stop the pills once we get settled together. I've been looking forward to starting a family for a long time."

She reported the conversation to Katharine, who agreed with her thinking. "No man's going to marry a woman he thinks can't have children for him," she reminded Neema.

Neema started to argue that Junior wasn't like that and, besides, she didn't know for sure that she *couldn't* have children. But she realized that she wasn't confident of either argument. She turned away and said nothing. Anxiety gnawed at her later as she thought about Katharine's words.

∽

Neema hadn't admitted to herself just how worried she was that her father might not show up to meet Junior when she took him out to Bagamoyo, even though Godfrey had agreed by phone to be there for the important occasion. She was relieved to see his car as she and Junior arrived in the old Lada just before lunch. Imani and Godfrey came out together to greet them at the front of the house.

After introductions, during pre-lunch drinks on the veranda, Neema relaxed as she watched Godfrey and Junior establish an easy camaraderie. They supported the same football teams and quickly got into a good-natured argument about the reasons for the losses in the most recent World Cup.

"But, man," said Godfrey, slapping Junior on the back, "you *know* Ghana should have beat Bahrain!" On this they agreed, but it didn't stop them from discussing it through most of lunch. After the meal ended, they drifted away to smoke cigars on the beach, leaving Neema and Imani on the veranda sipping tea.

"So, what do you think of him, Mama?" Neema asked.

"Well, Neema, I'm not marrying him. It's more important what *you* think of him, how the two of you get along," Imani said, settling back with her cup.

Neema set her tea down and examined her nails. "Well, obviously he's very good-looking." She bit off a bit of cuticle. "And we have a good time together. We have lots of friends and keep busy most evenings with them." She picked up a teaspoon and stirred extra sugar into her cup with more vigor than needed.

"Does he treat you with respect, Neema?"

Neema frowned and put down her teaspoon. "Well . . . sure. I mean, I'm a doctor, so of course he does. I'm sure he realizes my work is important, even if he makes more money in the private sector than I do in the Ministry. Yeah, of course he respects me."

"I wasn't just thinking of work, Neema," said Imani,

shaking her head, "although that's important. I'm thinking of whether he'll encourage you and support you when things don't go well." She looked at Neema over the top of her teacup. "Does he care how you feel about things?"

"Well, Mama, we don't have to talk a lot about feelings. We're busy and we have a lot of fun together." She hadn't prepared to answer these sorts of questions.

"Do you believe he'll be faithful in your marriage? Will he be a good father?" Imani asked more pointedly.

Neema winced, wondering whether this was a good time to tell her mother about her fertility fears. She decided against it. She still didn't know whether she'd be able to bear children, so why bring it up? And her mother's other questions had left her mildly annoyed. She pushed away her tea, barely tasted, and stood up.

"Let's go look at wedding dresses next week, Mama. Those are important too. Let's make this a big event. Right now I think I'll walk down to the beach and look for the men."

Neema and Junior married shortly after she finished her service at the District Hospital. They chose one of the historic churches on the waterfront, a legacy from the colonial era, for the ceremony, and several hundred guests attended the joining of the two important families. Neema's beaded white off-the-shoulder gown accented her height. Her three attendants, paired up with Junior's tuxedo-clad groomsmen, were decked out in dark red satin. The dresses, plus the afternoon light through the stained-glass windows and the vivid bouquets of bougainvillea and bird-of-paradise blooms, brought a brilliance to the dark stone floors and the old wooden pews. Creamy frangipani lent its sweet smell everywhere and the sanctuary was filled by the resonant tones of the organ.

"I was a little worried about your prospects, Neema," Godfrey said, with a vacant shrug, as they waited in the vestibule. "It's lucky you caught Junior Msese. Good to have him in the family. Kind of like the son I never had," he added, just before he put out his arm for Neema so they could walk down the aisle.

A convoy ferried guests between the church ceremony and the formal reception. An enthusiastic brass band in the back of a truck provided a break in the formality and led the wedding party to the reception hall. The procession took the long route, winding through twisting streets and around several roundabouts overgrown with scraggly palms.

The band disappeared once they got to the hall, however, and all was somber again. The guests sat at long tables covered in white linen cloths while black-clad waiters served multiple courses of roasted meats, salads, and vegetables. Neema and Junior sat at a table at the front for their meal, with a multitiered white wedding cake on the side. Once they finished eating, Neema moved to a dais, where she sat stiffly for a long time with her white wedding dress spread around her as a photographer took photo after photo. The guests mingled, chatting and offering congratulations to the bride and groom and their parents. But there was no music or dancing, and the evening ended early.

The day after the church ceremony, they traveled to Junior's family's village for more relaxed celebrations. Workers erected a big tent in the center of the village, and every available chair, stool, and bench was pulled there for the oldest guests and the parents of the newlyweds. Everyone turned out, wearing their finest traditional clothes. Children, clean and stiff in their best outfits, tried to wiggle onto the seats before they were swatted away by their elders. Temporarily chastened, they stood around quietly for five or ten minutes before they began to run and shriek again. Mothers, aunts, and older children kept busy trying to keep little ones from falling into the numerous cauldrons bubbling on the periphery or knocking down tent poles. Women transferred pots of stew, roasted meats, and vegetables to a table under the tent. Junior's uncle produced a battery-operated tape player, and the music blared as guests danced and sang.

"Ehhh," cackled Junior's grandmother, stirring a bowl of stew thick with chicken and tomato. "Soon the babies will come."

"That's what makes you a woman," intoned an old aunt loudly, tearing a piece of meat from a rib and washing it down with banana wine. "And our Junior is sure to have many children."

"Sure, his younger brother has three already," added another aunt from between mouthfuls of *ugali*. "With two boys, praise be to God."

On the other side of the compound, the men were engaging in similar speculation about fatherhood and how many children there might be. Junior smiled indulgently. This was not the place to talk about modern ideas of limiting the family to two children.

J oy and Daniel had no money for a church wedding, so they married in a simple ceremony at the registrar's office in Moshi. Joy's parents were there as witnesses, but it was too far for Daniel's mother to travel. After the ceremony the four of them went back to Joy's parents' home, where the village women had prepared rice, *ugali*, and a chicken stew for neighbors and friends who gathered to mark the occasion. The family was well liked, and at least a hundred people came by in the afternoon to eat and offer congratulations to the young couple.

The first problem Joy and Daniel faced as newlyweds was finding a place to live. They finally found a small room they could rent by the week in a mud-brick house, where two other families each rented slightly larger rooms. They'd received a foam mattress as a wedding gift, but otherwise they had very little with which to set up house. Joy's family gave them a cooking pot, which could be used over a charcoal fire behind the house. Daniel's family contributed a little chest for their few items of clothing. Friends contributed utensils, plates, and a few cups.

The second problem they faced loomed larger. Daniel had

had to give up his job as a delivery boy when he went back to the village for his father's final illness. He'd been replaced, and the hotel was not hiring any more employees. He managed to get a few odd jobs from time to time, but Joy's salary at the laundry was the only stable income they had. They could have managed on that, but then Joy found she was pregnant. They were happy to learn this, and it was not unexpected, but a child meant new demands and responsibilities.

Joy kept working at the hotel laundry until a week before she expected to deliver the baby, planning to take the legally allowed three months of maternity leave after the birth. She was healthy, and the government-run maternal health clinic in Moshi had provided her with extra iron and vitamins during her pregnancy. She loved going to the clinic and sitting there with other pregnant women. The experienced ones gave advice freely to the first-timers, who had already heard it all from their mothers and grandmothers, but Joy didn't mind that. She listened earnestly, smiling and nodding, taking it all in, determined to do everything she possibly could to make sure her baby would be healthy.

When she was about to start maternity leave, Joy had disturbing news — the hotel was closing. She tried to put the worry out of her mind as she and Daniel boarded a *dalla dalla* to travel to her parents' home for the delivery. Once she was settled, Daniel had to return to Moshi to take advantage of a two-day job he'd picked up.

Joy went into labor the next day. The birth attendant who helped was an old friend of her mother's and didn't demand a big fee. Surrounded by love, Joy, her mother, and several aunts warmly welcomed the baby girl, Emma, into the world.

Joy had grown up around new babies, but the instant and

overwhelming love she felt for Emma stunned her with its intensity. Swept away into an emotional flood of happiness, she lay with the child at her side for hours at a time, marveling at her perfect tiny features.

Daniel came out from Moshi a day after the birth and insisted on seeing and even holding their newborn baby, to the amusement of the older women. And Daniel had good news. His two-day job as a laborer on a building project in town was going to stretch for another two or three months. He'd go back to Moshi the next day. Joy had the good fortune to be able to stay with her parents for a few months, adjusting to being a mother.

The time at her parents' home passed quickly. Joy loved being with her mother, who doted on her first grandchild, but she felt uneasy to think that she was an extra mouth to feed among all the other children in her mother's care. After the first few luxurious days of rest following Emma's birth, Joy got up to help with the multitude of chores necessary to take care of the large family and her own new baby. It wasn't easy, but among grandparents, aunts, neighbors, and older children, all the work got done and all the children were cared for. And, as her mother remarked more than once, it was so sociable.

"Ah Joy, this is how it used to be in the village. Before young people started going into town for jobs. You see how well it works."

"Yes," said Joy, agreeably, "it does work well." But what she couldn't help noticing was that they hadn't moved forward one bit from the lives their own parents led in their villages farther out in the country. Her young siblings went to bed hungry some nights for want of food in the house. And, like her mother, none of her aunts could read. To Joy's disappointment, none of the siblings at home had even gone as far in school as she had. The sister just below her in age was about to marry a boy from the village and she'd soon produce more grandchildren for her mother.

So, Joy didn't feel reluctant to leave this sociable setting when it came time for her to go back to Daniel in Moshi. He was still in the little room they'd found just after they married. He used a bit of the money he made to buy a little cupboard and two chairs. He also bought a small pallet for the cousin, Amira, who returned with Joy. Amira was only nine and she'd just quit school. She and her parents were happy to have her go to town to live with Joy, where, in exchange for her meals and a place to sleep, she'd take care of Emma when Joy found another job.

Once Joy and Daniel were together again, they took Emma to the church for baptism. The congregation had grown and, amid congratulations, Joy picked up a rumor that the minister wanted to hire a cleaner. She and Daniel went straight to him to ask about it.

"Well now," boomed the rotund pastor, "you look like a sturdy girl. And I've known Daniel a long time. Is your own house clean?"

Daniel nodded vigorously. "Yes, Reverend, sir. Joy's a good housekeeper."

"Well then, let's try it," the minister replied. "Can you start tomorrow?"

Joy made a great effort to go regularly to the mother-and-baby clinics after she had Emma. She listened closely when the health education nurse talked about the importance of waiting several years between pregnancies and the idea made sense to her. But she was worried. What would Daniel say when she talked to him about the injections she could take every three months to prevent another baby?

"If you stop the injections, can we have more children?"

he asked anxiously several times after she told him. "And will anyone know you're doing this?" Daniel was far more reasonable than his own father had been. He agreed that having fewer children would be preferable to having the fourteen who had been born to his mother. Only three of the six boys survived childhood, but still, there wasn't enough land for each to have a piece. Daniel, as the second-to-last born, never had a chance at land or much education in spite of the fact that he was a boy. None of his older sisters went to school for more than a year.

Joy told him what the clinic nurses had said. "Yes, they say when I stop the injections we can have more. And by spacing them out, maybe we can save a little money in between children." In the back of her mind, Joy hoped that Daniel would come around to agreeing that two children were enough. She bolstered her case by adding, "We'll have a much better chance of sending all our children to school if we have fewer. And we'll have a better chance to make sure they have enough food, too." She let him think about that for a while, figuring he'd probably agree eventually to two children. For the time being, she settled for convincing him to leave a space after this first one.

She loved going to the baby clinic with Emma, wrapped in her blanket. Other young mothers gathered there, showing off their babies and chatting about the lessons they received from the nurses. It was fun to talk with them and share ideas.

"No, you should only feed the baby from the breast," Joy solemnly told a new mother whose grandmother was encouraging her to start feeding thin gruel, made with questionable water, to her two-month-old. The nurse, in a smart white uniform with a perky hat Joy admired, smiled encouragement at Joy when she heard her. Although it was getting worn, Joy kept Emma's *Child's Road-to-Health* card as clean as she could, wrapped in a fold of her *kanga* when she came to clinic. Some of the nurses showed surprise that Joy could read the card herself, including the graph. "This little mark here means the baby has gained weight," she said with a friendly smile to another new mother. Joy suspected that not all the nurses liked this. After all, who was she to read the baby's health record? But most encouraged Joy and she basked in their approval. Maybe being a nurse would have been just as satisfying as being a teacher.

Joy was absolutely faithful about coming in every twelve weeks for her injections, no matter the inconvenience it might cause. Emma grew stronger, and Joy pointed with pride at the marks on her card showing how she was gaining weight and getting taller.

One day when Amira was ill, Joy had to take Emma to the church with her. She swept, mopped, and dusted with Emma tied to her back, where the little girl was content for most of the morning. Eventually, however, Emma began to get restless. Joy thought ruefully that in the village, there would have been other children around to help with the baby. Just as she was about to untie the *kanga* and let Emma crawl around for a few minutes, a noise at the front of the church caught her attention. Someone was coming in the front door and Joy hurried forward to see who it was. A tall woman dressed in a fashionable business suit and wearing soft leather shoes with high heels stood inside the doorway, looking around boldly.

"*Habari ya asubuhi?*" said Joy with a small curtsy.

"*Nzuri sana,*" replied the woman nonchalantly. "*Habari yako?*"

"*Nzuri,*" said Joy, giving the obligatory reply. The woman came farther inside, running her eyes up and down the walls and across the floor as she continued speaking.

"I'm Ruth, the minister's cousin," she informed Joy. "Is he here?"

"No, but he'll be back after lunch," Joy started to say, just as Ruth spied Emma tied to her back.

"Oh, what an adorable baby!" she declared, reaching into her pocket for a sweet. Before Joy could say a word, Ruth had unwrapped it and was offering the toffee to Emma.

"Oh, madam, the baby mustn't eat sweeties!" cried Joy with concern before she could measure her response. Ruth paused and drew herself up, at the same time withdrawing the treat and causing Emma to emit a squall.

"Oh really? Well, in my experience all children love sweets. *I* think it would be just fine."

Joy blushed at the reprimand but was also determined to do the right thing for Emma. "Excuse me, madam. You're kind to offer, but the nurse at the baby clinic told us not to feed children sugary sweets."

"Well!" Ruth said, raising her eyebrows and nodding her head forward slightly. "I went to secretarial school so we didn't learn about those things, but I'm sure it wouldn't hurt her." She turned and started out the door. "I have many things to do this morning, so I'll be back later to see my cousin. You can tell him I was here. Good-bye." She was gone before Joy could say anything else.

Joy let Emma down off her back so the little girl could crawl around. Her jaw was tight with resentment and she frowned. Maybe she wouldn't tell the minister anything at all about the visit. After all, she was a cleaner at the church, not a secretary to take messages.

She stewed about it for the next few hours, thinking of things she wished she'd said to Ruth. She was relieved when the woman didn't return that afternoon and she hoped she'd never see her again.

∼

When two-year-old Emma was toddling around capably, Joy

and Daniel talked about having another child. Joy's job at the church didn't pay a lot, but it was steady. Daniel's building work had ended, but he'd managed to get enough odd jobs so they could tuck a little savings in a tin buried in the wall. Joy talked to the nurse at the clinic the next time she went in and they decided the time was right to stop taking the injections. It was a good time to have another child.

Several months later, Joy told Daniel with a smile that she was pregnant again.

11

NEEMA, 1987–1991

After she finished her district hospital service, the Ministry assigned Neema to a post in a hospital in Dar. Opened a few years previously, the building still looked new and clean, but it felt like a madhouse to Neema. Too few chairs were provided, and the noise from the throngs of patients was deafening as it echoed off the stone walls. Some doctors came late and took tea breaks without regard for how many people waited, leaving a clinic teeming with irritated patients, all wondering what the holdup was. To make it worse, patients had no access to toilets, save one across the grounds in another building. They constantly tried to get into the staff toilet, right next to Neema's examination room. When they found the door locked, they knocked on her door to inquire. It was maddening.

"You should bring these problems up at a staff meeting," counseled Junior when Neema complained at home. "How often do they have those?"

"Every three months is what I heard, but Matron cancelled the most recent one at the last minute and it wasn't rescheduled."

At the next meeting Neema learned that the clinic did

have working toilets that were intended for patients' use, but they couldn't be accessed because the hallway door leading to them was locked.

"That was for security during last year's health fair," said an older nurse. Everyone agreed this was no longer necessary, but no one knew who had the authority to unlock it, or for that matter, who had a key. It took several months to sort the problem out.

Most of the nurses in the hospital worked hard and cared about the patients' well-being. Some of them tried to offer Neema — one of the few female doctors in Tanzania — their friendship. But Neema took pains to keep her distance with nurses and she made it clear that her orders were to be followed without question. She no longer had to take first call on night duty, but from time to time she had to serve on backup call for both the adult and the pediatric medical wards. On these occasions she had to stay in the hospital hostel for the night.

One night she was called in the wee hours by a nurse on the pediatric ward. Annoyed to be awoken from a deep sleep, she wondered why a child would come in so late. She'd learned that most children arrived in the arms of a desperate parent shortly after dawn, once public transport resumed for the day. Almost no one had money for private transport. A more junior doctor should have been available at the hospital to take first call, but no one had been able to find him. Neema was in no mood to listen when the nursing sister called her.

"Doctor, I've started the usual antimalarial treatment for this child, but something doesn't seem right to me. I'd like to start antibiotics as well."

"Sister Chabuga, you know the protocol for treating these children. We don't treat malaria cases with antibiotics. Surely you're aware of the risks of overuse of antibiotics? What doesn't seem right to you?"

"Well, Doctor, he's comatose and completely nonreactive

to any stimuli I try. His mother says he's been like that for the past twelve hours. His neck isn't exactly stiff, but he reacts strangely when I flex it."

Neema sighed with exasperation. This nurse too often relied on her gut feelings instead of using objective examination signs. "Sorry, Sister, but that isn't a good enough reason to deviate from the Ministry protocol. Follow the protocol. I'll assess him and do a spinal tap in the morning if I need to. If anything shows up on that, we can start antibiotics then."

But when Neema arrived on the ward in the morning she found the beds reserved for acute pediatric cases empty. Sister Chabuga was off duty and the ward was quiet. Neema spied a single patient chart lying out on the counter. She glanced up the hall to see if anyone was watching and then, with a sick feeling in her stomach, she picked it up to see what she could learn.

It was the file on the child who had been admitted late the previous night. She turned quickly to the nursing notes.

The final entry was signed by Sister Chabuga: *Deceased 5:30.*

The blood drained from Neema's face, but she calmed herself and slowly flipped pages back to previous notes. Relief washed over her. This was almost too good to be true — the nurse had neglected to record the phone call she'd made to Dr. Moyo.

Neema made discreet inquiries in the next hour and learned that Sister Chabuga had gone off duty. Not only that, but she was scheduled to start her annual leave and she'd be gone for the next month. Here was another bit of luck. There was a chance the nurse would have forgotten the episode by the time she returned — children's deaths in the hospital weren't uncommon.

~

In the days following the incident, Neema seesawed between concern and complacence. It was unlikely that a nurse would report a doctor's mistakes, but it did happen occasionally. Sister Chabuga's failure to record her phone call would protect Neema but both women knew exactly what had happened. The thought of Sister Chabuga hovered as a dark, threatening cloud in Neema's mind.

∾

Two weeks after the episode she received a notice to report to the office of Dr. Lyimo, the hospital's senior medical superintendent. She walked through the crowded hallway towards his office, trying to slow her heart.

Mrs. Oboto, the department secretary, sat behind a desk covered with stacks of files cascading towards the edge. After greetings, she suggested Dr. Moyo should take a seat.

"The superintendent is with somebody else now. I had to squeeze in someone with an emergency, but he'll see you soon." Neema sat on the peeling plastic upholstery of the chair outside the door to Dr. Lyimo's office. She could faintly hear affable voices and laughter inside the inner office. Some emergency! After twenty minutes she cleared her throat and spoke to the secretary.

"Excuse me. Do you think maybe I should come another time?"

Mrs. Oboto shrugged. "Well, you can if you want, but Dr. Lyimo's a very busy man. And he'll be leaving this afternoon for two weeks' travel, so you probably should just wait."

The voices in the inner office continued and Neema shifted in the chair. After another ten minutes she was relieved to see the handle to the inner office door turn, followed by the emergence of a grinning young man, who closed the door behind him as he left the room.

"Thank you so much for fitting me in to talk to my uncle

this morning," he said, smiling at the secretary. "I'll be sure to say hello to your daughter when I see her later today."

Finally, five minutes later, there was a buzz at the secretary's desk. She looked over at Neema and spoke. "Okay. Dr. Lyimo will see you now. Please go in."

Dr. Lyimo sat behind a big desk, where he was perusing a schedule book. He rose to greet Neema. "Dr. Moyo. How are you? I'm sorry to make you wait. So much urgent business," he said with a quick shake of his head. "Do sit down."

Neema took the seat and waited in silence while Dr. Lyimo read over some notes he had on the desk. "Yes. Well. Dr. Moyo, it looks like you've been here a year and a half. Far as I can see, there's been no problem with your work, so congratulations on that." Relief washed across Neema, and she smiled and relaxed her grip on the chair arms.

Dr. Lyimo continued. "I called you in this morning because we've had a notification about a new position for you. The Ministry wants to shift you to a post in general medicine at the main teaching hospital. They'd like for you to start very soon. Actually, if possible, two weeks from today." Neema nodded and sat up straighter. "This will be a promotion for you, Dr. Moyo, so congratulations."

Neema inclined her head slightly. This *was* a pleasant surprise. It would be very satisfying to tell Junior about it. Maybe they'd plan something special for the weekend to celebrate. Her parents and Katharine would also be impressed. "Thank you, Dr. Lyimo," she said gravely. "I'd be pleased to take the new position."

Dr. Lyimo shifted forward and leaned his arms on the desk, smiling confidently. "Good. That's what I expected. Now, before I say good-bye to staff I always like to ask them about their experience here. That's one way I can learn about problems that need fixing. I don't get into the clinic much myself anymore, but we've always got to be looking to improve, you know." He gave a self-deprecating laugh. "I'd like to hear your thoughts about the clinics and wards you've worked in here. Any issues you noticed, suggestions for ways we might improve? Any problems?"

Neema sat back and bit the side of her lower lip, nodding slowly. She'd so often been frustrated with the clinic, but it was hard to know where to start.

"Well, the clinics don't start on time and that makes everything back up. By noon it's chaotic and the noise is terrible."

Dr. Lyimo smiled indulgently. "Well, that kind of delay is hard to avoid."

"Probably so," Neema said with a frown. "Maybe if staff had to sign in they'd get there on time."

Dr. Lyimo raised his eyebrows and cleared his throat. He tapped his pen on the desk. "Anything else?"

Neema shifted slightly as something occurred to her. She had an opportunity here. Before she had time to think it through, she spoke. "Well . . . maybe . . ." She hesitated.

"Please. Speak up. We can't improve without hearing about our problems," Dr. Lyimo encouraged her.

"Well, I don't want to speak badly of anyone and it's not a *big* problem . . . nothing that needs to be made official."

"That's okay. Go ahead. This is confidential."

"Well, you might want to tell Matron to keep an eye on Sister Chabuga. Just to be sure she follows protocols correctly." Then she smiled and changed her tone. "But all in all, I've enjoyed my time here. It's been a good place to work, Dr. Lyimo."

12

NEEMA, 1991–1993

Neema and Junior had settled into one of the new three-story blocks of flats going up in Dar-es-Salaam after they married. Traffic in Dar was more congested and chaotic all the time, with an ever-increasing number of used Japanese vehicles finding their way into the country. Neema used public transportation to get to the teaching hospital she'd been transferred to in her promotion. Junior spent almost as long — an hour each way — in his decrepit Lada to get back and forth to his job.

Although not wealthy, with their salaries they could live as well as or better than many of their friends. Several pieces of nice furniture, including a good couch, made their spacious two-bedroom flat on the third floor comfortable. A video player, which Junior's uncle had brought from Dubai as a gift, sat in front of the sofa. Electric power across Dar was erratic, but they accepted this philosophically, like everyone else.

Their house girl kept the place clean and had food ready every evening; if they weren't going out, they could relax once they got home. Sometimes they watched a video borrowed from a friend, and occasionally friends came over to join them. If the power failed, they gave it an hour or so to come back before calling it quits and dining out or going to bed early. On weekends they continued the social life they'd established with other young couples or visited their families.

One evening, a year and a half into their marriage, they returned home late after dinner with another couple. "Looks like Mary'll be having a baby soon," commented Junior as they got ready for bed.

Neema froze for an instant. She'd known for weeks that Mary was pregnant, and she cursed herself for accepting the dinner invitation when it would be so obvious. She needed to sound casual.

"Yes," she said with a shrug. "Say, did you see the new restaurant that opened on the Old Coastal Road? We should have gone there tonight. My fish wasn't very good. Maybe next weekend?"

Junior was not going to be distracted so easily. "Neema," he asked anxiously, not for the first time, "you did stop the birth control pills, right?"

"Sure," she responded nonchalantly, "but it often takes some months for the body to get used to not having the pills — you know, to reset." She started out of the room and called back over her shoulder, "Don't worry about it." She reentered a few minutes later ready for bed and gave Junior a suggestive smile. "We know what we need to do, right?"

But in fact, sex had started to feel like work, and she was worried. Since she'd stopped taking the birth control pills her menstrual pain had come back with a vengeance. She took care to hide it from Junior and even lied a few times about her state of health, taking to bed with excuses about having the flu when the pain grew too severe. She was glad he was an engineer and not a doctor or he might have been more suspicious.

He started asking frequently about having a baby. Worst of all were the comments he made about his brother, the younger one with three children. "He didn't seem to have any problem having kids," grumbled Junior. "How long are we going to have to wait?"

～

Worry about pregnancy was not the only stress for Neema during this time. Money worries weighed on her — it wasn't as plentiful as she expected it to be when she and Junior married.

"I try to keep track of what I spend, but we never seem to have anything left at the end of the month. And prices keep going up all the time. Anything that's imported — if I can even find it — costs a fortune! I really need more money for clothes. I need nice suits to wear to work. I can't go wrapped in a *kanga*!" complained Neema one evening as she and Junior ate dinner in their flat.

"Well, the country's had several currency devaluations," said Junior, spearing a forkful of chicken curry. "But quit worrying so much about it. I'll take care of everything."

"What about that salary raise you mentioned a while back — did you get it?" persisted Neema. Even with her promotional raise, Junior made almost twice what she did.

"Not yet," said Junior with a sideways glance away from her. "But I expect it'll come through soon."

"It *would* be very nice to have a bit more for clothes," said Neema with a little pout. "It's bad enough having to use public transport to get to work. At least I'd like to be dressed well when I get there."

Junior pushed back from the table. "Listen, I've got to meet some clients from work this evening. I could be very late, so don't wait up for me." He disappeared and then came out of the bedroom knotting a tie. "Is this straight?" He gave Neema a peck on the cheek as he headed for the door. "Don't worry so much about the money. It'll be fine soon."

But it wasn't. Neema looked at their bank account several

months later. It showed a regular amount going in every month from each of their salaries. There was a modest overall increase in the total they had — just not what there should be.

Then one day she was sorting papers at the desk in the house, deciding whether to discard or keep them, when she was surprised to realize she was looking at a pay slip from Junior's company. She looked at the amount on it, blinked, shook her head, and looked again. The pay slip was for almost twice what was going into their bank account each month from his salary. The date was only two months previous.

Junior was out of town, on one of the business trips he was taking more and more frequently, so she couldn't ask him immediately. But it was the first thing she mentioned when he came in the door the next week.

"Well, Neema," he said, stepping back from the hug he was about to give her. "I've been away for two weeks and that's the way you greet me? Guess I was hoping for something a little more affectionate."

Neema, arms crossed and eyes narrowed, continued to look at him. "Where has the money your company pays you gone? I've seen the pay slip."

Junior exhaled slowly and looked at the ground. "I've, uh, been meaning to tell you about this," he said while Neema glared at him. There was a long silence before he continued. "Well, Neema . . . it's my youngest brother. I've been helping him out now for some time. It's really a big favor to my parents. His school fees have gone up and I want to do my share to help the family."

"But why didn't you tell me about it?"

"I was going to. I was planning to, but you know how busy we've been and the right time just didn't come up." Neema let a silence grow until he spoke again. "Tell you what. Let's go out this evening and talk about it then. You choose the restaurant."

"Okay," she said finally, letting her arms fall to her sides. "But I don't like being deceived. Let me change my clothes and we can go."

Over dinner, Junior apologized profusely and pled his case. It was true, what he said: families expected those members lucky enough to have money to support relatives who needed help. Neema had seen this all her life. She listened to Junior for some time and reluctantly conceded his point.

But an uneasiness about her marriage was growing.

She met Katharine a few days later for shoe shopping and found herself defending Junior's actions. "Well, we all know it's a two-edged sword. Family's there when you need them, but you've got to be there for them when the tables turn." She gave a quick shrug and held up a pair of shoes with a high platform. "Can you imagine walking in these?" she said, handing one to Katharine to inspect. Then she paused and sighed. "I've known of a few young guys who moved to Dar and didn't tell their relatives their addresses — just to avoid having them show up asking for money or trying to move in."

"Mmm, yeah. I've heard stories like that," said Katharine. She put the shoe down abruptly. "Listen, Neema, I've got to go. I forgot about a meeting I have later this afternoon." She was gone before Neema could ask why she seemed to want to avoid talking about Junior these days.

Nearly six months later, Neema came across receipts lying on the desk from yet another trip to Dubai. They were for a toaster, a coffeemaker, and a blender from a duty-free shop. Where were these things? They hadn't ended up in their flat; he wouldn't have bought them for his parents, who already owned this stuff, and electrical appliances would be useless to his family in the village. But she had no heart for a confrontation.

She tried to shove the knowledge to the back of her head and ignore it. She'd pretend she hadn't seen the receipts.

The freedom from having to discuss difficult subjects with Junior, that freedom she'd once happily prattled about, had become an obstacle.

13

NEEMA, 1994

J unior rose through the ranks in his company quickly. His good education, hard work, and smooth personality helped. Neema could see why he was frequently selected to make trips abroad, to help the company grow, but she didn't like it.

"Do you really have to be away so much?" she grumbled.

"Aww, it's not that much," Junior protested. "I don't travel half as much of some of the guys."

When he was home, they didn't go out with friends as much as they had during the early years of their marriage. Junior seemed distracted, and he'd quit asking about starting a family. Neema was both relieved and worried. Her biggest worry was his lack of interest in sex. Did he have another woman somewhere?

She needed to unburden herself but, with the friends she'd made since marrying, conversations stayed on the surface. Talking to Katharine about the problem would feel awkward — Katharine had been Junior's friend before she was Neema's. Nonetheless, one night when Junior was away, Neema called her. Music and many voices in the background, the unmistakable sounds of a party, made it difficult to talk.

Over the general din, she could make out a male voice she was shocked to recognize.

"Katharine," Neema asked slowly, "what's going on over there? Is that Junior?"

Katharine didn't answer right away, then said in a rush, "Oh, it's just a group from work who're having dinner here tonight."

Neema heard a child's cry.

"Sorry, I've got to go," said Katharine. "Let's talk tomorrow." She hung up before Neema could say anything else. Frowning, Neema put the receiver down, sure that Katharine was hiding something. She couldn't shake the belief that she'd heard Junior. Confusion and anxiety battled in her head as she lay alone in her bed.

A few nights later, Neema and Katharine met for drinks at a new foreign hotel in town, amid bright colored lights and the sounds of a steel drum band. Katharine surprised her by starting off the conversation boldly. "How're things with Junior?"

"Well, honestly, I'm worried about Junior," Neema began. But Katharine's eagerness as she leaned in to catch every word felt unsavory. She faltered. "Well . . . I'm afraid he might have another woman."

Katharine looked her in the eye, looked away, and took in a deep breath. She looked back at Neema and spoke softly. "You know he wants children, Neema. How long are you going to wait before you tell him the truth?"

Neema sucked in her breath. "Can't you understand my side of it at all? You know how hard this problem's been for me."

"Sure, but what about *his* side?" Katharine shot back. "Why didn't you ever tell him the truth? You've known since before you married him." She shook her head.

Neema's nostrils flared. "But Katharine, *you* were the one

who agreed with me that I shouldn't tell him. Before we even decided to marry! And now you're criticizing *me*."

Katharine leaned back and crossed her arms. "That was back then. And it was years ago. Maybe I was wrong. And, Neema, you don't make it easy to disagree when you decide something."

Hot tears filled Neema's eyes as she stared at her old friend. "You have no idea how tough my life has been. You're just like everyone else who doesn't get how unfair things are for me."

"You've had a lot of advantages in life, Neema, but not everything's within your control."

Anger came to Neema's rescue. She sat up straight and narrowed her eyes at Katharine. "I guess I wouldn't expect you to understand how I feel. You come from a different sort of family. But I thought you were a better friend than this." She sneered and rose from the table. "Maybe I'll see you around." She turned on her heel and left the restaurant.

Only later did it hit her — she hadn't had a chance to ask why it sounded like Junior had been at Katharine's flat a few evenings before.

For a while, in spite of her unhappiness at home, Neema's work provided a reprieve. At least it kept her occupied. After a year at the teaching hospital, she'd admitted to herself how much she disliked being responsible for sick people. The fastest way to work her way up in the system was not as a doctor in a clinic. She applied for an administrative post and transferred to the pharmaceutical department in the Ministry of Health. Her unit was responsible for determining which drugs would be on the national formulary, purchasing these, and distributing them to hospitals across the country, from where they were sent out to small health centers. After a year she was promoted to deputy director of the department, with half a dozen people directly under her. Surely it was just a matter of time until she'd move up to become the director.

"I'll expect your reports to be submitted on time," she announced to the staff soon after she took the position of deputy director. "And if you need to talk to me about anything, make an appointment through our department secretary. Don't make any changes to existing procedures without consulting me first."

She settled into her office with a sense of satisfaction. She was off on the right foot. This position could grow into one with status. She liked the back door to her office, an incidental result of a renovation. It allowed her to come and go unnoticed by the staff. All in all, the job would be a great relief from the frustrations she'd experienced in the clinic.

She liked being the boss, too — or almost the boss. In theory she should report to the director, but as far as she could tell, he was seldom in the office. He hadn't given her any particular instructions or official training, but she was confident that she knew what to do.

Work helped to keep her mind off the problems at home, although the job brought its irritations. Consultants from abroad were forcing government institutions to shrink, writing reports criticizing personnel management — primarily the lack of accountability. Neema, along with others in the government, resented the advice of these "experts." Foreigners who didn't know Tanzania were dictating management policies! But to ignore their suggestions was to risk the loss of much needed foreign-aid infusions into the government.

Neema churned with irritation one afternoon as she read the latest edict resulting from consultants from abroad. A new freeze on hiring was going into place. How annoying! She'd hoped to replace a secretary who'd recently left her department and now she was going to have to get along without anyone in the position. She put the edict aside with a grimace and continued skimming through the pile of papers on her desk. She picked up a memo written by her immediate subordinate to the rest of the staff, on which she'd been copied. *Please note: Effective immediately, the weekly meeting to review costings will be moved from 8:30 to 8:45. This is due to traffic and the problems staff have getting here on time. —William Shangali.*

The memo was dated a month earlier and Neema guessed she'd overlooked it then. The meeting was not one she usually attended; nonetheless, a spark of indignation flashed and caught fire in her chest. She'd distinctly told the staff not to make changes in department procedures without consulting her.

Without any thought, she stood up and strode out into the main office where eight of her staff were at their desks, chatting with each other or bent over work.

"Mr. Shangali, will you please explain the meaning of this?" Neema asked sharply, thrusting the memo at him. He looked up at her with surprise and took the paper.

"Well, we changed the time of the meeting for the reason given," he said. He faltered as she continued to stare at him wordlessly. "Uh. It's worked out well. We waste less time at the meeting now that we're all there at the beginning," he said.

Neema narrowed her eyes. "That may be. But don't you remember what I told you when I first arrived here? I said no changes were to be made in procedures without asking me first."

Conversations in the room stopped and everyone watched silently. Mr. Shangali looked down at his desktop. Neema, in a severe gray suit, with her hair braided around her head like a helmet, looked like a military officer towering above the staff. One by one, they averted their eyes and looked down at their desktops or the floor until the whole room sat with hanging heads.

"You've overstepped your authority, Mr. Shangali. Don't do it again," said Neema through clenched teeth. She turned on her heel and walked back into her office. She shut her door firmly, but she heard someone let out a low whistle before chatter erupted on the other side of the door.

She sat down at her desk, face burning and hands shaking. How dare that man defy her orders! What about respect for her authority? How hard could it be to follow simple directions?

She stayed rigid with anger for a quarter of an hour. But her fury ebbed, and the shame that came with losing one's temper publicly began to creep over her.

She feared she'd lost face. She slumped and put her head down on her desk, trying to slow her breathing.

It was thirty minutes before she calmed her thoughts. It gradually came to her that she had something to do. Her mother was going to be in Dar that evening and they'd agreed to meet for dinner. She stood up slowly, cleared a few things off the desk, and left through the back door, relieved that she didn't have to see any of the staff as she went out.

Imani listened to Neema complain about William Shangali over dinner.

"Well, Neema, it doesn't sound like it was such a terrible thing he did," she said. She laid her knife and fork on the table and put her hands in her lap. She looked at Neema with a furrowed brow. "What's wrong with changing the time of a meeting by a few minutes?"

Neema frowned. "What's wrong is that I'm in charge in the office and I told staff not to make changes without talking to me first. Can't you see that it's important to establish who's in charge there?"

Imani looked at her silently for a while before she spoke.

Then she took up her utensils. "Yes, I understand that idea, but it's also important to try to help people who work for you to grow in their responsibilities — to give them some power. They don't have to be threats to you. They can be very helpful if you support them."

Neema's throat tightened. This wasn't what she wanted to hear. She tried again to make her mother understand. "I think I need to establish discipline in there. You can't imagine how lax they can be."

Imani gazed at her daughter and sighed. She changed the conversation to talk about unimportant issues with the house in Bagamoyo and they finished their dinner.

Neema went to bed alone that night since Junior was away again. She struggled to fall asleep as her mother's words replayed themselves in her head. She was positively not going to give William Shangali more power in the office. He probably *would* try to take her job if he had the chance.

But, alone with her thoughts, she admitted that she didn't feel any better after she'd disciplined him. She lay rigid for a long time, self-justifications and guilt chasing each other through her mind. At least she felt some control over the staff in her office. She couldn't say the same about her life at home with Junior.

On the Saturday afternoon of a week during which he'd said he had to be away for work in Dubai, Neema decided to go to a couple of shops she rarely visited, on the other side of town. She walked out of one with a new dress in a bag — and then she nearly dropped it.

Junior was standing under a large tree across the street.

She almost missed him, because there were several people in the little green square where he stood and he wore a shirt she'd never seen. He was laughing and feeding ice cream to a little boy old enough to run and jump around. A woman, whom she couldn't see well, sat nearby, watching and encouraging them.

Neema's limbs froze for an instant as her jaw dropped. How could he be there when he was in Dubai? She watched for a minute as her confusion turned to shock and rage. She could — no, she *should* — cross the street and confirm what she was seeing.

But the only explanation was mortifying. She wouldn't subject herself to that kind of humiliation.

She staggered back into a doorway and watched until Junior and the woman walked away in the sunshine, with the child between them. It was just what she'd feared — Junior had another woman. But what she hadn't counted on, and what nearly brought her to her knees with anguish, was the child.

The confrontation occurred when Junior came home a few days later, supposedly from Dubai. He didn't try to deny any of it. He was sorry, he said, but he was in love with someone else and had been for a long time — he just hadn't realized it. The child was his three-year-old son and he wanted to marry the mother, Marvice.

Marvice. That was a blow Neema hadn't even considered. Junior had never let go of her.

"I'm not going to agree to a divorce, Junior," she informed him icily, eyes flashing and fists on her hips. On this she was firm. They'd been married as Christians, and by Tanzanian law he could not take a second wife so long as he and Neema were married. She was not going to agree to the divorce that would allow him to marry someone else. And there was more: "I want you to move out of this flat immediately. I expect you to leave everything here except your own clothes."

Junior set his jaw and never wavered. "Alright, Neema, if that's the way you want it to be." He walked into the bedroom and started throwing things into a bag while Neema sat stiffly on the couch and stared at the wall.

Twenty minutes later, he emerged and went straight to the front door. Turning before leaving, he had a final comment. "You'll need to consider whether you can afford to stay here. You're going to be supporting yourself from now on. No court will make me pay you anything when you haven't given me any children."

14

NEEMA, 1995

Neema hadn't shared the details of her marital problems with her mother. She'd needed to tell someone, to relieve the simmering anger that threatened to boil over whenever she thought about what Junior had done to her. But every time she'd considered confiding in her mother, she remembered the uncomfortable questions Imani asked when she first met Junior. Now, with the final split, she knew she had to talk to her. She dawdled for almost two months after Junior left before she made the trip to Bagamoyo to deliver the news.

"Neema, welcome home," Imani greeted her, rising from the veranda as Neema walked up the path to the front of the house. The old swing Neema knew from childhood still hung there and she sank down on one of its cushions, comforted by the faded but still recognizable floral pattern and the familiar squeak as the swing rocked in the ocean breeze.

"Ahh, Mama. It's a relief to be out of Dar," said Neema. They sat in silence for a while.

"Tell me about your work," suggested Imani. "Is it going better now? Are you enjoying it?"

"Oh, Mama, I guess it's okay," said Neema with a shrug,

grateful her mother didn't ask specifically about William Shangali. She didn't want to think about that outburst. "I have to put up with the usual office problems. People are late with reports. Staff bicker and don't work hard. They complain about everything — and especially their salaries."

She warmed to the topic. "It's true that Ministry of Health salaries are too low — including mine! The only way to get enough to live decently is to go to as many meetings and trainings as possible — the per diems for going to those are pretty good. But the meetings . . . so dull! Last week I went to another one about improving the quality of the patients' experience at the hospital pharmacies." She yawned and rolled her eyes. "All this talk about serving the patient! How about those of us who run the system?"

Her mother didn't respond.

Juma, the servant who used to give Neema biscuits, stepped out onto the veranda with glasses of ice and soft drinks. "Welcome home, Miss Neema," he said, handing her a cold glass. "Still Fanta for you I guess?"

"Thank you, Juma." Neema took the glass and asked the expected questions. "How are you?"

"*Nzuri*, Miss Neema, *nzuri sana*" — very fine.

"And the children, how are they?"

"Oh, *nzuri sana*. The children are also *nzuri sana*," Juma said, then he paused. "But my wife, Dorothe, is only *nzuri kidogo*." Neema understood that an admission that Dorothe was only a little bit fine meant that things were not good at all. She was obliged to ask:

"What's the problem, Juma?"

"Her stomach is paining all the time now," said the old man as he poured soft drinks over ice for both women.

"I'm sorry. Did you take her to hospital?"

"I took her there last month. But we waited for many hours, and she felt worse and worse." Juma wiped up the condensation under Imani's glass. "We finally managed to see one of the doctors and got some tablets, but they haven't helped."

"Well, maybe Neema can take a look at her while she's here," said Imani, picking up her glass. Juma's face barely moved into a wan smile.

"Well . . . sure. I guess I can take a look at her," Neema agreed. "Perhaps later today you can bring her up to the house." Juma nodded and slipped back inside.

Imani leaned closer to Neema and cleared her throat. "Neema, I'd like to ask about Junior." She paused, then continued hesitantly. "You haven't said much about him recently. How are things with you two?"

Neema had come to talk about this, but once her mother mentioned it, her lifelong reluctance to discuss issues of the heart rose. She didn't answer, letting a long silence develop while her mother waited. Finally, Neema swallowed and spoke.

"I guess things aren't good, Mama." Her mother's face remained composed as she waited for Neema to continue. "I think, Mama . . . well, it looks like there's another woman in his life." Her mother nodded slowly, still silent. "In fact, it looks like he has a child with this other woman. We've separated." Neema closed her eyes briefly to hold back the tears that were forming. This admission was harder than she'd imagined.

Imani's shock showed on her face, but she remained silent for several minutes as she studied her daughter. Finally, she spoke. "Ahh, Neema. I'm so sorry." She reached out and picked up her glass, cradling it in both hands, but she didn't drink. For several minutes the only sounds were the sea, the creaking swing, and the calls of gulls. Neema swallowed a few times and struggled for self-control.

Eventually, her mother sighed and spoke. "Men have to show they can have children. It's always been like this."

"Yes," said Neema quietly, "but, Mama, what about me? I

want to have a child too." Tears overflowed and ran freely down her cheeks.

"Oh yes, I understand. Of course you'd like a child. That's always been the way as well." Imani paused and nodded gently. "But we have solutions for situations like yours. You know there are children in my village whom you could support and nourish. Their parents would welcome it."

Imani took a long swallow of her drink and Neema considered her words while she mopped at her cheeks. Her mother set her glass down and continued. "You could begin by supporting a girl as she goes through primary school in the village; then, when the time comes for secondary school, she could move to Dar to live with you. Let me think." She closed her eyes while the sounds of the waves, the swing, and the ice settling in the glasses filled another long pause. Then she opened her eyes and smiled. "I think I know just the right family, Neema. The father is a cousin of one of my aunt's cousins by marriage. They have . . . umm, let's see . . . it's three children now, I think. The eldest girl is said to be very bright, and I believe she's almost five. She could be starting primary school in a year or two."

The gulls overhead screeched and wheeled around in an overcast sky for some time as Neema thought about Imani's idea. It wasn't the miracle she wished for, but it was something. A little girl's love might fill the place that was hollowing out as she grew older. Her tears gradually stopped and she began to nod her head slowly. Her mother sat quietly, sipping her soft drink and giving Neema time to think.

"Mama, I think I'd like to do this," Neema said eventually. "I'd like to do this. Yes."

"Alright. It's been too long since I was back in the village. Let's plan to go out there and meet with the parents and their girl. Her name is Esther." Imani rose and started to go into the house. "Don't forget to look at Dorothe. I saw her two weeks ago and she didn't look good at all."

~

Neema drew in a sharp breath when Dorothe lumbered into the house later. The woman had always been petite and bird-like, but now she looked enormous. She shuffled along, obviously exhausted, in a large, shapeless dress. Most alarming were the deep pockets of sallow skin under her eyes. Neema turned away to hide her shock.

"How long have her eyes been yellow like this?" Neema asked Juma.

"Oh, for months now. Since I first took her to the clinic. But it's getting worse. The doctors don't seem interested. They gave us some tablets."

"May I see those?" said Neema, holding out her hand.

Juma handed over a small folded paper packet with five tablets in it. The name of a common mild pain reliever was scribbled across the front.

"Lie down, Dorothe," said Neema, indicating the low couch in the living room.

With a groan, Dorothe reclined, and Neema had a chance to see that although her middle looked big, her arms and legs were stick thin. She started to probe her abdomen and found just what she'd feared. Dorothe's apparent weight gain was all fluid; it was possible to feel numerous masses within her abdomen. Whatever the origins of this tumor, it was now far advanced. It would kill her.

Neema felt a flash of disdain for the unknown health workers who had examined Dorothe. Her condition had progressed to an end stage, but this didn't happen overnight; there would have been signs of serious disease months ago when Juma first took her in for examination. But at this point it was too late to do anything. Neema needed to find a way to move the unfortunate couple on so they wouldn't become her problem to manage. She didn't want them to think she could help, but she also didn't want them to spend their remaining time trudging from one place to another looking for help that didn't exist — what choices did she have?

"Juma, I'm going to write a note for you to take to the big referral hospital. Go tomorrow. They may be able to give Dorothe something that will make her feel better."

Dorothe heaved herself up and, supported by Juma, shuffled slowly out of the room. Neema hoped they didn't have to go through too many more fruitless examinations before they accepted the inevitable, but she wasn't going to be the one to tell them it was hopeless. She tried to put it out of her mind and to think about the upcoming trip to Ndungu instead.

There was still no phone service in Imani's home village, so the best plan was simply to show up. Neema and her mother agreed on two weeks when they could both go. Then there were gifts to buy for relatives of Imani, who would be expecting something from the wealthy family. They'd buy gifts for Esther's more distantly related family too, who'd be surprised.

The journey, with Imani's experienced driver, was uneventful. Neema hadn't been to Ndungu in years, and youthful memories flooded her as they moved inland. The smell of wet earth from the previous night's rains filled her throat. She recognized a few landmarks from childhood and she smiled as they sped by two closely spaced baobab trees. In the season when they had no leaves, she used to imagine they looked like grumpy old men marching towards the Usambara Mountains. They traveled northwest from Bagamoyo, on tarmac to Same town, where they stayed the night in a guesthouse. The only road to Ndungu went south from Same and, although it was only a hundred kilometers or so, it was rough and rocky and took several hours to navigate. They arrived before midday and pulled the car into the central village, under the leafy boughs of a jacaranda.

Vehicles such as theirs didn't often come to Ndungu, so excitement bubbled up on their arrival. Bibi Imani's parents were no longer alive, but cousins, aunts, and uncles gathered round to welcome the visitors. A lengthy discussion ensued about where the two women could sleep. A cousin suggested the tiny guestroom at the Sisters of Charity and ran over to organize a stay there for Imani and Neema. At least it would have running water. Plus, the Sisters had a small generator they ran for a few hours at night. Women bustled around to start planning festive meals for the guests.

Neema recalled her trips to the village as a child with pleasure, but, while the village hadn't changed, she had. In Dar, she got to see different people at work each day, take advantage of shops, and enjoy radio or video for amusement at night. In comparison, village life was painfully slow and dull. For long hours she walked around with her mother, greeting relatives with whom blood and marriage connections were distant and tenuous. But she didn't complain while her mother held important conversations with older people, slowly putting out feelers and laying the groundwork that would make a success of their plans for adoption.

At mid-morning, on the third day in the village, they went to Esther's parents, who by then had heard from several people about Neema's interest in supporting a young girl's schooling.

Outside the hut, Imani's call to announce their presence — "*Hodi! Hodi!*" — brought Esther's mother to the entryway. She squinted at Imani for only a moment before crying, "Oh, *Bibi* Imani! *Karibu, Karibu sana.* You're so welcome!" Her husband appeared a few minutes later, brought out stools, and set them in the shade of a mango tree.

"Please, sit and tell us all your news, *Bibi* Imani. And this must be your daughter — Dr. Neema. We're so honored to have you here. Esther! Esther!" he called. "Come and meet our visitors."

"Well, not really visitors," laughed Imani. "You know we are relatives."

"Oh yes. Let my wife get us tea and we can speak. Now where is that girl?" said Esther's father, just as a lively little girl skipped around the corner. She stopped abruptly, suddenly shy in front of guests.

"Esther, greet your *Bibi* Imani and Auntie Neema," commanded her father. The girl, in a thin and ragged little dress, stepped forward with her hand out as she bent her dusty legs in a small curtsy. "*Shikamoo*, Bibi. *Shikamoo*, Auntie." Neema and Imani exchanged satisfied smiles at the little girl's nice manners.

Esther's mother reappeared with tea. "Esther, run to Hassan's *duka* and get some biscuits," she said, giving the girl a folded bill.

Esther returned five minutes later with a small packet of biscuits, which her mother arranged on a plate. The adults sipped sugary tea from cracked but clean cups while they held a long discussion and tried to sort out the distant blood relationship everyone was sure existed between *Bibi* Imani and Esther's father. They finally agreed, with laughter, that they should all call themselves cousins one way or another.

Meanwhile, Esther played nearby with her two-year-old brother, creeping closer and closer to the visitors. Neither took a biscuit until Imani offered them, and then both smiled broadly. Neema brought out small gifts for the parents and children.

"*Asante sana*, Auntie," said Esther, admiring the colored ribbons and giving Neema a curtsy of thanks.

The next day, to Esther's parents' delight, Imani and Neema broached the idea of supporting the girl's schooling. After daily visits over the next week, Esther was running to greet Neema with her arms wide open when she appeared at the house.

"Auntie! Auntie Neema!" she yelled as Neema and Imani came to the door. Neema thrilled with pleasure when the girl threw her arms around her in a hug. The immediate future was bright. No one spoke of the idea that Esther might go to live with Neema in Dar at some future time, but it would not have seemed remarkable either. Neema and Imani left additional presents for Esther and her parents, as well as for the younger brother and the new baby they'd learned Esther's mother was expecting.

Neema returned to Dar feeling better than she had in months. The thought of the sweet four-year-old and the connection that would grow with her was even more powerful and soothing than she'd expected. Her marriage had failed, but anticipation of the little girl's love for her shined ahead like a candle in the dark. Things weren't so bad, and maybe they'd get better with time.

15

JOY, 1997

J oy knew Tanzanian law gave every woman three months off with pay when she had a baby — and her job would be waiting for her when she came back. At least she knew it was supposed to work like that. For workers like her, it didn't always happen that way, but she was counting on it. She lumbered through her duties at the church, right up until a few days before she expected to deliver.

"Good luck, Joy," said the minister as she left, taking her hand in his. "God will be with you."

"Thank you. I'll be back to work in three months," Joy answered confidently.

Later that afternoon, she and Emma crowded into a *dalla dalla* to go to her mother and father in the village for the birth, while Amira went home for a holiday.

Joy pitched in to help her mother with washing and cooking until her waters broke four days later on a Wednesday morning. They called the same birth attendant who'd helped Joy the first time. "Ahh. Wonderful! You've got a boy now," beamed the woman a few hours later, as she placed the baby on Joy's chest.

On Sunday, Daniel came out for the day to celebrate. They

named their son Elijah, after Daniel's father. The excitement around the house was a little less than the first time — Joy's sister already had two children of her own — but it was still a pleasure to be surrounded by the warmth of the large family. Emma, almost three years old, helped by fetching things and watching her younger cousins. Joy and Emma went back home to be with Daniel when Elijah was two weeks old.

When Elijah reached one month, Joy tied him on her back with a clean *kanga*, and she and Daniel walked to the church to show him off and have him baptized. Joy was proud of her little son and the congregants were welcoming — smiling, oohing, and aahing. The minister was friendly too, although he might have looked a little uncomfortable after the baptism when Joy reminded him that she'd be back for her church cleaning job when her leave was up.

She reminded him again two months later at the Wednesday prayer meeting. "I'll be coming back to work next week," she said politely, but he seemed not to hear her as he turned his head to talk to someone else. Joy glanced at Daniel. "I think he's just too busy to talk right now," she said. But she bit her lip and frowned.

Amira returned to the small room where the family still lived. She slept on her little pallet in the corner at night and happily took care of both Emma and Elijah. It cost very little to feed Amira and, as long as both Daniel and Joy were bringing in money, the household — crowded as it was — would function.

Joy walked confidently to the church the Monday after the prayer meeting, prepared to start work again. The church was one of the finer buildings in the neighborhood, constructed over several years as the money became available. It was made of concrete blocks, consisted of several rooms, and had a smoothly finished concrete floor, albeit with a large crack down the middle.

Her spirits sank straightaway when she found the minister's cousin, Ruth, in the anteroom to the chapel. She was setting things in order on the little table that served as the minister's desk in the corner. Joy couldn't help admiring the way the woman's hair was fixed in stylish twists held back with a wide band that matched her tightly fitted dress. The red of her lipstick was the same shade as the flowers in the dress, and her shiny blue high heels clicked authoritatively on the floor as she stepped towards Joy.

"*Shikamoo*," said Joy, with a slight curtsy. "Sorry to disturb you," she added. "I've come back to work."

"Oh?" said Ruth slowly, raising her eyebrows higher than Joy would have imagined possible. "Well, Reverend Emmanuel isn't here now." She looked more closely at Joy. "Aren't you the one who worked here before? Who had the little girl?"

"Yes, that's right," said Joy with a nod, dismayed that Ruth remembered the encounter. "The Reverend knows I'm coming and I don't mind waiting to see him."

Ruth looked skeptical and gave a wave of her hand. "Well, I'm sorry there's no chair for you, but you can wait on the bench outside the door."

The cool reception left Joy unnerved. What was going on? Her head drooped as she took a seat on the small bench outside. A rock, propped under one broken leg, shifted as she sat down and she had to jerk sideways to keep from falling over.

After a half hour, a girl, who Joy imagined was younger than she was, walked up to the door and passed through into the anteroom of the building. Joy heard the murmur of voices as the girl spoke with Ruth, but she couldn't make out their words. Another half hour passed as Joy waited with growing unease. Ruth went in and out of the door several times but ignored her. At length, Joy screwed up her courage and, when Ruth appeared again, she spoke.

"Sorry to disturb you, but can I start work now?" she

asked in the nicest voice she could muster. Ruth sighed and gave her a long look.

"Maybe you should come again tomorrow," she said with an impatient shake of her head. She turned her back and started across the road, then called back over her shoulder, "Reverend Emmanuel will be back then."

Joy slowly stood up, turned, and looked back through the anteroom and into the chapel. The girl was using the old broom with which Joy was so familiar to sweep the cracked floor where grime always collected. An equally familiar cleaning rag was tucked into her waist. She glanced out at Joy and hissed, "This job is mine now. Aunt Ruth gave it to *me*."

Joy, the blood draining from her face, turned away. There was absolutely nothing else she could do. She dragged her feet on the half-hour walk back to the little mud-brick room, trying to imagine what would happen to her family. How could the minister be guilty of this treachery? But then, it did fit with his odd behavior when she'd seen him the last time.

At the house, Amira was cooking *ugali* over coals in the yard with Elijah tied to her back and Emma underfoot. A frown creased her face as Joy entered the yard. Joy looked at the three people gathered there who depended on her and her heart sank even lower. She hadn't felt so helpless since she was a girl hearing that she had to quit school.

But she shook herself. At the moment, she needed to protect others from the bad news weighing her down. This, at least, she could do. She straightened her shoulders.

"I'm not starting back to work just yet," she said to Amira. "I'll work here today and we can catch up on clothes washing." Amira's frown eased and Joy managed a smile.

That evening was a solemn one. Daniel and Joy, both aware that Amira and Emma would hear everything they said, tried to keep their feelings in check. But Daniel went around all evening with his jaw set and Joy's few words came out in a flat monotone.

Only when Amira and the children had gone to sleep did Joy allow the tears to slip down her face. She took the small bundle wrapped in a dirty cloth from the hole in the wall, and she and Daniel counted their money. Joy was better with figures, so she worked it out. "I can buy five or six kilograms of maize flour with this . . . enough for a week or two if we're careful," she calculated. "We have a little oil left, too," she added when Daniel's face started to fall. "I'll start looking for work tomorrow. Maybe I can get a job as a cook. And we'll have whatever you can make doing odd jobs."

Thinking about taking some action made her feel a bit better, and eventually she and Daniel fell asleep.

A job as a cook! Wouldn't that be nice? Joy had once helped out as a cook for ten days in the kitchen of a visiting pastor for the church. The man and his family were Europeans and she'd been intrigued to see how things were done in their kitchen. At first the wife seemed unhappy that Joy was unfamiliar with their ways, but then, as Joy showed how quickly she could learn, the woman's attitude improved. She taught Joy to cook a few of the unfamiliar things they ate, like pasta and casseroles that went into an oven. Then she showed her a cookbook. Joy was proud to realize she could read enough to follow the cooking instructions, once she was introduced to measuring cups and spoons. These were just the fractions she'd loved as a schoolgirl!

"You mean you know how to divide in half or thirds?" asked the woman with surprise, and Joy nodded proudly. The days passed quickly and, even though she knew the job was temporary, she was disappointed when the visitors left the church and she had to go back to cleaning.

She thought back on that cook's job as she rose early the next day to start looking for work, going house to house and knocking on gates. She let her imagination run free and she wondered about the idea of working for *wazungu*. It would have both good and bad aspects.

Wazungu — white people from abroad — had a reputation for treating people who worked in their houses more leniently than local employers did. This was especially true for those who hadn't been in Africa long and weren't used to hiring people to work in the house. They often paid higher wages than Tanzanians and they paid them on time. On the other hand, many of them had unrealistic expectations and just didn't know how to talk to their house workers, since they didn't seem to have any where they came from. This was one of many puzzling things about them. Why would people with so much money wash their own clothes and clean their own houses? They also had odd habits and ideas about time, like getting upset if you came in a few minutes late. Working in their houses meant having to use English and serving as a translator for the ones who didn't know Swahili. Misunderstandings could arise. And sometimes they seemed so rude! Important greetings were often ignored as they rushed about their business.

As the afternoon lengthened, Joy's spirits flagged and she felt more keenly the urgency of getting any job at all that would bring in money. Recently someone in town had started a little training school for cooks and housekeepers, especially those who wanted to work for *wazungu*. But where was a person supposed to get the money to attend a school like that and get the certificate at the end unless she already had a good job?

Joy and her friend Fortunate had discussed this problem months before when they went together to the big open-air market in town. Among the narrow aisles overflowing with tomatoes, carrots, cabbage, yams, and beans, a thin boy was unloading a pile of mangoes to help his father sell from a wooden stand. As Joy and Fortunate talked about employment problems, he watched them.

"Mama," he hissed, to get their attention when his father's back was turned. "Mama, I can help." They looked at him.

"Little boy, you should mind your own business," drawled Fortunate with a laugh and a toss of her head.

But he persisted, saying, "I can get you a good certificate." Joy looked at him more closely. Perhaps he was not so young as his thin face made him look. "I can get you a certificate to help get any job," he repeated. "You need a certificate?" He glanced over to where his father was still busy with a customer, then he tipped his head back and used his chin to motion the women to move down the aisle towards the hanging sides of fly-specked beef. Joy and Fortunate looked at each other, shrugged, and moved off in the direction he indicated.

Standing in front of him, Joy saw that he was indeed older than he looked — maybe fourteen years. He was bold, too, once he had their attention. "I can get you a certificate for anything," he boasted. "Primary school, O-levels, A-levels, even a secretary course." As they stood there looking at him without saying anything, he pulled a paper out of his pocket. "Look," he said, "even Microsoft Excel." Joy took the certificate. It looked impressively official, bordered by a black line embellished with little swirls and curlicues. In clear, even type it read *This certifis that* _____ *has passed the course in MICROSOFT EXXCEL,* with spaces for a name and a date to be inserted.

Apparently encouraged by their scrutiny of the paper, he continued. "I can do it in color on special paper for a little more." Then, perhaps as an acknowledgment of their financial savvy, he added, "No more than the price of a few kilos of maize flour." Adding more flattery, he continued. "You must want . . . um . . . top secretary course?"

Fortunate did indeed look very interested. "You know the cook training school?" she asked him.

"Of course," he said with an arrogant nod.

"Can you do one for that?"

"Of course! Just write your name here for me." He handed her a grubby slip of paper and a pencil stub. "Give me the money and I'll meet you here tomorrow same time with the certificate."

Fortunate wrote out her name in block capitals. "And be sure you spell it right," she admonished, showing him who was in charge of the deal. But the pecking order was already established. The boy gave Fortunate a smirk.

"Give me the money first," he demanded boldly.

Fortunate's eyes widened. This was too much, and she set her jaw. "No," she said firmly, "I'm not stupid. No money until I see the certificate."

"Bah!" spat out the man-boy. "You're not serious." He turned to go. "I'll be here when you change your mind." With that, he strutted back to his father's stall.

Fortunate was put out. "That boy thinks he is a *bwana kubwa*," she said bitterly to Joy. "A big man, too big for his britches. He'll get into trouble."

Joy, though amused at the interaction, was also uneasy. She didn't like this scheme. She didn't say it to Fortunate, but she was bothered by what her friend wanted to do. It may have been just a piece of paper, but it was also a lie. And besides, what good was the paper if Fortunate got a job with it and didn't know how to cook? Or be a secretary? It twisted the idea of education. She remembered her father's words: *Mpanda hila huvuna ufukara.* Plant deceit and harvest poverty. She wasn't tempted to buy a fake certificate.

She thought about that market experience as she trudged home in the dusk. Without good news to report, the evening at home was quiet. The anxiety gnawing at her made no sound.

16

JOY, 1998

On the day she used the last of their money to buy maize flour, Joy went down to the river to wash the family's clothes. Listening to the usual gossip of the women, she heard something interesting. "Sure, that big house down on Uhuru Road — the one across from the tall termite hill — finally, it has a family in it," said a woman.

Joy knew the place. The house was owned by a wealthy Indian merchant, but it had stood empty for the past six months. It was rumored that no one would take it because the rent was too high. Joy listened closely as the woman continued. "The new tenants are *wazungu*, of course," she said with a satisfied grin, to show she knew what was going on about town.

"Now Yussuf and Mwaipopo will have to do something instead of lying around drunk all day and night," offered a second woman with a laugh.

"Sure, they've been lucky enough to stay on as guards for months with an empty house because the landlord's afraid of thieves breaking in," said the first woman.

"Ha!" cackled the second woman, "as if Yussuf or

Mwaipopo would stop a thief!" The women all broke into laughter.

Joy cocked her head and stopped her scrubbing for a second. This new *wazungu* family could be a chance for her. She'd been turned down at all the houses and hotels where she'd applied the previous week. It was getting harder to pretend to be positive. She'd already cut her own food down to half and she couldn't stand to think of Emma crying in hunger. The girl was getting bigger every day, and so was her appetite.

She quickly wrung out the clothes, murmured something to excuse herself, and hurried home to take off her soiled *kanga*, glad she'd been wearing it to protect her dress. She smoothed her hair into a neat bun and slipped her feet into some plastic flats. Then she walked fast down the rutted road to the big house, rushing past a young Maasai boy wrapped in a blue-and-red-checked *shuka* who was trying to herd a half dozen skeletal cows through the neighborhood.

She knocked at the big, solid metal gate when she reached the house. "*Shikamoo*," she said with a curtsy to the old man who unlocked and opened a small entryway cut into the larger gate. She'd been taught to greet all elders with a "*shikamoo*," no matter what their station. Although it was unlikely that this guard, who looked like he'd been drinking, would have any influence in the house, she couldn't be sure. They went through the greetings as Joy tried to peer into the compound, past the driveway and into the front garden.

"Does this place have a cook yet? Or a housekeeper?" she asked the guard in the most positive voice she could manage.

"Yes. There's a girl here now — hired a few days ago to work in the kitchen."

Joy let out a discouraged sigh — she was probably too late. But at least she could ask about any other work that might be available. The guard was skeptical.

"Well, can I at least knock on the door and talk to the lady of the house?" persisted Joy. "Maybe she'd speak to me."

And maybe Joy's "*shikamoo*" paid off, because the guard let her enter the compound. "*Hajui Swahili,*" he warned her unnecessarily — she hadn't expected the woman to know Swahili! She passed through the small entryway, walked up the gravel drive, and knocked as firmly as she dared on the front door.

A small woman with short brown hair and spectacles, slight, as many *wazungu* women were, opened the door. Joy wondered briefly why these women were so often thin when they must have plenty to eat. It made them look ill. The woman said nothing but looked expectantly at Joy.

"Hello. Good morning, Madam. How are you?" asked Joy, with a bow. "Excuse me for disturbing you." The woman still said nothing, still looked expectant, and didn't inquire how Joy was, which was disconcerting. But she looked pleasant enough, so Joy continued.

"I'm looking for work in the house and I wonder if you have any," she said carefully. The woman's face changed. She inclined her head a little and smiled.

"Well . . . actually . . . hmmm. What sort of work are you looking for in the house?"

Joy had to listen closely, as the woman had a funny accent. She swallowed, curled her fingers lightly into fists at her sides, and spoke carefully. "I have cooked for Europeans. And I can clean and wash and iron, take care of clothes." The woman raised her eyebrows just a fraction and pursed her lips slightly as if thinking. Then she nodded.

"Please come in and let's talk." She stood back and waved Joy through the door.

The living room was huge, with two large couches and several comfortable armchairs with cushions. A number of small tables were scattered around and Joy wondered how many people lived here. Up a few steps and through a large archway, Joy saw a dining room with a table and eight chairs. A hallway led out of the dining area and she could glimpse rooms coming off both sides of the hall. She expected they'd go to the kitchen to talk and she glanced around surreptitiously, wondering where it was.

But the woman indicated that Joy should sit down in one of the living room chairs, and then she sat down opposite her. She smiled again when they were settled. She sat back comfortably in her own chair while Joy perched on the edge of hers with her hands folded neatly in her lap.

"Can you tell me your name," the woman asked in a kind voice, "and more about the work you're looking for?"

"I am Joy," she answered in a low, polite voice, bowing her head slightly. "I would like to be a cook and housekeeper."

The woman cocked her head but kept looking straight at Joy. She nodded again. "I see," she said. "Can you tell me about your experience?"

Joy explained that she'd worked in the kitchen of the visiting pastor, without mentioning that it was only for two weeks. She told the woman she'd worked at the church as a cleaner, but after the recent birth of her second child, someone else had taken the job.

"Where are your children now," asked the woman, "and how old are they?"

"They stay with a girl from my village who lives with my family," Joy explained. "Not far from here. The firstborn is three years and the baby was born three months ago."

The woman nodded, then asked what dishes Joy could cook.

"Umm, chicken and chips or roasted chicken with vegetables. Beef stew," started Joy uncertainly. "Pasta. And curries. Salads." She faltered, and the lady tried to help her.

"Rice and beans?" she prompted, to which Joy nodded vigorously. "And can you follow recipes from a book?" the woman asked.

"Oh yes," said Joy more assuredly. "I'm sure if you have it written down, I can make it." This seemed to please the woman.

She explained to Joy that she and her husband were Americans.

Ahh, *that* explained the funny accent, thought Joy, pleased with herself for picking this up. She struggled through the woman's swallowed vowels to learn that she and her husband were both doctors, teaching at the medical school and hospital, they had two young sons, and they'd lived in different countries of Africa before coming to Tanzania. Then the woman told her about the salary, which was a great relief to Joy. She'd dreaded asking.

"We'd pay once a month, not weekly. We're busy and we don't want to have to deal with cash for the staff every week." Joy nodded her understanding. "And we don't give any loans to staff, so please don't ask."

It was a better salary than Joy had ever made. She instantly decided to wait until she actually started work to ask Madam whether she could possibly make an exception just once and give her an advance after the first week. Joy couldn't imagine how it could be too much trouble to deal with money in any circumstances when one had plenty of it, but that was part of the strangeness of *wazungu*. As far as getting paid monthly rather than weekly, she and Daniel could get used to that.

"I'd like you to start around eight each morning," the woman continued. "We come home for lunch and would like you to have that ready for us." She went on, "You'd be responsible for all the cooking, cleaning the house, and for washing and ironing our clothes. Oh, and we have a washing machine."

A washing machine was an unexpected treat, but otherwise the description of the work was much as Joy expected. As Joy nodded, the woman kept talking. "I don't need you to sit around here. Once you are finished with everything each day you can go home."

That surprised Joy. In the hotel laundry the staff had always tried to look busy all the time, even if there was nothing to do. And Joy never left the church before the official quitting time, even if it meant she sometimes pushed a broom around a clean floor for what seemed like hours. Joy thought pleasantly about how she might use extra time at home.

Then the woman spoke again. "I hired a girl a week ago on a trial basis," she said. "I told her it would be a two-week trial, but I am not happy with her." She paused and Joy wondered why she was not happy, but she was not going to ask a bold question that was not her business. "I'd like to let her go and have you start right away."

Joy's concern on hearing this must have showed on her face because the woman added hastily, "Of course I'd pay her for the second week." Joy hesitated, said nothing for several seconds, and glanced sideways. "Is there a problem with this?" asked the woman, looking puzzled but not unkind.

Joy's heart was pounding. This job was more than what she'd hoped for. But there *was* a problem that the woman apparently didn't understand. Joy licked her lips and spoke reluctantly. "I don't want her to think I took her job, Madam. This is a small town and she might try to cause trouble for me or my family. It's better if she finishes her two weeks and I come again after she's gone."

"Well . . ." said the woman slowly. She looked displeased with this proposal and Joy wondered if she'd made a mistake. There was a long silence as the woman frowned and bit the inside of her cheek, keeping her gaze on Joy. "Alright," she finally said. "What if you come here on Monday morning one week from now to start? We'll try the arrangement with you for two weeks and see how it goes." Joy relaxed and gave an inward sigh of relief. Now all she had to do was get her family through the next two weeks. She could do that.

17

JOY, 1998–2000

Joy was three months into her new job the first time she finished work early. The afternoon sun shone high in the sky. Would it really be okay to leave? She turned off the iron and looked at her list. Fresh linens on all the beds, mud removed from Mr. James' shoes, house clean and swept, the week's bread resting on the counter under a clean cloth, and the night's dinner on the stovetop ready to be heated.

She walked through the house and didn't see anything else to do. The oldest boy's room was a mess, but Madam insisted she should not pick up his things. "They'll never learn to take care of themselves if it's all done for them," she said with a grimace as she and Joy surveyed the clothes littering the floor of his room one day. Joy was surprised Madam felt this way, but she agreed with her. She closed the door on the mess and went home early.

Emma danced with delight to see her. Joy got out the toys, a sack filled with pieces of plastic dishes and containers. Joy had collected these odds and ends, useless for holding food but good for playing with. Emma's tongue protruded slightly as she concentrated on nesting the bowls in each other or stacking them as high as she could. Joy had been trying to teach the little girl to balance a plastic dish on her head, and they laughed for so long that she was surprised to look up and find the sun low in the sky. Daniel would soon be home for dinner.

"I like this job," Joy said to him that evening as she washed her hands carefully before sitting down next to the bowl to share a meal. Daniel often ate the evening meal before Joy and the children, but sometimes he and Joy shared the bowl. In these cases Joy took out a little bit to give the children later to be sure they'd have enough. Daniel didn't mind — he encouraged it, and it was one of the things she liked about him. He listened that evening as she talked about her work.

"They have bulbs in every socket and plenty of windows, so the house is really light inside," she said, shifting to a more comfortable position on the ground where the bowl sat. "There are three toilets and only four people live there! The couches and furniture all look new. It's nice." She paused for a moment. "And they must have over a hundred books on the shelves," she said, as she reached out and formed a small ball of *ugali* with her right hand the polite way to eat. "When Madam saw me dusting those books and looking at them, she said I could borrow one if I wanted."

Wazungu all lived in big houses, and Joy and Daniel had walked by plenty of them. Actually *being* in one every day, however, being in it alone for hours, was a new experience. At first she'd found it lonely, but she gradually became accustomed to it and learned she liked the peace and quiet. She could organize her time as she liked and no one stood over her watching everything she did.

Madam suggested that Joy could ask for help from Yussuf or Mwaipopo if needed, but of course she hadn't informed them that Joy might request help. They were often asleep out in the yard, and it took some effort, not always successful, to try to rouse them by shouting. At least she'd not noticed them drinking anymore.

She grew used to the family's dogs and lost her fear of them. Not that they were coming into the house, which, Joy noted with approval, Madam did not allow. She had been told by friends that some *wazungu* not only allowed their dogs to come inside but let them get on the furniture, which was just shocking. The dogs of this household were always outside in the garden and they barked if anyone came to the gate. This helped Joy feel more secure in the big place. She had a friend who'd been alone in the house of her *mzungu* employer when thieves came. Had it not been for the fact that her friend was beaten badly, she might have been accused of organizing the burglary herself. Such inside jobs were not uncommon, though not among Joy's friends. All household staff dreaded a break-in because the police, eager to "solve" the crime and be done with it, would often try to pin the blame on one or more of the house workers.

After Joy got her first few monthly salaries, she and Daniel moved into a better house built of concrete block, rather than mud bricks, with a tin roof that wouldn't leak no matter how hard it rained. They rented by the week, and Joy carefully kept track of the money Madam paid her each month to be sure she still had some at the end of each pay period.

The new house was really just one room with a separate closet, but it was considerably larger than the one they'd had before. And concrete blocks were nicer and cleaner than mud bricks. Two other small families each rented large single rooms in the house and a family of seven had the final two adjoining rooms. The house didn't have a toilet, but there was a proper pit latrine in the back with a door that closed with a latch. A cement pad on the side of the house served as a convenient base for a cooking fire and, best of all, a standpipe next to it meant that Joy didn't have to take a bucket down the road to buy water or fetch it from the river. The tenants agreed on a system they considered fair to pay the water bill the landlord brought each month. Electricity flowed to Joy and Daniel's room through a meter that functioned when they punched in a number from a coupon they bought every few weeks or so. Of course, they didn't use it too often and almost never had any credit left by the end of Joy's pay period.

Joy stuck a few bright pictures to the walls in her family's room, and she collected several old but still useful crates and flat boards. She arranged these to make a low table that she covered with a piece of cloth. Some of her furnishings were castoffs from Madam. Joy was often surprised by the things Madam threw away, although she'd heard of *wazungu* who threw away a lot more. She'd been nervous when Madam came in unexpectedly while she was taking some colored pictures and plastic ornaments from the trash bin, but Madam looked the other way. After that, she occasionally left things in a pile and told Joy she was welcome to take them, "if she could use them." Of course, she could use most things and, if she couldn't, she knew someone who could.

As she and Daniel finished off the bowl she slowly continued sharing her thoughts with her husband. "But some things I don't understand."

"Such as what?" asked Daniel, cocking an eyebrow.

"Well, why do they write everything down instead of just telling me? Do they think I can't remember?" Joy found a note on the table every morning listing what she needed to do for the day. Madam was often in the house when Joy arrived, not yet having left for work. She could easily have told her, but still, the note was there. Sometimes it led to confusion, like the time Mr. James had written to "make peanut butter and ham sandwiches" for lunch. It *had* seemed odd, but then she'd never eaten sandwich ham and she'd heard that some Americans ate peanut butter and jam together, so she spread the ham with peanut butter and put it on the bread to make a sandwich.

"Oh dear," said Mr. James when he picked it up at lunch. But the note was still on the table, and after reading it again he laughed, recognizing his mistake.

Madam and Mr. James seemed to write notes effortlessly and to find it a good way to communicate. She learned that they expected her to write her own notes in return. She had to admit it was handy when she left before they came home. Or when she came late because of a mother-and-child clinic visit. They showed her where there was a stash of recycled paper she could use and a good supply of pencils.

Dear Madam, her labored print read on the note she left. *Diner in oven. Plese look in frig for salad. Will come tomorow early to mak beds.* Or, *Yussuf say he want to talk to you* — and of course, this note would fill Madam with dismay. Joy and Madam had had a conversation about communication with Yussuf a few months after Joy started work.

"Joy, how would you like to supervise Yussuf and Mwaipopo?" Madam suggested brightly that day. Madam tried to avoid dealing with either of the guards. Strange that she didn't seem to enjoy being the boss. Yussuf spoke no English at all and Joy thought he had very little common sense. Mwaipopo, on the other hand, seemed bright, but he was sullen, in addition to not knowing any English or understanding Madam's limited Swahili. Madam had kept both of them on since they'd been at the house for several years, but Joy could see how much they annoyed her. Joy was required to do all the translating for Madam, and the long rambles the men produced when she seemed to expect a yes-or-no answer tried Madam's patience. She'd shift visibly from one foot to the other, waiting for the reply. Especially troublesome were the times when the two guards had petty disagreements with each other, such as about who might have failed to return the shovel to the shed, or who had broken the chain on the bicycle they'd convinced Madam to buy them to get back and forth to work.

"You understand supervision, right?" persisted Madam when Joy hesitated to agree to take it on. "It would mean that you'd be like their boss. You'd talk to them and tell them when we want something done, and they'd ask *you* when they want something instead of asking us."

Joy looked at Madam, both puzzled and curious. What difference would this "official supervisor position" make when she already had to translate everything anyway?

Madam continued. "You'd give them their salaries each month, coordinate their leave time, and work out any disagreements they have."

Joy hesitated, still feeling skeptical, and Madam, possibly misunderstanding the hesitation, persisted. "We'll increase your salary a bit to cover the extra responsibility."

Joy swallowed and bit her lip. Being the boss of two men who were both older than she would be a challenge. True, she had more education than either of them did; she could read and write. If only she'd been able to finish primary school! Surely if she had that extra education she'd have more confidence. As it was, though, she feared they'd never be satisfied to have her, younger than either of them and also a woman, sort out their problems. She wished Madam would deal with them herself. Her father used to tell her that the path to the hut of a great chief is well worn. Did Madam not understand this? She and her husband were the chiefs here. On the other hand, a salary raise would be great. More money would mean extra food for her family or new shoes for the children. In some ways, the challenge of supervising was even appealing.

Daniel understood her misgivings about supervising the two men, but he liked the idea of the extra money. "I think you should agree to do it," he said with a shrug. "Maybe I can come and help sort things out if there are problems between Yussuf and Mwaipopo." Joy nodded, although this wouldn't go over well at all with Madam, who was always polite to Daniel but didn't seem to like having extra people hanging around the property. The ways of *wazungu* were strange. The next day she agreed to supervise Yussuf and Mwaipopo.

Joy had a chance to earn her salary raise a few weeks later. *Please have guards clear away rubbish next to back fence,* she read on her note one morning. A mess of rusty tin cans, old bottles, and wires was piled up next to the back fence. Maybe there was a soft drink bottle in there, but it was unlikely; those bottles were worth more than the drink that had been inside them and the guards always took any they found to a little *duka* for the deposit. After she hung up the laundry, Joy looked out by the front gate, but Yussuf, who was supposed to be working the day shift that month, wasn't there. She walked around the house and found him lying under the big mango tree in the back garden.

"Yussuf," she called, relieved when he raised his head a bit. She hated having to shake him awake. "Yussuf, I need to talk to you." Yussuf continued to lie on his back as he met her eyes briefly. Then he insolently turned his face away. "Yussuf, Madam wants you to move that pile of rubbish next to the back fence," she said, standing over him and talking to the side of his head. He continued to gaze across the ground, into the distance. Satisfied that he'd heard her, but uncertain whether he was going to cooperate, Joy turned and walked purposefully back to the house, holding her head high in case he was watching. She thought she heard him snicker behind her as she went.

The pile was still there the next day and Madam asked about it at lunchtime. "Did you tell Yussuf to get rid of it?"

"Yes, Madam. He is going to do it," she said, not wanting to admit he'd ignored her and clenching her teeth at the thought that she'd probably have to do it herself.

"Good. And, this afternoon, can you please buy some avocados for tonight's dinner from the lady on Lema Road?"

Later that afternoon, Yussuf let Joy out the front gate. She found a new fruit stand, closer to the house than Lema Road, and made her purchase in half the time expected. She was thinking about the problem of Yussuf as she walked back to Madam's with three perfect avocados. Passing the two-meter-high termite mound across from the house and arriving at the big front gate, she was surprised to find she could push it open and enter the compound. The lock was hanging open inside on the hasp.

"Yussuf!" she called, images of a burglary rushing into her head. "Yussuf! Where are you?"

To her relief, the house was locked, with no sign of a break-in. She used her key to enter, then snatched up the spare gate key and went out to lock up the compound. She was in the back garden looking for Yussuf when she heard the clanging of someone pounding heavily on the big metal gate. She hurried around to check. Yussuf's sheepish face appeared through the little window in the gate. Her relief was replaced with a flash with anger. Every guard knew not to leave a gate open that way, even for a few minutes.

"What do you think you're doing?" she demanded with a harshness few had ever seen from her. "I just found the gate open and walked right into the front garden! Madam could sack you for this." The shamefaced Yussuf started to offer an explanation, but Joy was too angry to listen. She turned and walked into the house, closing the door forcefully behind her.

An hour later, she looked out the back window. The pile of rubbish had been removed.

～

Another strange thing about *wazungu*, in Joy's opinion, was the relationships between husbands and wives and who did what in the house. Madam seemed to assume, if she weren't around, that Joy could ask Mr. James to make decisions about dinner or the house or other domestic things that men didn't think about. And yet, Joy and Madam had shared a laugh just the week before about men's inability to select ripe fruit.

Joy had been at the clinic and Madam tried to get Yussuf to go to the end of the road and buy two avocados "for today," as those that were ripe and ready to eat immediately were known. The seller must have recognized an opportunity to unload a couple that had already turned to black mush and Yussuf brought these back. "Ugh," said Madam, tossing them out the back door to the dogs just as Joy came into the kitchen. Her sigh was good-natured and said she should have known better. She smiled ruefully and confessed her mistake to Joy.

"Men don't know nothing about these things," agreed Joy, and she and Madam shared a companionable laugh.

Nonetheless, Joy observed that Madam and her husband made a lot of household decisions together and they didn't seem to have clear roles in the house — especially when it came to planning meals and sometimes even how to cook foods. "James will show you how we like the chicken roasted," said Madam casually to Joy the first week she was there. She flitted out of the room as Joy's eyes widened with surprise. Joy was skeptical when Mr. James told her he'd show her how they liked the potatoes mashed. He seemed to know what he was doing, but she'd certainly never seen a man in the kitchen mashing potatoes before. She gradually came to accept it, however, and learned that she could equally well ask Mr. James about the dinner as she could ask Madam. This turned out to be convenient when Madam wasn't around. If she asked when both were there she occasionally witnessed some disagreements in their cooking methods, but she learned to laugh along with them about these. "We'll just see how this turns out," Madam said with a wink sometimes when Mr. James had got his way with the method.

"Yes," Joy said again to Daniel, as they used little balls of *ugali* to clean out the last bit of sauce in the bowl. "*Wazungu* have some strange ways." Then as she rose to start the washing up, she looked over at him sideways. "Maybe you'd like to clean up tonight."

He laughed, and she felt the satisfaction of having a good husband.

18

JOY, 2001

"Joy, could you go to the market for us today?" asked Madam one morning, bustling around in her usual hurry to leave for work. Joy wondered again why she was so concerned about being late, since she was the boss. It looked undignified to rush around so much. "You know what we buy, and Peter could drive you." Joy hesitated; she didn't want to make mistakes with Madam's money, and maybe be blamed if something went missing. But "the market" meant the big open-air market where farmers brought produce and hanging sides of meat to sell directly to customers, and Joy was pretty sure that Madam was already making mistakes with her money at that place — being overcharged. On the other hand, there would be advantages to doing the shopping for Madam. She might pick up a few things for her own family, too, while she was there. Prices were better than at the small corner stands where she usually had to shop. The problem with using the big market regularly for her shopping was that getting there by foot or local transport took more time than she had. As though reading her mind, Madam suggested, "You might as well do your own shopping at the same time."

Joy considered the idea for a few minutes. Not all women trusted their cooks to do the big weekly shopping, but if Madam was willing to give her the money, then this could benefit them both.

She agreed to take on the task and soon it was a weekly routine. She walked proudly through the market with her three large baskets, which grew steadily heavier as she and Peter, Madam's driver, moved down the aisles and made purchases. It was fun to laugh and banter with the market sellers when Joy had money tied up in the waist of her *kanga.* Indeed, the sellers soon learned that she had plenty of money, but Joy didn't let them take advantage of her. She enjoyed the respect she earned by having the means to bargain. She kept a list with all the totals so she could show Madam where the money went, and she meticulously separated her own purchases from those for Madam's family.

"Yes, I want you to divide the beans into two piles, one with two kilos and one with a half kilo, and I need separate receipts for each," she insisted, even if the man behind the counter acted like she was making extra trouble.

"Thanks, Joy," nodded Madam, barely glancing at the scraps of paper that served as receipts when Joy came in with baskets spilling out fruits and vegetables. "This is great, and I can use Saturday mornings now for something else."

That was a funny way to think of time, mused Joy. Was it really something to be *used*? She remembered her father laughing about some *wazungu* coming to a village and demanding to know when their meeting would start — when it was perfectly obvious that the meeting would start when everyone got there! Maybe it made some sense, though. She herself knew where the sun would be when her children started asking about food, or where it would be when everyone got to the church on Sunday morning and the preacher started. If she wanted to get home early, she should start the bread rising first thing on arrival at Madam's and only then go to the back of the house to start making beds and sweeping. And if she organized her work so that she didn't bake bread on the same days she did the laundry, she could wash the sheets first thing and have them dry and folded by mid-afternoon — assuming it wasn't raining — and then she could go home early. Madam was happy to let Joy organize household duties her own way. Having control over when she did tasks was satisfying. But she still didn't think of time as something to be used.

After two years at Madam's, when Joy had shown she could do the family's marketing and got used to the family's ways, Madam suggested that she take on another job she and her husband didn't enjoy — the weekly trip to the shop in town for items that were processed or imported, such as pasta, cheese, or biscuits. This involved considerably more money and often some decision-making, since stock at the shop was irregular and couldn't be relied on. Joy never bought at this shop for herself and wasn't used to what the items should cost.

"But, Joy," Madam said reasonably, "you cook for us with these foods and you'll learn about the prices." It was true — Joy used them all the time in Madam's kitchen.

On the first day that Joy was to take on this new duty, she appeared for work in one of her nicest dresses with a matching scarf neatly wound around her hair. "Wow," said Madam with surprise, "you're dressed up today."

"It's today you want me to go to Deepak's shop, right?" asked Joy, wondering, not for the first time, why Madam didn't make more effort to dress as nicely as *she* could. She often went out in worn clothes that Joy thought were too loose and ill-fitting. She could understand wearing old clothes around the house, but surely Madam could do better when she went out, considering the money she had.

"Well, sure, I asked Peter to take you there this afternoon," replied Madam, looking puzzled, maybe wondering about the connection between a trip to Deepak's and Joy's dress.

"Sorry to disturb you, but I'm thinking that maybe it's a good idea if you come with me this first time," suggested Joy hesitantly, since Madam looked rushed. Joy hated to ask Madam for anything when she was rushed.

"But Peter will take you," reiterated Madam. "I don't think I need to go too, do I?"

"Well," faltered Joy, "maybe it's good if you introduce me to Mr. Deepak."

"Ah," said Madam, understanding dawning on her face. "I see." She sighed. "Okay. Let's do it right after lunch."

Joy was relieved. Madam, because she was well educated and moneyed, could walk into any shop, deal with landlords, tradesmen, or officials, and be treated with respect. Even by the Indian merchants. She must have noticed that the Indian community tended to stick together and didn't intermarry or mix socially with the African community. Maybe she didn't understand the way that some of them looked down on the Africans. Just a few months back it had happened when Madam asked Joy to arrange repairs to the leaking faucet in one of the bathrooms. This required a call to Mrs. Chatterjee, the wife of the wealthy Indian landlord who owned the house.

Joy hadn't wanted to call Mrs. Chatterjee, but she knew she had to. She hoped the telephone would malfunction, as it often did, and her heart sank when she pushed the buttons and the call went through.

"Where's Madam?" Mrs. Chatterjee demanded rudely after Joy had identified herself, apologized for bothering her, and stated her purpose. "Can't she call me herself?"

"*Tafadhali*, please," Joy tried again. "She asked me to call you to tell you we need the leaking faucet fixed."

"Well, we'll see. It must not be very important or she'd call herself," Mrs. Chatterjee had responded with ill-concealed disdain.

"Okay. Thank you. Good-bye," said Joy, chagrined and hanging up in humiliation.

Then at lunch Madam had asked, "Joy, did you call Mrs. Chatterjee?" Joy nodded assent and Madam continued. "When will she send someone to fix it?"

"She didn't say," replied Joy.

"Well, did you ask?" Madam responded in a reasonable tone.

"Maybe tomorrow," Joy had said, looking away from Madam, unwilling to admit she'd tried and failed to get Mrs. Chatterjee to take her seriously.

"Hmmm," was Madam's comment as she bustled down the hall looking for something.

When no one had shown up to fix the leak after three more days, Madam told Joy again to be sure to call Mrs. Chatterjee.

"Madam, I think it's better if you call," said Joy apologetically. "I think it will get fixed faster if you call." Madam had frowned with annoyance but made the call. The leak was fixed that afternoon.

So, on the day of the shopping trip, Joy sighed with relief as she straightened her scarf. Thank goodness she wouldn't have to deal with the shopkeeper by herself! She collected the shopping baskets and got into the car to go to Deepak's with Madam.

~

Deepak's was a small shop with five narrow aisles. Goods were stacked high and packed tightly on the shelves, and many of the canned and preserved items weren't familiar at all to Joy. There was a big chest freezer at the front with a clear glass top that could be folded back. Inside were meats like sandwich ham, bacon, and sausages, as well as treats like ice cream. A large cooler filled with dairy products and soft drinks sat next to the door. Madam introduced her to Mr. Deepak and, to Joy's surprise, he was very nice to her — and he spoke Swahili perfectly. He helped the two of them to find everything on the list, and Madam handed over the money.

"Joy will be doing our shopping by herself in the future," Madam said with a smile, and Mr. Deepak nodded pleasantly. Within a month, Joy looked forward to the weekly trip and wondered why she'd ever been nervous. And, according to Madam, when she made an occasional trip to the shop herself, Mr. Deepak always asked about her.

19

JOY, 2002

J oy often saw Madam's boys reading in the afternoon after school or on Saturday morning when they had no school. One day, when Sam left his book out on the dining table and went outside to play, Joy picked it up to look at it. She frowned. Could this possibly be schoolwork? The book's cover had a picture of various sorts of small animals, dressed in little jackets, hats, or trousers, and some wearing boots. From what she read on the back cover of the book it seemed these animals organized themselves into armies, fought wars, built cities, and traveled the seas on big ships they captained. She'd seen fantasy stories that were picture books, but there weren't any pictures in Sam's book and there were a lot of pages. It seemed like a lot of book for a boy Sam's age. An old granny in the village had told all the children folk stories about animals when Joy was a child, but she didn't expect to see these sorts of stories written down in books. Books, aside from picture books, were supposed to be collections of knowledge about history or geography or science. She decided to ask him about it.

"Sam, is this a book you read at school?" she said, when she caught him in a rare quiet moment.

"Oh no," he said with a laugh. "That's just a book I'm reading for fun." He scrunched up his face in concentration. "You see, there's a group of bad stoats who are trying to take over the castle from the hares and otters." He continued in a rush, trying to describe to Joy a complex tale about unfamiliar animals that made little sense. Almost as quickly as he began, he ended and ran out of the room, shouting, "You can read it when I'm finished!" Joy laughed at his enthusiasm but she still wasn't sure about the book.

"Madam, what is a stoat?" she asked later.

"Ah," laughed Madam, after a momentary puzzled frown. "Sam must've been telling you about his book." Joy nodded. "Well, a stoat is a small animal, but very fierce." She furrowed her brow. "I guess it's like the honey badgers here." Joy continued to look uncertain. "Sorry. I have no idea what that animal is called in Swahili. Maybe something like a giant rat?"

"But that's a long book for such a small boy to read," said Joy, shuddering at the idea of a giant rat, but more interested in the fact that Sam was reading the book than in exactly what a stoat was. "When did he learn to read so well?"

"Ahh," said Madam. "The boys do love to read. I think it's because we've been reading to them since they were very small."

"You mean since they were babies?" Joy asked in surprise.

"Well, probably since around age one, when they first began to try to talk. They always liked the pictures even if they didn't understand the stories too well." Joy looked interested and she continued. "You know scientists say that reading to children, even if they can barely speak, is one of the best things you can do to get them interested in learning."

"Oh really?" said Joy slowly. "I like this idea, Madam. I would like to read to my children."

Madam went to the shelf and poked through the books there, then pulled off three or four picture books that the boys had enjoyed a few years before. Handing them to Joy, she said, "You're welcome to take these, Joy, and keep them."

"Thank you, Madam. I'm going to do it," said Joy as she took the books. She carried them home and started that night.

Within a few weeks, she was snuggling with Emma and Elijah in the middle of the floor mat under the single light bulb nearly every night. Emma had started what was becoming an everyday plea. "Mama, will you read to us tonight?"

Joy laughed. "But we finished that book last night."

"Doesn't matter, Mama," said Emma. "'Lijah and I want to hear it again." She looked to her younger brother for support and he nodded vigorously.

"Okay," said Joy, since she enjoyed the reading almost as much as the children did. "Okay, but lights on for an hour only. Electricity is expensive. We don't have much credit left on the meter and I don't have another coupon."

Then she added, "And you have to clean the room before we start."

The few books she had were simple, with lots of pictures and few words. She wished she had some in Swahili, although she figured the children would learn a bit of English from the books she got from Madam. She loved pointing out things on the pages and hearing the children's questions. They often repeated these over and over, which made her laugh.

"Why do *you* think the little boy did that?" she'd ask. She marveled at how many different responses the children could come up with. It would be nice to have more picture books with African children. Maybe she'd be able to find some in the future. For now she was glad to have any children's books at all. Daniel rigged up a shelf on the wall in their room and she carefully stacked the books there.

～

Joy was worried. She stood at the kitchen sink after a Saturday dinner party at Madam's, sloshing warm soapy water over the plates, looking up occasionally to watch four geckos clinging to the outside of the kitchen window screen with their big spade-like feet. Their tongues whipped out so swiftly to catch their mosquito meals that the insects seemed to disappear by magic. Once in a while a newly hatched termite, trying its wings, was snatched from the air. She stared at five perfect elliptical eggs backlit by the outdoor floodlight in the translucent belly of one of the geckos. She snapped back to the present, realizing the visit her youngest sister, Sara, would make the next day was weighing on her mind. She had a bad feeling about it.

"What do you think she wants?" Joy had asked Daniel that afternoon when she learned of the upcoming event. "It must be important since she sent a message ahead of time. She wants to be sure we're here when she comes."

"I don't know, Joy," said Daniel. He grimaced. "I've heard some things around town about Heri. I hope she's not coming to give us bad news about him."

Joy's brother Heri had not done well in school and he'd quit after a few years. He hadn't married and he was still living with his parents. He didn't have a job and he wasn't contributing to the family's upkeep. She'd heard her parents complain about the fact that he sometimes disappeared for days with other young men they didn't like.

She looked at the window again. The geckos were gone. She finished rinsing the last plate and stacked it to dry.

∼

Sara arrived late Sunday afternoon. She was ten years younger than Joy, still a little girl when Joy had started work in the laundry; Joy never felt she knew her well. One thing she and the whole family did know was that Sara idolized Heri.

Emma and Elijah were excited at the idea of seeing their aunt. "Maybe she'll bring sweeties," Joy heard Emma suggest to Elijah.

"Well, don't ask her," said Joy. "And if she does, no matter how many she brings, you're only allowed one piece a day."

Since Sara didn't come until late in the afternoon, Joy let Emma and Elijah go out to play with neighbor children rather than waiting at home to greet her. Joy, Daniel, and Sara had already had a chance to drink a cup of tea and catch up on small talk by the time the children raced into the yard. Seeing their aunt, they pulled themselves up straight and advanced respectfully to greet her.

When she saw them, Sara pulled out a small packet of sweets. Emma and Elijah began to dance with excitement and begged to have one on the spot.

"You can have it now or you can have it later," said Joy. "But remember what I said. It's the only one you get today." Elijah took his right away, but Emma scowled for several minutes with the effort of making such a big decision. "I'll have mine later," she finally said.

"Oh, you're too strict," said Sara. "Sweets won't hurt them. They're just children."

Joy started to frown, but before she could say anything, Daniel spoke.

"*Asiyefunzwa na mamaye atafunzwa na ulimwengu* — Learn it from your mother or you will learn it from the world. Didn't you ever hear that saying, Sara?"

Daniel caught Joy's eye and gave her an easy grin. "That's what my mama used to say when she punished me or had to tell me something I didn't want to hear." He turned to Sara. "I'll bet your *baba* said it too. It's hard to say no to your kids — but it's the only way to raise good ones." He smiled at Joy. "Joy's a great mother."

Mollified, Joy turned to Sara. "Would you like more tea?" As she poured it, she tried to move the conversation to the question that had been on her mind. "I'm glad to hear all is well with you, but is there more? You haven't mentioned Heri. How's he doing?"

Sara sighed. "Actually, that's what I wanted to talk to you about. *Baba* didn't want to ask you, but Mama and I were sure you'd help."

Joy's heart sank. She glanced over at Daniel and leaned forward to hear what Sara would say.

"I'm afraid it isn't good news about Heri. He's had such a hard time and things just haven't gone well for him."

Joy's heart sank further. She wished Sara would just come out with the news.

"A few nights ago, we learned that he'd been arrested."

Joy tried to suppress her gasp. This was much worse than she'd imagined.

"The police claim that he was involved in a break-in. I'm sure it isn't true, but now they want almost 100,000 *shilingi* to release him. We don't have the money."

Joy and Daniel both sat in stunned silence for several moments. Panicked thoughts raced through Joy's head. The amount they needed was roughly what she made each month, but far more than she and Daniel had saved. And they'd worked hard to build up the little savings they had.

Sara looked around the yard and back into the door to the house. "I noticed you've got several pieces of furniture and even a number of books," she pointed out.

Joy looked over at Daniel. She wanted to cry. He kept his gaze steadily on her, but she couldn't read his thoughts. It was her family. He cleared his throat.

"We don't have much savings either," he said hesitantly. "Of course, we'd like to help, but I'm just not sure how much we can offer." He continued to hold Joy's gaze.

Joy felt a rush of love for this man. He was trying to

support her, but letting her make the decision. She had about 20,000 *shilingi* in a tin hidden in the wall. She wanted to keep it for the children's school. Emma was supposed to start in a few months. This was agony. What should she do?

She folded her arms across her chest and looked down at the ground. She made a decision and looked up at her sister. "I have 10,000 *shilingi*, but I keep it at Madam's house for safety. I can't get it until tomorrow."

Daniel sat perfectly still and didn't even blink at these falsehoods.

Sara's face fell. "Couldn't you sell some of the books you have?" she pleaded.

Daniel stood up and crossed his arms. "No. We will not sell any books. We won't do that. We're giving you our savings and that will have to be enough. We're sorry about Heri. Very sorry. But this is the best we can do."

Sara swallowed, then rose and turned stiffly to Joy. "Thank you for your help, Sister. Where can I pick up the money?"

"I'll bring it to you tomorrow," said Daniel.

~

Joy and Daniel talked late into the night about the problem. "I hate to lie and I hate to not help them more," she said.

"You did the right thing, Joy," he said soothingly. "Tomorrow I'll take them half of the money. Then you take the tin to Madam's and see if you really can keep it there."

"I will. I will for sure. But it hurts to see Heri get into this trouble. What happened to him?"

"I guess he really should have learned more from his mother."

~

Madam's children were about five years older than Emma and Elijah. Joy liked the boys, who were polite and respectful to her. She approved of their manners, but she saw that Madam and Mr. James had to work at teaching them.

One afternoon, angry voices — Madam's and the older boy's — exploded in one of the back bedrooms, followed by a slammed door. Joy went about her business and pretended she hadn't heard anything. Later, she went into the living room to clean and found Madam slumped in one of the nice chairs, drinking a cup of tea.

"Do children in Tanzanian families become rebellious and difficult when they get to be around thirteen years old?" Madam asked Joy wearily. "And what do you do about it?"

"Hmm," said Joy, pondering this for a moment. Madam looked shaken — and no wonder. Children shouldn't shout at their parents the way her son had. But she knew children went through rough patches on their way to adulthood.

She nodded and smiled at Madam in understanding. "Ah yes," she said. "Yes, that is the time they need lots of extra love at home."

Madam swallowed some tea and seemed to consider this for a few moments before she spoke slowly. "I guess that's right. Raising children isn't easy. It's hard to know why they sometimes go wrong, but I think you're right about the extra love."

Later that night, talking before they fell asleep, Joy told Daniel the story. "Hmm," Daniel said, drifting off. "Seems like people and families are pretty much the same everywhere.

20

IMANI, 2002

Tensions often ran high at the National Assembly in the capital of Tanzania and sometimes they spilled over onto the veranda at Bagamoyo. Imani, sixty-seven years old but still strong and active, had retired a few years earlier at the mandatory age, but she continued to work as a special-hire consultant to the government.

"Oh, *Bibi*, there's no one like you to talk with about the problems in government. Your veranda's where a lot of our ideas get hashed out before they ever come to the Assembly floor."

It was true, thought Imani, and she was proud of the fact that policymakers still gravitated to her Sunday afternoon gatherings. Godfrey had been absent for years, a minor foot-note in the country's history and little more than that in Imani's life.

The anti-counterfeiting bill had been debated for months when it came up on the veranda one afternoon. "It's just common sense," snapped one member of the Assembly, slamming his drink down on the table. "These counterfeit drugs are pouring into countries all over eastern Africa. Traders sell them on the street corners and in the marketplaces. It's just a matter of time before they end up in the legitimate pharmacy shops too. It's outrageous and it's going to kill people! This bill is our best chance to stop it."

"Sure, man," sighed an equally frustrated legislator. "It sounds like common sense and of course we want what's best for the people. But it's not that simple. If we pass this the way it's written now, it'll stop us from getting generic medicines." He paused and looked around to be sure others on the veranda understood this. "You know these are the only affordable options for Tanzania. We have to rely on them. Now wouldn't the big European pharmaceutical companies just love to see us forced to buy their overpriced drugs?" He rattled the ice in his glass. "Hmph. You're not going to see the leaders in India or China falling for this."

"No," said the first man with a shake of his head. "They'll continue to make their own medicines and find ways to sell them here — genuine and counterfeit both!"

A third politician spoke. "You're right about the generic drugs from India and China. And there's another thing — that bill will make it impossible for us to build up our own drug manufacturing here in Tanzania." He slapped his palm on the table and scowled. "And that's something we really need."

"How can people recognize the counterfeits?" Imani asked, genuinely curious but also hoping to defuse the tension with a purely practical question.

"Ah, *Bibi*, that's just it. Essentially, they can't — or it takes some expertise," said the man who'd slapped the table. "These crooked manufacturers are ingenious. The packaging looks identical to the real drugs. They even include fake batch numbers." He let out a long sigh. "The only way to recognize them most of the time is small defects in packaging, like printing on a blister pack that rubs off with a wet finger." He rubbed his own wet finger on the table top to demonstrate. "Or sometimes the clue is spelling mistakes and typos in the package information sheets."

"And what's actually *in* the tablets?" Imani asked.

"Well, the drugs might be dangerous substances. Or they might be legitimate ingredients cut with chalk or talc — or they might be nothing *except* chalk or talc," explained the man with disgust. "Either way, it's bad for the patient who takes them."

"Where do they come from?" persisted Imani, increasingly horrified by the implications she could imagine.

"Oh, they're usually made in India or China," the man snorted with disgust. "They work their way into our county after trips across many borders. You know — small bribes there can get just about anything across." He grimaced and took a long swallow from his glass. "There's a huge amount of money to be made off these drugs. That's why it's so hard to control the problem."

"I guess there's little we can do about the sales by itinerant market traders," said Imani. "But surely we can trust the drugs purchased by the Ministry of Health. As long as the private pharmacy shops are required to get their drugs from official sources, the supplies ought to be safe. We just need to educate people not to buy medicine from market traders."

Imani hadn't lost her passion for education and she especially liked the discussions when her old friends and colleagues from the Ministry were present.

"*Bibi* Imani, don't you have a granddaughter in a village school in Ndungu?" asked a colleague one Sunday afternoon. "How's she doing?"

"Ah, thank you for asking. My granddaughter's at the top

of her primary school class now in Ndungu, if you'll excuse my boasting."

Her colleague chuckled. "It's the *bibi*'s privilege to boast. Congratulations!"

Imani smiled with deep satisfaction. Esther's progress was a continued pleasure to both her and Neema. "Yes, we visit there every six months or so. Last time we learned that she'd come first in maths."

"Maths is well taught in our schools," said a young man. "Even in rural schools. What I worry about is English language."

"But *Mwalimu* Nyerere was right to insist on primary education in Swahili," said one of the older men. "This binds Tanzanians together in a way that never happened in Kenya — just look at how fractious that country is!"

"Sure," insisted the young man, "but the problem is that primary education in Swahili doesn't prepare our kids well for secondary school in English. That abrupt switch to English leaves lots of kids struggling."

At this, Imani couldn't suppress a loud sigh. "But have you been in the secondary schools? Many of the teachers there have such poor English that they're still teaching in Swahili."

"That's exactly the problem!" responded the animated young man. "Our textbooks are all in English. I had a world history textbook in English with a teacher who mostly used Swahili."

An old friend of Imani's jumped in to the discussion. "Look, English is needed to compete in East Africa — and in most of the world. I've argued for years that primary school teaching should be switched to English. Surely this would better prepare our students for the twenty-first century?"

"No," said Imani. All heads turned towards her and everyone listened. "What we need is better teachers at both the primary and secondary levels. We *should* continue to teach

in Swahili in primary school. It's our national language —
part of our identity as Tanzanians. But we also need English.
The students should start studying it early with teachers who
can speak and write it well. Teachers who've demonstrated
proficiency — not just waved a certificate." She shook her
head.

"Oh, *Bibi*," said her friend, "you'd be horrified to know
how much cheating goes on — and teachers are often part of
it. Students make payments for good marks all the time."

There was a silence. Many of the people on the veranda
were old enough to remember the way *Bibi* Imani had been
passed over decades before for a position at the national level
in the Ministry of Education, although she never mentioned
it herself. They were all uncomfortably aware that educational standards had dropped and corruption in schools had
grown.

Imani rose to go inside and order more tea, thinking again
about her granddaughter. Maybe it was time to bring Esther
to Dar for school.

∼

One afternoon the talk turned to per diems.

"You mean to tell me that you think high-up government
officials should be paid just for going to meetings?" Imani
challenged a young woman on the veranda. "They even call
them 'sitting allowances'. Extra pay for sitting in meetings,
doing their jobs. That's just government-approved corruption.
Mwalimu Nyerere never did this kind of thing."

"I don't see it that way," grumbled the young woman. "If
our salaries weren't so low, this wouldn't be an issue. We
deserve to be paid for our work."

"I agree," said the fat uncle, who still came to the house in
Bagamoyo to join veranda talks. "If NGOs want us to go to
the meetings, they ought to pay a fair day's wage. These

nongovernment organizations all have their own agendas and they each think their priorities are the most deserving."

"Maybe, but it's come to the point where attending meetings is viewed as a source of income," replied *Bibi* Imani with a sigh. "I've seen instances where heads of units were away at meetings that had nothing to do with their jobs, while the work in the unit practically came to a standstill." She took a biscuit from the tray and offered one to Fat Uncle. "But sure, you have a point about the NGOs. They come in with their own agendas and pay far too little attention to what Tanzanians want."

Imani paused to nibble at her biscuit, but she wasn't finished with this subject yet. "And the per diem culture has made it difficult to do good community development projects. The foreign NGOs want to show quick results to their own governments, so they pay villagers to dig their own wells or latrines. They call this 'community development,' and now villagers won't lift a finger to help themselves without a payment."

"I suppose it's better than paying foreigners to do the work, though, isn't it?" said Fat Uncle with a smirk.

"Maybe," answered an old friend of Imani's. "But, either way, who's going to maintain the things once the NGO leaves? The villagers feel no real ownership for the projects. What kind of community development is this? One of the best projects I've seen was done by a local man and his wife who returned to Tanzania with a little money after years abroad. His home village wanted a covered area with cement market stalls. So these two bought the cement and materials and donated them to the village, but refused to hire anyone for the labor. Ha! Everyone grumbled, but eventually the community got organized and did it themselves. Then they came up with a plan to improve the village schoolhouse — they only asked for a few supplies and they did all the work themselves. You can bet they take good care of it now."

"Sometimes I worry that the influx of foreign money has done as much harm as good," sighed Imani. She knew Neema was always on the lookout for allowances and that she'd probably have agreed with Fat Uncle and the grumbling young woman if she'd been present. She felt vaguely ashamed for her daughter.

J oy was walking home along the rutted road she took six days a week between her house and Madam's. Across the fields, Kilimanjaro's peak emerged from a band of clouds. Joy's father insisted that the snow on top of the mountain was less than when he was a boy, but today there was a fresh fall of cold white on the top. Down below, where Joy walked, the ruts in the road were rock hard and buried under a thick layer of dust. Even the leaves of the bougainvillea hedges lining the road were coated with the beige powder. This road would turn to sticky mud soon, once the rains began. She reflected for a minute on whether it was harder keeping the family's clothes clean in the dry season or the rainy season. But these thoughts took only part of her mind; behind them there was a growing unease. The previous Sunday morning, Daniel had gone to see his mother and sister in his home village, Ndungu. Joy wanted to go with him, but taking the whole family was too costly.

Daniel had planned to get there by nightfall on the Sunday he left. He expected to spend a few nights and come back home on Tuesday or Wednesday. When he didn't show up on Wednesday, Joy was more disappointed than worried. "When's *Baba* coming home?" Emma had asked petulantly.

"Today," Joy had answered with an easy smile. But when Emma asked the same question on Friday, worry allowed irritation to break through. "Today," she snapped, and then felt ashamed of taking out her anxiety on Emma.

Uneasiness left her even more moody on her half-day of work Saturday morning. At home on Saturday evening, once the children were asleep, she was in tears.

She awoke Sunday morning after a fitful night, resolved to ask Madam for help. Amira was away, so Joy went next door.

"Grace, I've got to go out. Can you keep an eye on Emma and Elijah, playing near the pump?" she asked. Her heart warmed a little at the readiness of Grace's smile as she agreed. But fear overtook her again as she walked toward Madam's, worrying about what she'd say. Madam knew that Joy supported the family because Daniel had no regular job, and Joy wanted Madam to think well of Daniel. She knocked at the door with a dry mouth.

"Joy," said Madam with surprise, a Sunday morning cup of tea in hand. "What's going on?"

"I'm sorry to disturb you, Madam," Joy said softly, standing on the threshold. She didn't want Madam to think she'd presume to enter the house when she wasn't working. "I need to ask your help." She paused to let Madam take in this possibly unwelcome fact, then continued. "Daniel went to his sister's a week ago and he's not come back."

Madam frowned and stepped back. "Come in, Joy, and tell me about it."

"Joy? What's going on?" said Mr. James as he came into the living room from the hallway. They sat down in the chairs Joy dusted regularly but rarely sat in herself.

"Go ahead," said Madam when Joy hesitated before starting to talk. The story came out slowly, with all the details of places, days, and times. Madam rubbed her temple and interrupted with a wave of her hand. "So, you expected him back on Tuesday?" Then, without waiting for an answer, she said, "I guess there's no way to contact his sister?"

"That's right, Madam," said Joy.

Madam hesitated a minute, exchanging looks with her husband, then asked, "Does Daniel drink?"

It wasn't unexpected; after all, Madam didn't know Daniel. But it still hurt to imagine she thought this way about him. "No, Madam," she said softly, "he doesn't drink." After a pause, she said, "I'm afraid something happened to him."

Madam and her husband exchanged looks again. Mr. James stood up. "Let's see where this village, Ndungu, is," he suggested, pulling a map out of the bookcase. "What's the biggest village near to it?" They all bent over the map, which he'd spread on the dining table. "Hmm, I think this is it, right?" he asked Joy, pointing at marks on the map that meant little to her. She flushed with embarrassment at her inability to interpret the map better.

"Well, it's not that far," noted Madam. "Looks like only about three hundred kilometers."

"Well, sure. As the crow flies," said Mr. James. He turned to Joy with a half-smile and a little eye roll. "She doesn't really understand maps very well," he said, with a gesture towards his wife. "The roads are what we have to look at."

Joy bit the inside of her cheek, thinking about how far it was. She knew the way, but she didn't think about distances in kilometers. She thought about how many hours or days it would take to get there by foot or bus. She figured James understood the state of disrepair of the roads. He frowned in concentration and studied the map. "Trouble is that sometimes the roads shown on these maps don't actually exist." Finally, he looked up and smiled at Joy. "You know the transport options and I think we can figure out which way he went. Maybe we should take the car and look for him."

Joy let out her breath. This was exactly what she'd been hoping for.

Joy and Mr. James got into the Land Rover and started down the road Joy figured Daniel would have used on the first part of his trip.

They quickly left Moshi and entered into a tangle of narrow dirt tracks, none of which had any markers. A pickup truck appeared suddenly out of a maize field, its bed jammed with people — many sitting up on the sides and hanging on by fingertips only. Several chickens were tied by their legs and lay haphazardly on the top of the cab, more or less secured by flapping jute ropes. The deeply rutted roads twisted and interwove, but Joy knew these little roads. "Go that way," she pointed. Then, "Here!" as they suddenly emerged onto a bigger road. "Here's where he would have caught the first *dalla dalla.*"

Mr. James pulled the car up onto the tarmac. Minivans, driven by testosterone-fueled young men, whipped by, honking continually and passing whenever they could get up the speed. With no regard for oncoming traffic, they were often the cause of accidents. Joy had heard Madam forbid her older son from using them. Mr. James let out a few whistles and cursed a couple of times as they appeared out of nowhere and raced by.

After thirty minutes, Joy pointed again and called out, "Turn here!" Mr. James barely made the sharp right onto another rutted dirt road.

"Whew," he sighed, with obvious relief, as they left the heavily trafficked tarmac.

They bumped along for another half hour before Joy sat up straighter and leaned forward. A figure off in the distance hobbled towards them. "I think it might be Daniel," she said, leaning forward as close as she could get to the windshield and biting her lower lip. "It looks like his red jacket!"

Mr. James pressed down harder on the accelerator in spite

of the rugged road. "It's him!" shouted Joy, closing her eyes in relief. "That's him! Thanks to God, that's him!"

They slowed as they came upon the limping man, and Joy threw open the car door and leaped out to rush to Daniel. His face broke into a broad smile, but his knees started to buckle as he moved towards Joy. Mr. James got out of the car to help, but Joy was out sooner, throwing her arms around Daniel. In the face of the heartfelt reunion, Mr. James shifted from one foot to the other and looked out in the distance.

"Are you alright? I wish we'd brought some drinks and something to eat. You look like you could use it," said Mr. James.

Daniel nodded. Then, in weary sentences, leaning against the vehicle, he started to explain what had happened. Joy broke in to translate for James every now and then.

He hadn't started home until Thursday, because he was delayed by an incident in the village. Once he left, he caught the first *dalla dalla*, but then, thinking he could save time, he took a remote footpath towards the next bus transfer point. Thieves had jumped him. He'd been left only mildly beaten but without any money, too far away to walk back to the village. He could only walk towards home. Astonishingly, he still had his red jacket. But since the assault he'd been walking for almost two days without food, and he was tired and hungry. Plus, his leg was sore where he'd been kicked.

"Oh Daniel, Emma will be so happy to see you!" cried Joy several times, showing an emotional side that she'd never shown Mr. James or Madam before.

Then, remembering Daniel's comment about the initial delay, she asked, "But, Daniel, why didn't you leave until Thursday?"

Daniel grimaced and anger clouded his face. "Oh Joy, it's a long story and hard to talk about. I'll tell you in the car." Mr. James helped Daniel get up into the vehicle, and as they bumped their way home Daniel told her what had happened, what he'd seen and heard from Auntie Mina, with Joy occasionally relating bits of it to James in English.

On the Tuesday Daniel was to leave for home, one of the older women in the village, a dear family friend known for years to everyone in the village as Auntie Mina, came to talk to him. The problem was a young girl named Esther — the eldest daughter of Afaafa, who was a distant relation of Auntie Mina, as indeed many people were in the small village. Esther was a bright girl. Thanks to support from a remote relative on Afaafa's husband's side, a well-off doctor in Dar, she was not only able to start school but was still attending at age twelve. It was a good arrangement, and everyone believed that the girl had the potential to go far.

But on Monday morning she didn't go to school and seemed withdrawn and troubled. Auntie Mina found her crying alone down at the river and pressed her for an explanation. Eventually, between outbursts of tears and whimpers of shame, she told the old woman what had happened

"I'm scared. Something terrible . . . An old man . . . an old man . . . forced me," the girl sobbed. She dug into her pocket, bringing out a tight fist that she unfolded to reveal a few *shilingi* notes. "What do I do with these?" she asked. "If I buy anything, my parents will begin asking questions. They'll begin suspecting. I'm so scared," she wailed as Auntie Mina's face crumpled in horror.

The old man had given her the two notes when he was done with her, and told her to keep her silence. "One word out of you about this," he said, "just *one word* and I'll get the head teacher to expel you from school." Since then, her mind had been a roiling muddle of fearful thoughts: fear of what might be happening in her body, fear of being found out, fear of an unsparing barrage of blame, shame, ridicule, and wrath, and fear of being expelled.

"But where did this happen?" Auntie Mina had asked the girl.

"At his house," she replied.

Auntie Mina was shocked. "You went to the old man's home?"

"I didn't know it was his home, Auntie. The head teacher told me to go there after school."

Auntie understood this. The girl had been taught not to question authority, and she would do as told.

"Where was the head teacher?" she'd asked, attempting to get the details straight.

"He wasn't there, Auntie. The old man told me to come in and wait for him. As soon as I set a foot in the house, he pulled me in further, locked the door, and raised my skirt." The girl was overwhelmed as she recounted the terrible moment she realized what was about to happen to her. She let out a long wail. "Oh, you can't tell my parents!"

The older woman held her and murmured soothingly. "No, Esther, I won't tell your parents," she said. She thought long and hard as she comforted the girl. "I won't tell anyone unless you agree first. But I know someone who might help. I know a very good man."

The suggestion sent Esther into a panic. "I can't tell a *man* what happened!"

"No. Don't worry," soothed Auntie Mina. "Daniel's not like the other men in this village, Esther. He won't blame you. He's a good man. And he doesn't live here anymore. Let's see if Daniel will go reckon with the man."

So Auntie had related the entire story to Daniel. But when she asked him to talk to the authorities, Daniel didn't like it. "I know it's wrong, and it makes me sick, what happened to the girl," he said. "But if I go to either the old man or the head teacher, they'll know she told us and they *will* expel her. And they'll probably make up a story to tell her parents as well and accuse her of lying." He shook his head, bitterly frustrated. "No one will take my word against a head teacher's, and certainly they won't take the word of a twelve-year-old girl. And in the end, the head teacher will still have his position. Is this going to make the situation better or worse?"

Daniel and Auntie Mina talked about what to do for two days. They could not find a solution. A head teacher was just too powerful in a small village.

Joy, with a deepening sense of horror and shame, had been stopping Daniel occasionally as he told the story so that she could relate it to Mr. James in pieces. Sometimes she and Daniel talked between themselves for long stretches as Joy asked him to explain things. Mr. James tried to ask a few questions himself, and this usually resulted in more prolonged discussion between Joy and Daniel. Joy's distress and disgust grew as the conversation continued.

By the time Mr. James reached their house to drop them off, all was quiet in the car. Daniel and Joy went to the neighbor to get the children, and that reunion warmed Joy's heart. But late that night Daniel, awoke to the sound of Joy sobbing next to him. "Oh Daniel, I feel helpless! I can't think of one thing we can do for that girl. What if it were Emma? We need to be able to take care of our children! School shouldn't be a place they're afraid to go to."

22

JOY, 2004–2005

The incident with the girl in Daniel's village reminded Joy of how lucky she was — she had good parents and a loving husband. She walked home from work thinking with satisfaction that her two-child family was just right. She'd started the injections again to prevent another pregnancy after Elijah was born. Daniel had no objections, and he'd even come to agree with Joy that two children was a good number.

Tonight, Elijah was celebrating his seventh birthday. Madam had agreed that Joy could use the oven the day before to bake a small cake. Emma had used a few *shilingi* to buy a colorful toy for her younger brother, and Joy was looking forward to a special evening with her family. She had some small candles to put on the cake and she could picture her children's eyes shining in the light. So, in spite of recent weariness, she was eager to get home. She walked as quickly as she could. The rains had come and the mud threatened to suck her shoes off her feet as she went along, forcing her to curl her toes hard to keep them on.

She thought again of her family, complete now, thanks to the government clinic she'd continued to attend faithfully over the years. Sometimes she was disappointed to find that a nurse she'd grown fond of was no longer there. If the new nurse was especially friendly, Joy asked her about the previous one who'd treated her. This often led to stories of staff turnover, along with complaints about the work conditions and the low salaries paid by the Ministry of Health.

These complaints jarred with the stories her father told in her childhood — stories about people who'd worked willingly with little or no pay to build the country. She needed to believe the nurses who took care of her family did their best to make the system work. She hated hearing rumors like one a friend passed on that the regional medical officer marked up prices in the dispensary and siphoned off the extra. She refused to talk to the friend for a while. If she noticed clinic staff were unhelpful, she attributed it to all the work they had to do. She waited patiently for her turn in crowded clinics and behaved respectfully.

Nurse Mkata had worked at the clinic for years, yet she didn't have enough money to cover her daughter's school expenses. She was careful with money, but the needs of her children for food and clothing were always growing. She looked to the clinic for an opportunity to supplement her income — taking advantage of the fact that there were women who attended the public clinic who would prefer to attend a "private clinic," paying a little for contraceptive injections to avoid the wait at the public facility.

The clinic nurses extracted the contraceptive drug for injection in a syringe from a small bottle of a solution that looked like water and held enough to treat about ten women. It was easy for Nurse Mkata to draw up enough medicine for five doses, squirt it into an empty bottle, pocket this, then inject some saline into the first bottle to make up the volume she'd pilfered.

Nurse Mkata's neighbors appreciated the private service she began to offer. The nurse not only bought a new school uniform for her daughter, but she bought more food for her family. She stole from random bottles to make it harder to detect what she was doing. There was little danger of the district supervisor catching a problem. He came around for monthly visits but stayed only long enough to poke his head in the door, find something to criticize, then lecture the clinic head about it for a few minutes. Once finished, he jumped back in his vehicle and raced off to the next stop. There was no accountability in the management system. The attitudes from the top trickled down to the workers at every level.

Joy had gone for her regular injection shortly before Elijah's seventh birthday. She smiled to see that her favorite nurse, Sister Mpanda, was on duty. The sister picked up the nearest bottle and gave Joy the jab in her hip. "Ooh!" Joy said with a barely perceptible wince as the needle pierced her skin. But it didn't really hurt, and Joy and the nurse smiled at each other. They'd often talked about how important these jabs were to Joy's family.

So it was a shock to Joy, two months later, to find she was pregnant — the last thing she wanted! No wonder she was so tired. Madam caught her crying quietly in the pantry one day at lunch.

"What's the matter, Joy?" Madam asked as Joy tried to use her apron to wipe tears from her face.

It was embarrassing to be crying at work, and Madam's inquiry only made it harder to pull herself together. "Oh, Madam," she said, her voice breaking, "I'm pregnant again."

"So . . . this wasn't something you wanted?" said Madam. Joy was surprised by her apparently real concern.

Joy shook her head. "No. Daniel and I wanted to have two

children. With two we could give them a good life. We could send them to school and be sure they had enough to eat." She sniffed up additional tears and wiped her eyes again. "I've been taking injections every three months at the clinic to stop this from happening." A wave of dismay washed over her and she began to cry again. "How will we ever manage school for three children?" Madam nodded slowly in understanding as she reached out and put her hand on Joy's arm in sympathy.

Daniel wasn't happy about the idea of another child either, but there was nothing to be done about it. The pregnancy progressed without any problems. Week by week, Joy saw her body changing, and as the baby started to move, her heart softened towards the prospect of another child. Sister Mpanda was always at the clinic to take care of her when she went for checkups.

"Well, the injections don't always work," she admitted with a frown. "But it seems like we've had several failures in the last few months." She smiled reassuringly at Joy. "Let's just be sure to take good care of you now so you'll have a healthy baby."

Having a healthy baby was the main thing, but in low moments Joy worried about all that lay ahead. It helped a bit when she and Madam talked about her plans.

"Joy, we need to arrange for someone to do your work when you leave to have the baby," she said one day as Joy was growing large. Memories of what happened at the church came back to Joy, clouding her face with anxiety.

"Of course, we want you back after your three months' leave, Joy," continued Madam. "Your replacement will just be temporary. But we need to find someone. Do you have any ideas?"

"I think I can find a girl. I'll get her to come the week before I leave so I can show her everything."

"Good," said Madam, obviously relieved.

When the time came, Madam took pains to explain to the replacement that this was temporary and she'd have to leave once Joy came back to work. Madam even wrote it down on a paper and asked the girl to sign it.

~

Joy delivered the baby in Moshi at the public hospital. She wasn't the only one who found the baby girl exceptional. She came into the world with soft curls on her perfectly shaped head and glowing velvety skin. Daniel came to visit a few hours after the birth and they named the girl Zahra, after his mother. She slept peacefully, sucked contentedly, and cooed. Joy relaxed into the blissful state she'd enjoyed after her first child was born. Lying on the mattress feeding Zahra, Joy watched her tiny nose and mouth moving infinitesimally, and she was overwhelmed by love for this baby she'd imagined she didn't want.

The three months passed quickly, and the time came to go back to work at Madam's. Joy tied Zahra onto her back in a *kanga*, and the baby slept quietly as Joy went about her duties, stopping once in a while to nurse her.

~

One morning, three weeks after Joy returned to work, Madam's note was more scribbled than usual. Joy had to make an effort to read it. *Please make up guestroom for two. No one here for lunch. Spanish chicken for six people for dinner. Tell Yussuf to weed driveway!*

Visitors from abroad frequently came to stay with Madam's family for a few days or weeks. Joy liked having visitors in spite of the extra work because they were usually nice. They asked questions about her family and her life, and they often left small tips. She wondered where these two were coming from. She guessed they wouldn't be there until the afternoon since no one was home for lunch, but thought she might as well get everything ready early in the day. She adjusted Zahra on her back and went out to start readying the little guesthouse in the back.

Around three o'clock, she heard the big metal gate clang and the crunch of wheels on the driveway gravel. From the front door she saw Madam climb out of the Land Rover's front seat and a man and woman get out of the back.

"Joy, these are our guests, Julie and Frank. Joy is our housekeeper," said Madam, as the driver started to unload their bags from the back. Joy gave a little curtsy, put out her hand to shake, and was about to welcome the guests in English when Frank greeted her first in Swahili.

"Oh, very nice," said Joy with pleasure. Her smile broadened as the man continued speaking, using fluent Swahili phrases to make small talk. Julie spoke fluent Swahili as well, asking about the baby as she peeked around to look at Zahra, tied to Joy's back.

"But how do you speak such good Swahili?" asked Joy.

"We lived here for two years just after Independence," said Frank, clearly enjoying Joy's surprise.

Over the next few days, they settled in and Joy took opportunities to talk with them. They made just enough mistakes in Swahili to give them all something to laugh about and Joy loved to help them when they struggled with words.

"You mean you were in Tanzania together forty years ago?" Joy asked one afternoon. It was hard to tell how old some *wazungu* were. Julie had brown hair, but Frank was a pale blond man with uneven skin tone. Spectacles hid his eyes and a mustache covered his entire upper lip.

"Yep. We'd just married at the time," said Frank. "We both volunteered as community development assistants."

"My *baba* knew some community development assistants

years ago," Joy said. "He used to tell me about them when I was little."

"Really?" said Frank, raising his pale eyebrows. "Where does he live now? Do you think we could visit him?"

Joy stood straighter at the idea of taking visitors from abroad to meet her father. He'd love it!

"Why don't you go out there on a Saturday?" suggested Madam. "Peter can take you all in the car."

They left at ten on the chosen Saturday. Frank insisted they stop at a shop, where he picked out soft drinks, biscuits, samosas, and other fried treats to take along.

Joy's parents and siblings were waiting for them when they pulled up. Little stools were lined up outside the hut. Traditional greetings put everyone at ease, and when it became clear that Frank and Julie not only spoke Swahili well but had many stories to tell from the past, everyone relaxed and sat back to have a good time.

"Well, I guess we don't know any of the same people from back then," Frank agreed, after a long hunt for mutual acquaintances, "but tell me your best story about a volunteer."

"Well," drawled Joy's father, scratching his head. "Hmm. I think it would be about a young man who was here to help with surveying for roads." He smiled in remembering and settled more comfortably on his stool. "I saw this guy outside the Moshi post office building. He had a punctured tire and he was trying to raise his truck with a nice little mechanical jack. You know the type?"

Frank nodded.

"Well, of course I offered to help the man, but he wasn't having any of it. He said he could do it himself. Not unfriendly, but just very sure of himself, you know? He got the truck up on the jack and squatted down to wrestle the tire off. Then he stood up to throw it into the back of the truck. He hoisted that thing with a big swing and let it fly — maybe just to show how strong he was. But," he slapped his knee and chuckled, "it hit the truck bed and knocked the truck right off the jack." Frank joined him in a guffaw.

"I don't know what he said, but he yelled something in English and I can guess it was a curse. What was really funny was the look on his face when he turned and caught my eye." His guffaw died back to a chuckle. "I tried to keep a straight face, but it was just impossible. He stopped dead and looked at me like a thundercloud. Then he started laughing too. Of course, I offered again to help, and this time he accepted it." Joy's father grinned ear to ear, as did Frank. "Later he bought me a beer and I found out what he was doing in Tanzania. That man was the first European I ever talked to."

The women, including Julie, went into the hut to prepare tea to go with the snacks. Frank stayed outside and shared a few of his own stories about the early years of the new country.

Inside, Joy was astonished at the bond that quickly sprang up among the three women as they prepared tea and arranged the snacks. Was it because they shared stories of their children? Julie told them what a surprise she had when she found herself pregnant with her last born, twenty-five years ago. It was years after she thought she'd had her last and she'd been dismayed at the news. "But oh, what a blessing that child has been! I never imagined!" Joy smiled, wondering if Julie suspected that Zahra had been a surprise to her too.

The women took the tea outside. The snacks disappeared as though by magic with the whole family and a few neighbors to consume them.

The men told a few more stories from the old days, and Joy's father shared the last one about another *mzungu* man he'd met years after the first. "He kept asking which snakes were bad," he said. Joy, her family, and the neighbors all burst into laughter at this. Every child old enough to speak a sentence knew to kill any snake he had the bad luck to encounter!

"Ah Joy," said Frank on the drive home. "That was a wonderful afternoon. Your father's a good man. I like your family very much."

Joy, with Zahra in her arms, her new friend Julie next to her, and Emma and Elijah behind her in the Land Rover, smiled. Her *baba* was indeed a good man.

23

NEEMA, 2003–2005

Neema had managed to stay in her flat as the years went by, although she worried about money all the time. She was promoted from her position as deputy director to serve as acting director three years after she joined the Pharmaceutical Unit, when her boss moved to another department. Well, "promoted" — maybe, she often grumbled. As an "acting" she didn't get the salary of an official director, and her sitting allowances weren't as high. She'd been supporting Esther for eight years now, and she couldn't help but resent that expense sometimes. She could count on Imani to help out if needed, but she definitely didn't want to ask her father for money. He blamed her for the separation from Junior, which she avoided discussing with him — not too difficult since she rarely saw the man.

"I'm sure to be moved up into position as official director any time," she said on a visit to Bagamoyo while Imani listened, as always, to her daughter's talk about herself. "After all, I've had nearly ten years of experience in the unit and more than half of it as acting director. And I've been the principal investigator on published research papers, which ought to be in my favor."

Imani looked away. Neema had always insisted that her name be on any research that was even vaguely related to the Pharmaceutical Unit. In one instance, the editor of an international journal had questioned Neema's actual contribution to the work, and Neema had complained bitterly to Imani when she had to justify herself.

"How do your colleagues in the unit view the possibility of your promotion?" asked Imani.

Neema frowned in annoyance — the other people in the unit were her subordinates, not her colleagues — but she sensed her mother wouldn't like to hear that. "I'm known for being tough, of course," she said stiffly, "but I'm sure everyone thinks I'm fair."

Imani raised her eyebrows but made no comment.

Juma shuffled out with drinks for the women. Every time Neema saw him, she was struck by how much he'd aged since his wife died several years before. "Are you sure you shouldn't replace him with someone younger?" Neema had asked Imani once, and she was taken aback by her mother's anger.

Now Imani thanked the old man and settled back into her seat. "You know, Neema, there's been a fair amount of instability in several ministries recently, due to the rash of corruption scandals plaguing us. Several foreign aid organizations have pulled out of the country. I believe some higher-ups avoid making official appointments so they can escape blame if things don't work out — or when the political winds shift. So we often have more acting than official heads. And some people like the safety of being an 'acting.'"

"I suppose so," said Neema, "but I'm ready to move up. I've earned it."

∾

Sometimes, alone in the evening, after a drink or two, Neema wondered if Junior might be following her career. It would be gratifying if he heard she'd been moved up to the director's position. Over the years, through a few mutual acquaintances, she'd kept tabs on his life with his new family and she assumed he kept track of her. She made sure the right people knew she'd done well, counting on it getting back to Junior. It was good to hear that he hadn't done as well at his job as everyone expected. It was also satisfying to learn that his new "wife's" position in the Ministry of Education had little status. Surely he must regret the way he'd treated her.

Meanwhile, she waited for her promotion.

Neema had been avoiding Katharine for several years when she ran into her late one afternoon at the shops on the Slipway. After a few seconds of awkwardness, Katharine smiled and spoke.

"Hello, Neema. How are you?" Her smile looked genuine and she sounded like she actually cared. Neema had never forgiven Katharine for taking Junior's side in their marital problems. But she remembered with nostalgia what she and Katharine had shared in mutual struggles through training and their early years as doctors. And it wasn't just the work they'd shared — they'd had fun, too. So, she took a deep breath and answered.

"I'm fine. How are things for you?"

"Good." Katharine smiled. "Shall we have a drink?"

The two sat together for an hour, talking about their jobs and various happenings in the Ministry of Health. They skirted around personal matters for a while, but eventually Katharine mentioned that she'd married another doctor. She volunteered nothing about children, and Neema couldn't resist asking.

"Yes. I have two. A girl and a boy," Katharine said, and

then, to Neema's relief, she changed the subject to talk about her parents. They had dinner, and Neema found herself starting to be captured again by Katharine's charm.

After that evening, they started meeting every few months to catch up. Little was said about Junior and his new family, but the subject wasn't off limits either. Neema never asked directly, but she believed that Katharine saw Junior from time to time. She calculated what she told Katharine about her job and personal life to be sure the right things would get back to Junior.

"Oh Neema, I'm sure you'll be made director any time now. I heard the new Permanent Secretary wants to fill the position and you're the obvious choice for it."

"Yes, I think you're right. I'll be earning considerably more, too, now that some of the freezes on hiring and salaries have been lifted. I won't say I never thought I'd rise this high, because I did expect to. I just wasn't sure when. I'm ready for it now."

Some things hadn't changed: Katharine coyly pressed for more information. "And will you be sharing this news with someone special?"

"Ha, Katharine! I've been seeing several men and really must make some choices," Neema lied with an arch smile. She did occasionally meet a man for dinner, but none of these meetings developed into anything. She spent her evenings and weekends alone unless she was at Bagamoyo.

Neema got the message one rainy afternoon that Dr. Moses Kavimbi, the newly appointed Permanent Secretary, wanted to see her. She smiled. At last she was going to get the news she was waiting for. She arrived at his office on time and was greeted politely by his secretary. To her satisfaction, she was ushered directly into his office.

Dr. Kavimbi was an older man with gray hair. The fluorescent ceiling lights reflected off his wire-rimmed spectacles as he came around from behind his desk to greet her. He gave her a warm, broad smile and when she stretched out her hand to shake, he surprised her by taking it in both of his.

"Dr. Moyo. How are you? It's a pleasure to meet you in person."

"Thank you, sir. I'm fine, and how are you?"

"Oh, just fine, Dr. Moyo, just fine," he boomed. He turned the two armchairs in front of his desk to face each other. "Let's sit," he suggested, continuing to talk as they settled into their seats. "I've heard that you run a very efficient department as acting director and we're so grateful for that." He smiled again. "Of course, we expected it — you *are* your mother's daughter!"

At Neema's look of surprise, he chuckled. "Oh yes, I was very young myself, but I knew enough to look up to *Bibi* Imani. She was a great heroine to my older sisters and, young as I was, I did get to meet her. I knew enough to appreciate the work she did for this country. Truly she is a good woman! How's she doing? Still living in Bagamoyo?"

"Well, she's fine," Neema said with a smile, which broadened with satisfaction at his recognition of her mother. "She's in good health, and yes, she still lives in Bagamoyo. I see her often."

"Oh yes. I'm sure you do, good daughter that you are. She must be proud of you. I hope she's surrounded by grandchildren." Neema winced but hid it with a nod, waiting for the conversation to move in the direction she expected.

"I want to thank you for the job you've done serving as acting director. As I said, you've done it well and we all appreciate it." Dr. Kavimbi let a short silence develop while Neema basked in the praise. "And I want you to know that we realize how much work it's been. You've had to do the job without a deputy to help you over the years. That's been tough." He gave her a chance to acknowledge this, which she did with a solemn nod before he continued. "So, I know you'll be happy to learn that we've finally found the right person to take the position of director and you'll no longer have to shoulder that burden. I know you're going to enjoy working for Dr. Shilio. Like you, he has a background as a medical doctor. He also has a degree in chemistry that makes him well qualified for this position. With both of you in the department, the work ought to be much more manageable."

Neema felt the blood drain from her face and she swallowed around a suddenly dry mouth. She tightened her grip on the arms of her chair. Had she heard him correctly? Did her shock show? Perhaps it did, because Dr. Kavimbi rushed onward before she could speak. "Dr. Moyo, I do want to say again how grateful we are for your service. We couldn't have asked for more." He glanced over at the door and then offered a smile. "And I especially want for you to remember me to your mother."

He stood up, pushed back his chair, and stroked his chin. "I think she may recall me if you remind her of my sisters, Amili and Eunice." He waited for her to rise.

Unsure what else to do, she forced her stiff limbs to move and ignored the nausea in her stomach. As she rose, he put his hand on her back and started to guide her out of the room, talking steadily. "I hope to come around to visit the department soon. I'm trying to make personal visits in order to greet as many of the heads of departments as possible in our ministry. I doubt I'll get to your department by Monday when Dr. Shilio will start, but I'll be there eventually and I look forward to meeting you again back in your official position as deputy director." He added with a mirthless laugh, "Oh dear, you can imagine I have quite a job ahead!" As he showed her out the doorway, the final thing she heard was, "Looking forward to seeing you again soon, Dr. Moyo."

Neema stood dazed outside the office for a moment until

she commanded her feet to move. She walked past the secretary and into the hall. Even without Dr. Kavimbi's reminder of her mother, it would have been impossible not to think of her. She was flooded by a recollection of the tearful emotional scene years ago on the afternoon of her mother's great anger in Bagamoyo. A fierce anger of her own swept through her, leaving her scalded.

She walked stiffly back to her office, where everyone had left for the day. Once there, she collapsed at her desk and put her head down, trying to gather her thoughts and let the anger defuse.

Slowly it came to her that she needed to get away. She wrote a message for the secretary she shared with the department, stating that she'd be gone for a fortnight for a family emergency. But she didn't need to give any reason. Let the department remember that she was the boss — she was still acting director until Monday. She tore up the note and started to clear her desk. But why not leave it piled high with papers for Dr. Shilio to sort through? She took only a few personal items and left the office abruptly. She wasn't going to be there when Dr. Shilio arrived to take the position, nor, if she could help it, when Dr. Kavimbi came around for his departmental visit. She walked down to the parking lot, grateful the building was empty. She stopped at her flat to pack a small bag, then drove straight to Bagamoyo.

Neema arrived late in the day, and it wasn't until the next morning that she told her mother the story. *Bibi* Imani's face and, in fact, her whole body drooped as Neema told her about the conversation with Moses Kavimbi. "And did you actually know him and his sisters a long time ago?" asked Neema. "I'm surprised you could have been friends with him."

"Well, yes, Neema. They're a good family and I did know his sisters well. Moses isn't a bad man." Neema scowled, but Imani ignored it and continued. "I'm sorry, Neema. I wish it hadn't gone like this."

"But, Mama, don't you think this is unfair? That I was passed over just because they wanted to give the post to a man?" Surely her mother would agree with her on this!

"Sure, Neema, women have always had a harder time getting ahead." Imani gazed out at the ocean with a slight frown, then back at her daughter. "But there may be many reasons it worked out this way."

There was silence for a moment before Imani sighed, straightened up, and grimaced. "I *am* sorry, Neema. But now that you're here, let's try to have as pleasant a time as possible."

Neema frowned, annoyed at her mother's lack of sympathy. She couldn't quit thinking about the injustice she'd been dealt, and it was not a restful fortnight at Bagamoyo.

By the time Neema returned to work two weeks later, the rawness she'd felt was starting to be covered over by a tough and bitter scab. She resisted efforts to engage in the team atmosphere that Dr. Shilio was trying to build in the department. She did exactly what was required of her and not a bit more, maintaining an aggressive air of aloofness with her head held high.

Dr. Shilio spent his first few weeks studying the mandate of the department and getting to know the staff and their roles. No changes would be made right away. Neema would continue most of her duties, including ordering drugs and interacting with the suppliers who'd worked with the Ministry for years.

~

Two months after Dr. Shilio started, Neema met with Mr. Mark Tibaijuka, one of the vendors who arranged drug purchases for the Ministry, when he dropped by the office one morning. She'd ordered drugs from him for a few years and always found him agreeable. She appreciated the tactful way he conveyed his sympathy about her diminished position in the department.

"Well, Dr. Moyo, they sure missed an opportunity here. There's no substitute for the long experience you've had." He shook his head slowly. "There's just no way to understand some decisions made in the government, I guess." He frowned with concern, then brightened. "So, why don't we have lunch today? I've got some interesting new ideas to talk to you about."

"Okay," she said, nodding indifferently. "How about the Slipway? There are a couple of good restaurants there to choose from."

"Well, how about if we make it someplace small and quiet instead?" he said. "Too many people will want to stop and talk at those Slipway restaurants. You're a well-known person."

Neema nodded to acknowledge this and then suggested with a shrug that he select a place.

She'd never met this man outside the office before and she was surprised to find he drove a BMW — and a new model at that. "Well, it's no more than you ought to have," he laughed good-naturedly when she commented.

She gave a wan smile.

The restaurant was an exclusive one that she'd heard of but not visited before. The high prices impressed her, but she made no comment. As they ate, she asked about Tibaijuka's family and, when he asked about hers, she talked a little about Esther. He reiterated his sympathy concerning the choice of director.

"But you're still in charge of purchasing, right?" he asked. "You've got that all to yourself still? You're in charge of signing purchase and payment orders?"

"Sure, for now. I think the new director may be planning to split up these tasks and allocate them differently in the future, but for now I'm doing it the way I always did."

"Well, that's great then. There's an opportunity I'd like to suggest to you, and it sounds like now is the time for it."

"Oh? What's that?"

He leaned in closer. "Of course, you know that artemisinin combination therapies are set to become the first line treatment for malaria next year here in Tanzania."

"Of course. ACT is a great therapy. It's already being used in many places in the country — just not as first line yet."

"Sure. And I guess the government still hasn't decided which manufacturer they'll deal with in the long term." He shrugged. "But you know all this. I'm just afraid that when ACT becomes first-line treatment and orders go up, the prices may go up too."

"Maybe." Neema shrugged.

"Well, I've got a possibility of getting a large shipment right now at a great price from one of my old suppliers."

"Mmm. So?"

Mr. Tibaijuka leaned in closer, pursed his lips and nodded his head as though he were thinking aloud. "With the right purchase and payment order, working with the right party, one could make a nice little supplement." He kept his eyes directly on her as he spoke. "In your case, you know, this would kind of make up for what ought to have been yours anyway — I mean if you'd got the promotion everyone knows you should have had."

Neema took in a sharp breath, wanting to be sure she was understanding. "Are you suggesting I'd sign purchase and payment orders for one thing and another thing would actually be delivered?"

"Could work like that. You sign both purchase and payment orders now, right?"

"Well, yes," Neema said, nodding slowly.

"It would mean that you'd have to work with a supplier you know and trust — like me. He'd have to transfer the difference in the real price and what's shown on the payment order back to you. No one would be hurt by this, and we'd actually be saving some money for the Ministry in the long run."

"And the drug? It's actually from a good company that you know?"

"Oh yeah. Sure. A very good Chinese manufacturer I've been dealing with for several years."

"How much money are you talking about?"

He named a sum that made Neema widen her eyes. At this point she wasn't going to see a salary raise at all, and this deal would help make up for that loss. She thought about the financial frustrations she'd endured over the years and how she'd had to be so careful with money in order to maintain a lifestyle she'd rightfully earned. She thought guiltily about how she'd neglected Esther. It was time to bring her to Dar, and that would require extra funds.

"Is this a one-time deal?"

"Sure. Let's start that way, but we can see what might develop over time. It'd be important that you have a special account for this." He smiled at her while she studied his face.

"Are we the only ones who'd know about this? I don't want to get anyone else in the department involved."

"Of course." He reached into his coat pocket and drew out a paper that he unfolded while keeping his eyes on her. "Here are a few details you'll need. You can look it over later and let me know if you have any questions." He leaned back, crossed his arms and smiled again. "Shall we get you back to work now, Neema?"

∼

She looked the paper over carefully that night. All the details of what she needed to fill out on a purchase order and a payment request were here. She'd need to set up a new account to receive the kickback payment, but otherwise it was a simple matter. One thing she liked was that the amount she'd make was roughly the difference between her current salary and what she would have made as director had she been paid fairly over the past years for the work she'd done. It was very satisfying to think she'd get what should have been hers.

She was going to do the deal for the drugs.

Just before she fell asleep, something that had been niggling in the back of her mind came clear: Tibaijuka had called her by her first name as they left the restaurant.

24

JOY, 2006

"Daniel, wouldn't it be nice to take the whole family to Ndungu for a holiday?" asked Joy. "Your mother's never seen Zahra and she's getting bigger every day."

"Sure, I'd love for Mama to meet Zahra," said Daniel. "It'd mean a lot to her, and she's getting older all the time." He frowned. "But the cost of taking the whole family would be high. Do you really think we can do it?"

"Only if we start saving for it," said Joy with a smile.

By putting a little bit each week into a tin, Joy showed Daniel that it could be done. They reached their goal after months of effort. Madam agreed to Joy's request for a week off — enough time for a short visit — and they finished making their plans.

As the sun came up on a Saturday morning, the family was settled in the first of the *dalla dallas* and buses they had to take. It was packed, as were all of these vans that ferried thousands of people around daily. The drivers rented them for a day at a time to cover set routes and they made their money according to how many people they could jam in.

Emma and Elijah, twelve and nine years old, were dressed in their best clothes. Beside themselves with excitement, they vied for who got to hold Zahra on the seat and who got to sit next to the window. Zahra wore a new pair of little purple shoes. These were a treat that she didn't really need, but cheap goods from China were everywhere now, and Joy relented and bought them when Emma pointed out that the purple was the exact color of the jacaranda flowers the children loved. Zahra put them on immediately and couldn't quit touching and looking at them.

The older children skipped and walked quickly to keep up with their parents as they traversed dirt paths to make the transfers from *dalla dalla* to bus and back again. They danced with excitement when Daniel bought them each a soda from a vendor selling at the bus window. Zahra rode securely tied to Joy's back in a *kanga*, her little legs now long enough to dangle out the sides of the wrap. By catching an early morning bus from Moshi, they arrived at Same town in time to catch the last transport out to Ndungu, arriving just after nightfall, eight hours from the time they left home.

Daniel's parents made room for them in their hut near the village center, making it convenient for everyone to visit and see the latest addition to the family. The leafy boughs of a jacaranda provided a purple umbrella above and Joy couldn't quit smiling — it was fun to see her family as the center of attention. As she carried water, washed clothes, chopped vegetables, and stirred big pots of *ugali*, she laughed with pleasure to see her children run around with their cousins, shrieking through the village. Little Zahra tried to join, but her legs were short and she couldn't run well in the shoes, which she refused to take off. She screamed with delight when older children hoisted her up on their backs. At the end of each day the children were so exhausted they fell onto mats on the hut floor and slept without moving.

~

The only shadow in those few days was learning about the girl who had caused Daniel to delay his trip home the previous year. Joy made a point of looking for Esther to see how she was doing, but the women she asked just shrugged. No one was willing to talk about it.

"Auntie Mina," she said when she had a private moment with the old woman, "What happened to the girl, Esther?"

Auntie's face clouded over and she sighed deeply. "She refused to go back to school. Mostly she stays at home now and helps her mother."

"What do her parents say?" asked Joy. "Daniel told me the girl was receiving special support for school from a rich relative in Dar." She couldn't help thinking how much she wished she'd had that kind of support. "What do her parents make of her refusal to take advantage of that chance?"

"They don't understand it. They don't know what happened to their sunny girl to turn her into someone who's afraid of everyone. She has no friends now, either." Auntie hesitated. "I'm afraid the parents believe she's been bewitched."

"But what about the relative who was supporting her?" Joy persisted. "What does she think?"

"Ahh," said Auntie. "Well, we'll soon see about that. She used to come out here once or twice each year to see Esther. She made a visit right before the problem began. Then she didn't make it out here last year. So, Esther's parents haven't seen the woman since it happened, about a year ago. They just kept hoping the problem would right itself. They finally sent a message and asked her to come visit so they can tell her about the problem." She cocked her head. "In fact, Esther's mother told me she's supposed to come today or tomorrow. They're nervous about the meeting."

"What a shame," said Joy, turning to go back to her chores. The wasted educational opportunity was terrible but, as a mother, she viewed the trauma to the young girl as much worse. Both filled her with sorrow.

Auntie Mina had one more comment. "Just don't say anything to anyone about what happened. Of course, Daniel knows and he told you. But for Esther's sake don't mention it to anyone else."

"No worry," said Joy. "I don't want to make the poor girl's troubles worse than they already are. I saw what happened to a friend from my own village. She fell pregnant after a rape. She had to leave the village and never came back. No one helps a girl who's been raped."

Late that afternoon Joy saw a big car enter the village. Two women, as well as a driver, were visible through the darkened windows. "That must be the relative who's been supporting Esther," she said to Daniel.

On Tuesday morning, the fourth day they were in the village, Zahra woke up cranky. Daniel's attempts to improve her spirits by tossing her into the air led to muttering from some of the women about the proper way to treat little girls, but Joy and Daniel laughed this off. Still, the roughhousing didn't improve Zahra's mood. Joy was busy all day and only that night did she see that Zahra was quiet and without any energy.

"Feel her head," she said to Daniel. "She seems hot to me." Daniel frowned and placed his hand on Zahra's forehead.

"She *is* hot," he agreed. "Let's see how she is in the morning. If she's not better I'll go buy some medicine. There's a *duka la dawa* in the next village over."

That night, Zahra vomited twice and moaned frequently. Joy lay beside her, feeling helpless.

The first thing Wednesday morning, Daniel set off for the

village three kilometers away. At the little shop that sold medicines, he described the child's symptoms to the shop-keeper. "I think she has malaria," he said. The shopkeeper nodded in agreement.

"Here," he said, handing a small box to Daniel. "This is the best. Smash the tablets in water. Give the child two now and two more at midday, then two around sunset. This should take care of it," he said confidently. Daniel handed over his money, took the tablets, and ran all the way back to Ndungu.

Once there, he raced back into the hut, where he and Joy smashed two tablets in water and, tilting Zahra's head back, managed to get her to swallow them. By that time, the neighbors all knew that Zahra was ill. Everyone was concerned and offering advice.

"Feed her," insisted one mother.

"Don't let her eat," countered another.

Joy and Daniel heard raised voices a few meters outside the hut and they went out to see what the commotion was about. One of the village elders, a traditional healer, was arguing with Daniel's mother.

"You should not trust the medicine from that *duka la dawa*," he said heatedly. "I can make a tea from the best tree bark that is very good for malaria."

Daniel's mother seemed skeptical. "I've seen several people worsen after using the healer's concoctions," she said in a low voice to Joy and Daniel. "I don't want to offend a respected elder, but I'm worried about taking his advice."

"Let's see how the tablets work first," Joy suggested. "Then maybe we'll try the tea." The healer clicked his tongue in disapproval but stopped arguing with the family.

Zahra grew steadily sleepier over the morning and by midday, when she got the second dose of medicine, Joy was panicked. The nearest health center was only five kilometers away, but everyone in the village insisted that going there was a mistake. "Don't waste time at that place," agreed all the women. "There're no medicines to be had there and often no staff, either." The mothers, gathered around the hut, were firm: "You need to go to the District Hospital in Same right now."

"Wait," said a young woman in a red kerchief. "I heard that one of those visitors from Dar — the ones who came to visit Esther's family — is a doctor. I'll go get her." She took off towards Esther's house.

Zahra lay on a pallet in a hut while Joy sat by her side, caressing her gently, bathing her with water, and fanning her with a piece of stiff cardboard that Daniel's mother found for her. Sweat dripped from Joy's face onto Zahra. Daniel paced around the hut and stuck his head in every few minutes to see what was happening to his little daughter. Where was the doctor? Joy got up every five minutes and went out to pace with Daniel and look around. By the time the red-kerchiefed woman appeared at the door of the hut Joy was near tears, but a spark of hope flared in her heart when the woman spoke.

"Joy. Joy," she said. "This is Dr. Neema Moyo, from Dar-es-Salaam. She's agreed to examine Zahra."

25

NEEMA AND IMANI, 2006

When Neema got the message from Esther's parents asking her to visit Ndungu as soon as she could, she knew she was overdue.

"Mama, I know I should have gone out there before now. You don't have to remind me that it's been a year since I've gone." Imani looked at her sharply and Neema rearranged her pout into a half-smile. "And, thank you for offering to go with me. It'll be a far nicer trip in your car than in mine."

"Why did Esther's parents say they wanted you to visit now?" asked Imani, ignoring the implied complaint about the car.

"They didn't give any reason. Just said there was something important they wanted to discuss."

Neema frowned. She hadn't intended to neglect Esther. Maybe she was ready to bring her to Dar, especially since she'd received the nice sum from the deal with Tibaijuka. Maybe she could buy a nicer car, too, although she needed to be careful — people might wonder if she made a sudden change in her spending habits. And she ought to try to make the money go as far as possible. Dr. Shilio was making management changes in the unit, and another deal with Tibai-juka might be tricky.

∾

Neema and Imani arrived in Ndungu on a Monday, in the late afternoon, and the village looked the same as it always did. A group of villagers gathered around the big car and made them feel welcome. Esther's parents appeared almost immediately with their greetings, but Esther was nowhere to be seen. Despite the warm treatment and the excitement caused by visitors arriving in a big car, Neema sensed a wariness in the women who greeted them.

"Thank you for coming, *Bibi* Imani and Dr. Neema. We'll have time to talk tomorrow," was all Esther's parents said as they helped the visitors settle in.

"Mama, do you think there's something wrong here?" Neema asked her mother later that night when they were finally alone in the guestroom of the Sisters of Charity.

"I don't know, Neema. I do have the feeling that everyone is rather restrained — like there's something hanging in the air that isn't good." She shrugged. "But I guess we'll find out tomorrow. Let's go to bed."

But Neema didn't sleep well. Where was Esther? Why hadn't she come running to greet her as she always had in the past?

∾

On Tuesday, around mid-morning, Neema and Imani walked across the dusty village to visit Esther's home. To Neema's relief, Esther herself came out of the house, bringing tea. But it took her only a moment to see the change in Esther. Not only did she not come running to greet them, but her posture was more like that of an old woman than a young girl. She kept her eyes on the ground and didn't look the visitors — or even her parents — in the eye. She'd lost weight and her clothes hung on her slight frame. As she approached Neema, she managed a timid half-smile, still without eye contact, and she accepted but did not return a hug. She spoke politely when forced to respond, but the childish exuberance of the past was completely gone. Esther disappeared back into the house as soon as everyone was served tea. As they sat back and sipped the hot sweet liquid, Neema spoke.

"Esther seems very quiet. How's school going?"

Esther's parents looked at each other and her father nodded at his wife to speak.

"That's what we wanted to talk to you about. That's why we asked you to come visit." Neema and Imani glanced at each other and frowned.

"What's the problem?"

Esther's mother swallowed, shifted in her chair, and began. "About a year ago, shortly after your last visit, Esther quit going to school all of a sudden. She wouldn't say why, even when we insisted she tell us. At first she said she felt too sick to go and she stayed in bed for many days." She paused and rubbed her brow. "Over the next few weeks she gradually got out of bed and started doing some chores around the house. But she said she didn't want to go back to school. She wouldn't give any reason." She looked down at the ground, then up at Imani, teary-eyed. "Nothing we said would change her mind and she refused to talk about it. In fact, she didn't talk much to anyone about anything. She did her chores and even took on new ones since she had time." Tears ran down the woman's cheeks. "I'm sorry, this is very hard," she said softly. "It hasn't changed in months. Now, if she's not doing chores she stays around the house, doesn't play with her friends, or visit with anyone outside the family. At first, she hid when her friends came by to see her. Now they've quit coming. Once in a while she sees old Auntie Mina when she visits, but that's it." She paused again to wipe her cheeks, then shook her head sorrowfully.

Neema leaned forward in her chair. "But you must have ordered her to tell you what's the matter," she said. "She's always been an obedient girl. How could she not give you a reason for her behavior?" She shook her head in disbelief.

Esther's parents both shrugged as they looked at each other, and then her father spoke. "We're very sorry about this, but we have no explanation. I even went to the school to ask if her teacher knew anything, but he said no — he knew nothing. No one at the school could give us any reason. Even the head teacher denies any understanding of it. He thinks maybe she was . . ." The father paused and swallowed hard. "Well, he thinks maybe she was bewitched." With this admission, tears filled his eyes.

Esther's mother took over again. "We've kept the money you were sending for school expenses and we can return it to you."

"But we're concerned about Esther," said Imani, her voice rising. "The money's only one issue. What about Esther?"

The four adults sat in silence, no one knowing what to do or say. Eventually, Esther's mother remarked that they had prepared a meal for the visitors. She got up and went inside to gather plates and cutlery. She and Esther came out together and the two of them served a banana stew over rice.

Esther took her plate and started to sit apart from everyone else.

"Esther, wouldn't you like to come sit here next to me?" asked Imani softly.

The girl didn't say a word and she kept her head down, but she did move her stool just a little closer to Imani's. There was almost no conversation during the meal, and Neema and Imani left soon afterward.

The two women spent what remained of the afternoon walking around the village, stopping to make calls on people they knew. They tried to bring up the subject of Esther with several people, but no one would talk about it. The sense that something was wrong in the village grew stronger as the afternoon ended and the evening waned. "Tomorrow, I'm going to talk to Auntie Mina myself," announced Imani that night. "I've known her for a long time, and I think she'll tell me what's going on."

∼

It wasn't hard to find Auntie Mina on Wednesday morning. Imani went alone since Neema didn't know the woman. After lengthy greetings, Mina prepared tea. The two women conversed for a while, catching up on the lives of mutual friends and acquaintances who'd moved outside the village. Only after those discussions died down did Imani finally broach the subject of Esther. Auntie Mina sighed deeply and seemed to weigh her thoughts. Finally, she spoke.

"I've been silent about this because I made a promise to Esther. But considering your place in her life, I wonder if it's really a favor to her to keep you in the dark. In fact, you may be the only one who can help her." The old lady looked off in the distance. "I'd hoped she might heal with time, but it's not happening. In fact, things are getting worse. Maybe you could take her out of this village."

Then, slowly, Auntie Mina told Imani what had happened.

Imani's mind churned with rage and disgust as she heard the story. She struggled to find words. "I can't believe that a teacher in our schools was involved in this — and yet . . ." She thought back to discussions of corruption in the schools on her veranda and she wrung her hands. "I knew there was cheating and payoffs for grades but I never imagined this! Why didn't I insist Esther come to Dar where we could have kept a closer eye on her? Oh, Auntie, I just feel old and helpless sometimes," she cried. "Can you imagine what *Mwalimu* Nyerere would have thought?"

"It's painful to see," agreed Auntie Mina. "But let's not forget that there's always been evil in this world. Men have always taken what they want from women. This is not something new." She sighed. "And I'm afraid there's more. You need to know something else." She swallowed. "The people here believe this village has been bewitched."

"Yes, Esther's father mentioned that," said Imani. She didn't have any faith in sorcery herself, but the concept could be very powerful in village life. "You don't think they'd harm Esther, do you? To cure the bewitching?"

Auntie Mina looked with deadly seriousness at Imani. "It could happen," she said slowly. "It *has* happened in this village in such cases."

Imani slumped for several minutes, twisting her hands together. Finally, she sighed and stood up. "Thank you for your honesty with me, Auntie. Let's see what can be done. We need to make a plan."

Imani returned to Neema, knowing there was no easy way to give this news to her daughter. "Esther was raped, Neema. She was raped by an old man with the help of a teacher at her school and that's why she won't go back there."

Neema's eyes widened in horror. "But this is terrible! Didn't her parents go to the school about it? Why didn't they tell us what happened?"

"Neema, her parents don't know what happened. Try to imagine how the girl felt. You didn't grow up in a village like this, but I did. Many people would blame the girl — or just assume it was somehow her fault. Esther herself probably feels she did something wrong. She was so ashamed, she made Auntie Mina promise not to tell anyone." Imani shifted on the bed where she and Neema sat in their room. "And Neema, I'm really worried about what could happen to Esther. Apparently, people think she's bewitched. In these little villages, terrible things can be done to women and girls who are bewitched to try to prevent them from turning into witches."

Neema started to reply, but there was a noise outside the window.

"*Hodi,*" called a woman outside, announcing her presence. "*Hodi.*"

"Yes, we're here. Please come in," said Imani in response to the woman in a red kerchief who was catching her breath outside the window.

"*Habari ya asubuhi,*" said the kerchiefed woman with a small bow. Once greetings were exchanged, she explained her purpose. "I'm sorry to disturb you, but I think you are a doctor?" she said, looking at Neema.

"Yes, I'm a doctor," said Neema, holding her head a little higher. "I'm Dr. Neema Moyo."

The woman gave a deferential nod. "The young grand-daughter of my neighbor has fallen ill. We're all so worried. *Tafadhali, naomba* — please. Can you come see her?"

"Of course," said Imani, standing up before Neema had time to reply. "We can come right now, can't we, Neema?"

"I guess we can," Neema said with a shrug, rising from the bed.

With the kerchiefed woman in the lead, the three women made their way quickly across the village to the hut where the sick child lay. A number of people were gathered outside near the door, talking in low voices. As Neema and Imani approached, a man stepped forward from the group.

"Daniel," said the kerchiefed woman to the man, "this is *Bibi* Imani and Dr. Neema."

The man stretched his hand out as the kerchiefed woman added, "Daniel is the child's father." Then she stepped into the hut, from where Neema could hear her talking to someone.

"*Shikamoo*," Daniel greeted Neema and Imani solemnly.

"*Marahaba*," replied Imani, inclining her head to acknowledge the respect.

"My little daughter, Zahra, is sick. Thank you for agreeing to examine her," said Daniel. He turned to an older woman standing behind him and introduced her as the *bibi* of the little girl. After those greetings were completed, he led them into the hut.

Neema stooped to step inside and was immediately assaulted by the smell of wood smoke and a slightly musty odor — no surprise, since a number of people were obviously staying in this tiny room. A small child who looked to be about two years old lay sprawled on a grass mat. A teary-eyed woman was bathing the child's body with water and fanning her with a piece of old cardboard. The woman rose when Neema entered the hut. "*Shikamoo*," she said with a curtsy.

"I'm Dr. Moyo," said Neema, somewhat brusquely. "I guess you're the child's mother."

"Yes. I'm Joy," was the reply.

"What happened?" asked Neema.

The mother spoke in a tremulous voice. "She was fine yesterday morning, but she fell sick by late afternoon. She slept poorly last night and vomited a couple of times. She feels very hot."

"Hmm," said Neema, grimacing as she knelt on the ground to examine the child.

The little girl was burning with fever and her heart rate was high. Neema tried to put aside her frustration at being expected to do an examination in such primitive conditions with no instruments. The girl's neck flexed easily without stiffness and her abdomen felt okay. In the poor light of the hut it was difficult to tell, but, judging by the color of her inner eyelids, she didn't seem to be anemic. She tested for any response to pain and the little girl barely moved. That made Neema's heart quicken. The child most likely had malaria — and she was definitely slipping into a coma. She turned to Joy.

"Have you been using a bed net?" Neema asked her briskly.

"Yes. Faithfully," said the tearful woman, looking stricken but struggling to appear dignified.

"And have you given her any treatment?"

"Yes. We bought tablets at a shop near here this morning. The man said they were the best for malaria." She pulled a box with green lettering from her *kanga* and Neema read on the front *ACT – Artemisinin Combination Therapy*.

"Good. This *is* the best drug for malaria. I think your daughter will start to improve. But meanwhile she's very ill and there's nothing more we can do for her here. It's best if you can get her to the District Hospital in Same. Is that possible?"

Joy gave a discouraged sigh and was about to say something when Imani, who had followed Neema into the hut, spoke up. "Of course. My driver can take her in our car. He can leave immediately."

Relief flooded the anxious mother's face. "Oh, thank you, madam," she said with a breaking voice. "And thanks be to God."

"We'll go right now to alert the driver," said Imani.

Neema followed her mother as they walked rapidly back across the village. "We should go with them, Neema," said Imani. "Gather a few things for the night quickly and let's go. The family may need some financial support and I intend to give it. We can decide what to do about Esther when we get back."

26

IMANI AND NEEMA, 2006

The big car was ready to go within twenty minutes. Imani sat in the front passenger seat and Neema settled behind the driver. As soon as they pulled up at the hut, Joy emerged, and Daniel followed with the sick child in his arms. Joy climbed into the backseat with Neema and Daniel tenderly lay his sick daughter on the seat with her head in Joy's lap. Then he clambered into the far back of the vehicle and they were off.

With shaky hands, Joy managed to get another dose of medicine down Zahra's throat in the car. This reassured Neema a little bit but it had no effect on Zahra, who started making an eerie moaning sound. A few minutes later, the child had a seizure. Joy screamed and broke down in sobs.

"Daniel, she's burning up with fever," she cried. Neema watched Daniel lean over the seat to stroke his daughter and try to comfort his wife with gentle touches, but his face was set in fear. Imani, in the front seat, urged the driver to go faster if he could.

Thirty minutes later, they came to a small wooden shack that served as a *duka* for the sparse huts in the area. Imani shoved money at the driver. "Go in, please, and buy three large bottles of water," she urged him.

"We'll use them for wetting this cloth to cool Zahra," Imani told Joy, handing her a small towel from the front.

The driver ran in, ran back out a few minutes later with the water, and jumped behind the wheel. They rode on, lurching over the bumpy road, the car filled with silent, heavy fear. The grim-faced driver muttered under his breath when they hit the bigger potholes, but he pushed the car as fast as he could.

Neema helped Joy keep the towel wet and applied to the burning little body, and they took turns fanning Zahra with the cardboard Joy had used earlier. Neema barely noticed the water splashing over the car seat and onto her clothes and feet. She watched helplessly as Zahra became deeply unconscious, emitting low moans and occasionally twitching with a seizure. Neema had seen plenty of gravely ill people, both adults and children, but to be trapped, sitting side by side with a mother radiating raw fear for two hours as she watched her child slip away, forced her into parts of her mind she didn't want to go. The drive seemed to go on forever. The mother's vulnerability was terrifying. Neema couldn't avoid thinking about her own barrenness, and a tiny needle of relief pierced her as she realized it was a vulnerability she'd never have to experience.

The Same hospital was just off the main road through town and the driver pulled right up to the front door. He ran around to the back to open the rear of the car so Daniel could jump out as Joy got out of her seat, struggling to lift Zahra with her. Daniel took Zahra in his arms, and he and Joy ran together into the hospital. Imani and Neema hurried close behind them.

Within a few minutes, the nurse on duty took blood samples and inserted an intravenous drip into Zahra's arm. A senior nurse came in to talk to the duty nurse as she gave

Zahra an injection in her thigh. The senior nurse did her own examination and frowned. "I'm going to get the doctor," she said, hurrying out of the room.

Joy answered questions, explaining what had happened and what she'd witnessed of Zahra's behavior over the past forty-eight hours. "I've given her three doses of malaria medicine from the *duka la dawa*," she said; the nurses exchanged glances, nodded, and seemed to be reassured.

Zahra lay in a small bed in a room with a dozen small beds, most occupied by sick children under the watch of worried mothers. Imani stood by Joy's side and frequently put her hand out to steady the woman. Neema didn't say a word or interfere with the hospital team, but stood at the foot of the bed. Several nurses gathered around Zahra, one checking her pulse and blood pressure and another bathing her with cool cloths. Joy's face seemed to fall apart as Zahra's breathing became very irregular, with occasional gasps and long, slow exhalations.

The doctor appeared. The nurses introduced him to the parents and to Dr. Moyo. He nodded and turned to Joy. "Do you have the medicine you gave her?"

Joy pulled it out of her bag with trembling hands to show him. He studied the box for several seconds, then took out the little paper inside and read it over. "Where did you buy this?" he asked.

"From a *duka la dawa* near Ndungu," Daniel answered solemnly for his wife, who was sobbing quietly and biting her fists now, too overwrought to speak.

"A proper shop? Not just a trader?" persisted the doctor.

Daniel nodded. "Yes, it was a proper shop."

The doctor turned to the nurse standing next to him and spoke in a low voice. "Look at this — at the package insert. The name's spelled wrong. It says *Artminsin*. And look at the symbol on the insert — it isn't right either and it doesn't match what's on the box. I don't trust these tablets. I'm afraid they're counterfeit."

He handed the paper to Neema. "Look, Dr. Moyo. You see exactly what I mean, don't you?"

Neema took the insert and looked at it. Her eyes widened and she stiffened, started to speak, and then clamped her mouth shut. Why hadn't she looked more carefully when the little girl's mother showed her the box in the hut? She'd not thought at all of the possibility that the medicine could be fraudulent. She handed the insert back to the doctor, who crumpled it in his fist.

Imani, standing on the other side of the nurse, grasped the side of the bed for support.

The intravenous fluids and drugs running into Zahra's arm were finally getting into her bloodstream, bolstering her and going after the parasites multiplying there.

But it was too late.

Within a half hour, Zahra took one last gasp, then went still. Neema couldn't take her eyes off the wailing, grief-stricken mother. When their eyes met, she saw a pain whose dark depths she couldn't fathom.

The nurses pulled a screen around Zahra's bed as the other mothers in the room stood back, silent and respectful. Imani and Neema moved back too and left the parents together at the bedside. The only noise in the room was the keening of the bereaved couple. One little purple shoe had fallen from Zahra's foot and lay on top of the sheet.

Imani wondered how she'd made it through that night. Sorrows seemed to grow greater as she aged, and this time it felt like their weight might crush her. In some ways, Zahra's death was harder to bear than that of her own child years before. This little girl had been alive long enough to show the world her personality, to make her own tiny imprint on many people who'd miss her and whose lives would be changed. And it wasn't fate, but deliberate evil that was responsible for this tragedy.

Imani did what she could to help the grieving couple. She organized transport for them to accompany the body to Moshi, where they lived, and she assured the couple she'd organize the trip back to Moshi for their two older children as well once she reached Ndungu. She was glad to be of service and grateful that she had the money to help. The death seemed to have affected Neema deeply. Her daughter had withdrawn and barely said a word since Zahra died.

Joy and Daniel left the next day, huddled together in the rear seat of a vehicle hired by Imani. The child's body lay across their laps, wrapped in a white sheet.

Imani and Neema headed back to Ndungu in Imani's car. Neema seemed less withdrawn than she had the night before, and Imani tried to talk about what had happened.

"Mmm. Yes," said Neema. "Malaria can strike so fast. No one knows why some children develop the severe forms while others have only mild symptoms. Those parents might not have used their bed nets properly. They seemed like they weren't very well educated." She paused a moment, stretched, and yawned. "Although they did manage to get drugs quickly for the girl in the village." She shook her head. "So many parents wait too late to start treatment."

Imani felt a chill. Neema was unnaturally cold. Was it because she was a doctor who had seen many deaths before — even in children — that she was this way? With a flash of antipathy towards her daughter, she spoke more harshly than usual.

"Neema, those parents did everything they could possibly

do. It was bad medicine that killed the child." Shaking her head, Imani added more calmly, "I don't know how that stuff gets into the shops."

"It gets in when itinerant traders sell it," Neema said stridently. "I wouldn't be surprised if the father bought those tablets directly from a market trader and never even went to a proper *duka la dawa*. He could have been lying to the doctor at the hospital."

Imani felt ill and she rubbed her head. She didn't want to talk to her daughter anymore. Instead, she started turning over in her mind how she would deliver the tragic news back in Ndungu. Should she mention the counterfeit medicine? Something had to be done about that or there might be other deaths. Would it be kindest to tell the child's grandmother the whole truth immediately?

A number of villagers, including Zahra's grandmother, crowded up to the vehicle as they pulled into Ndungu. Imani got out and walked with the grandmother into her hut. Tears poured down the faces of both women as Imani told her what happened at the hospital.

After a decent interval, Imani left and slipped back across the village to take refuge at the guesthouse. She was exhausted by all that had happened since she arrived in Ndungu a few short days before. Still, she intended to pursue the question of the medicine at the *duka*.

"Neema, you may not believe the medicine came from the *duka la dawa*, but we have an obligation to check. We're going there first thing tomorrow. We can't take a chance that this might happen to someone else. Now let's both get some rest."

~

After breakfast the next day, Imani had her driver take them to the shop where Daniel said he bought the medicine for Zahra.

Neema dreaded the visit but could think of no way to avoid it. She'd spent a restless night telling herself not to worry. Assuming the medicine actually came from the shop, it was likely that the owner got it from some itinerant salesman. In fact, it might be satisfying to catch the shopkeeper who'd made such a transaction.

But a part of her didn't want to learn more.

The shop was only a few minutes from Ndungu by car. It was a single tiny room, much like any other *duka la dawa*. A wooden glass-fronted case that also served as a counter extended across the width of the shop. Inside the case, behind the glass, a few small boxes and bottles were neatly arranged. A simple wooden chair behind the counter and two shelves on the wall above it with a few more neat stacks of small boxes completed the furnishings. Tinny music blared from a little radio on the floor.

A balding middle-aged man got up from the chair behind the counter and turned down the sound as the two women entered. The three exchanged greetings and the shopkeeper spoke.

"How can I help you? You need some medicines this morning?"

Neema and Imani had talked about how they would approach this, and Imani spoke first.

"Yes, we'd like some antimalarial tablets. My grandson has been ill with fever for two days now, so we think it's malaria."

"Yes, that's probably right," agreed the shopkeeper solemnly, stroking his chin, then reaching into the case. He pulled out a box printed in green across the front. "This is the best drug," he said, handing the small carton to Imani.

Neema recognized the box she'd seen in the hut and again at the bedside in the hospital. She took it from Imani. It looked perfectly normal at first glance, just as it had in the hut two days ago. She studied it more carefully this time, noting the sell-by date, which was okay. Her throat tightened as she read in fine print on one end that the drug was manufactured in China. She opened the box and took out the package insert. It was exactly like the one she'd seen at Same hospital. Her mother must have read that fact in her face.

"It's the same medicine, isn't it?" asked Imani anxiously. "What a shame we didn't know. We might have been able to find another *duka la dawa* on the way to Same with a different brand. Perhaps we could have given good medicine to the little girl sooner."

Neema kept her face down for a few seconds as she clenched and unclenched her jaw a few times. "Where did you buy this?" she finally asked, looking up and directly at the shopkeeper, dreading his answer but holding her head up.

He frowned. "It came from the Ministry of Health, of course. That's where I get all my stock. Why are you asking me? And who are you?"

Neema ignored his questions. "Do you have the bill of sale?"

He rummaged through a drawer behind the counter and drew out a paper. "Yes. Yes, I do," he said, thrusting it at her. "Just look at it."

Neema did look and she looked hard, hoping to find any indication of a forgery. But the document looked authentic. Her mouth dried and sweat collected under her arms as she scanned the paper. She'd never actually seen the boxes of ACT she and Tibaijuka arranged to bring into the country, so she didn't know what they looked like. She grasped at a straw — maybe this wasn't what they'd imported. Tibaijuka had said his source was reliable.

But she felt sick. Why hadn't she examined the shipment that she and Tibaijuka imported? Why had she trusted the man?

The shopkeeper was staring at her and waiting for a

response. She had to say something. She struggled to move her tongue in her dry mouth.

"These drugs are not good, sir." She thrust the package insert at him. "Look at the errors in spelling and the symbols. This medicine may be defective."

"But I bought these drugs properly," protested the shop-keeper, folding his arms and straightening his back. "Who are you?"

Imani took a step forward and put a hand on Neema's arm. "Sir, please don't be worried. Dr. Moyo works for the Ministry of Health. You've provided us with what we need and she'll follow up. This bill of sale shows that you followed proper procedures and you're not in any trouble. Now, is there someplace we can make a copy of this paper?"

Mollified, but still frowning, the man pointed across the street at another shop where a hand-lettered sign on a board read *Copy/fax*. She and Imani walked over to the shop and, after waiting fifteen minutes for the shopkeeper to start his generator, they copied the bill.

When they returned to the *duka la dawa*, the shopkeeper, clearly shaken, handed them a bag with five boxes of tablets in it. "This is all I have left," he said. "You can take it, but you need to pay for it just like I did," he added with a scowl.

Imani handed him money and the two women left with assurances to the shopkeeper that they'd get back to him, that he shouldn't worry, but that he mustn't sell any more of the tablets if he happened to find more boxes in his shop.

Imani shook her head slowly as she and Neema got back into the vehicle. "Oh, Neema, just imagine. Counterfeit medicines coming from the Ministry itself. This makes me ill. One more example of corruption in our country. You must be devastated. I'm glad you're in a position to look into it."

Nausea rose in Neema. She struggled to hide her shaking hands from her mother. "I'll deal with this as soon as I get back to Dar, Mama. Can we just let it go for now? Let's get back to what we came here for. Let's concentrate on what we can do for Esther."

Imani sank back in the vehicle's passenger seat with a long exhalation. "Okay. I'm glad you're thinking about Esther's future. I have some ideas about that."

27

JOY, 2006

Joy and Daniel buried Zahra in a small cemetery near fields of tall green maize in Joy's childhood village, overlooked by Mount Kilimanjaro. As they walked away from the burial site along the hard-packed mud road, the procession of neatly dressed mourners broke up. Madam and Mr. James attended and filled their hands with dirt to throw on the casket at the end of the ceremony, but they did not accompany the mourners back to the village. There, women laid out dishes of greens, bowls of *ugali* with beans, and stewed bananas, all cooked that morning to feed the mourners. Daniel tried to mingle with the guests, but Joy couldn't do it.

She retired into a little windowless addition that her father had put up to provide extra space for the four children still living at home. Emma and Elijah sat solemnly next to the house, getting up every now and again to go inside to sit with their mother. Other friends and family came in a few at a time so that Joy was not left alone with her grief.

Joy stayed in the house for nearly a week, while waves of pain, each as overwhelming as the last, washed over her.

Sights and sounds around her were wavy and dreamlike, as if she were deep underwater and drowning in sorrow.

Outside the house, her father sat for hours, protecting her from some of the people who came around to see her. "Daniel told us about the bad medicine that Zahra got from the *duka la dawa* near Ndungu," said an old man who had been at the funeral, "and we should think of something to do about it. Corruption will kill this country." But Joy's father countered this.

"*Mzee*," he said, clenching a fist, "don't you think I'm angry about what happened? Sure, I'd like to hurt that man that sold Daniel the bad medicine." But then he relaxed, his face softened, and he spoke more gently. "But corruption and evil have always existed. We can waste our lives trying to get rid of them from the top. What we have to do is build the best families and villages we can, in spite of it. We have to teach our children the right ways to try to make sure they don't add to the evil." He wiped a tear away from his eye. "And when we get hit by the bad things, all we can do is try to move forward. My heart breaks for my daughter, and right now helping her is what I need to do."

Joy eventually emerged from the dark house with Daniel, flanked by Elijah and Emma. The sun was warm on her face and it was comforting to hear the shouts of neighbor children at play. The waves of grief continued to flood her unpredictably, and each left a vast, washed-out emptiness behind.

Elijah and Emma were subdued and cried frequently and pitifully. Two more weeks passed and Joy slowly began to move about more, fetching water and sometimes helping with the cooking for the family.

"Joy, do you think you should go back to work soon?"

asked Daniel one day, an edge of anxiety in his voice. "Madam sent a message a few days ago. She said to take your time, but I think she'd like to have you back soon. I know it's hard, but maybe it would be good to get busy somewhere else."

"Can't do it," was all Joy could reply.

Her father found her outside the next evening on her own, sitting and weeping on the bank of the river where she'd spent so much time as a girl.

"Joy, it pains me to see you this way."

Joy said nothing, but she looked up at him as he squatted on the large rock the women used for beating the clothes.

"I want to tell you a story," he began. "Do you remember your mother at all?"

Joy shook her head no and her father continued. "She was a wonderful woman. When I met her, she was a beautiful, happy girl who worked hard. I could hardly believe it when she and her family agreed for us to marry. She made every single day a celebration for me. The day you were born was the happiest of our lives. She took care of us and she loved you with all she had. You were only about eighteen months old when she died." Here he grimaced, and tears formed in the corners of his weathered eyelids. Joy put her hand out to touch his arm. "But what you don't know, because I never told you, is that I lost more than your mother that terrible day. She passed giving birth to a little boy. I lost them both." He trembled slightly and Joy kept her hand on his arm. "So, Joy, I do know something of the pain you're feeling now." They sat in silence for several minutes as he collected himself. "I felt like the sun would never warm me again . . . like the world was a black and cold place and it would always be that way." Joy squeezed his arm gently.

"What saved me was having you, Joy. You were too young to understand what we'd lost. You woke up each day with a smile or a laugh. I didn't want to see you lose that. You reminded me every day that life was worth living and that the sun would warm me again."

Joy's eyes had filled as she listened. "But, *Baba*, did it ever stop hurting?"

"No, Joy, it has never stopped hurting. I think about your mother and our little boy every day. But I also find new reasons to be glad to be alive every day. I love each of my other children — and that eases the pain."

The faces of Emma and Elijah slipped into Joy's mind and settled there. Then she did something she hadn't done since she was a very small girl. She threw herself into her father's arms and sobbed without control. It was a magnificent relief. She slowed down finally, with some hiccups, and looked up to see that Daniel had joined them with Emma and Elijah. They entered the embrace and the five family members held each other, sitting in silence for a long time.

Then Joy kissed her two remaining children, stood up, and put out her hands. They all walked back to the house together.

~

Over the next week, Joy found that talking to her father about a lot of things was helpful.

"*Baba*, I've lost faith in our country. I've learned so many things I don't want to know. It seems like teachers aren't what they're supposed to be. Government officials are rude and corrupt. What happened to the ideals of *Mwalimu* Nyerere? Was all that talk about Independence and unity in the country just lies?"

"Ahh, Joy," her *baba* said with a sad smile. "Yes, you're grown up now. I did want you to love this country and all it stands for and I know that you have. Don't give that up." He paused in his repair of an old wood plow he still used. "I do believe in what *Mwalimu* Nyerere stood for. I believe in his ideas, even though it's hard to make them work. So much depends on a few people at the top to do the right thing — and sometimes they become corrupt." He smiled at his daughter. "I wish I could have protected you from all this — but then you'd never have grown up. Believe what you do matters, Joy. That's what hope is. Keep it. That's the best strength anyone can have."

Joy, Daniel, Emma, and Elijah went back to their rented room in Moshi so Joy could go back to work. Daniel had removed Zahra's few small clothes so that Joy didn't have to see them. Their household had shrunk to four.

The neighbors were all there to welcome them back. For the first few weeks friends came by every day to visit, bringing food to share. Joy walked Emma and Elijah to school on their first day back so she could explain to the teacher where they had been. Then, finding she wanted to be with them as long as possible each morning, she continued for several months to walk them to school before continuing on to work.

At Madam's, Yussuf let her in the gate and nodded respectfully. There were condolence cards from Madam's sons, who were in secondary school in America, as well as from some of the visitors Joy had taken care of as houseguests at Madam's over the years. It was some comfort to carry out familiar routines and, if she sometimes had to stop to wipe away tears, she did it and then moved on.

The first time she went back to Deepak's, she was surprised and moved when Mr. Deepak came out from behind the counter and took both her hands.

"I'm so sorry for your loss, Joy," he said simply. And she wondered how she could ever have been afraid of this kind man.

Her father was right. There was still much goodness in the world. It mattered what she did.

28

NEEMA, 2006

I t was mostly due to the efforts of Imani and Auntie Mina that Esther left Ndungu with Neema and Imani a few days after the incident with the child who died. Esther still wasn't talking much.

"I'm very sad to see her go," said Esther's mother softly, "but perhaps it's for the best. Maybe the change will bring the old Esther back to life."

"I think she'll be happy living with Neema," said Imani with a reassuring smile. "After she gets settled, Neema will enroll her in a nearby school. We'll send word to you on how she does."

∼

Having Esther in her home wasn't like Neema imagined it would be.

"No, I haven't enrolled her in school because she still says she doesn't want to go," Neema complained to Katharine. "I really don't know what she does all day in the flat. I guess she watches TV, and she must talk to the house girl sometimes. She used to be so sweet and affectionate, always running to me for a hug when I visited. Now she barely speaks to me. Not only do I not get a hug — I get dead silence."

In their new relationship, Katharine didn't criticize Neema and she remained silent now, although her eyes widened as Neema continued. "Maybe I should threaten to send her back to the village. But I guess that would just make me look like a failure."

Within a month, the strain was becoming too much for Neema every day. She tried being more forceful.

"Esther, we have to enroll you in school again. You're going to fall behind even more than you already have if we don't."

Esther said nothing and Neema persisted. "You'll like it, Esther. You were always such a good student. I was so proud of your marks. Don't disappoint me this way."

But the girl sat with her head hung low, refusing to respond. Neema watched tears slipping down Esther's face — again! — and sighed. She turned on her heel and left the room.

The glum atmosphere in the flat continued, and Neema decided that a few days in Bagamoyo might do them both good. At least there would be others there to share the burden.

∼

"Oh, Mama," sighed Neema. "It is such a relief to be here with other people. It's really getting me down to be around Esther all the time with her constant silence. It's depressing."

Imani studied Neema for a few minutes before she spoke. "Well, Neema, it may be depressing for Esther too. Have you tried to talk to her about why she won't go to school?"

"Well, no, I haven't. Although I did remind her how far behind she was going to fall if she didn't go. I figured she wouldn't want to talk about what happened to her in her village — that she'd rather just forget it."

"Neema, a little more compassion from you might help," Imani said with narrowed eyes.

Neema sniffed. "Well, Mama, I didn't expect to get criticism from you. I'm trying to do the girl a favor and she's not making it easy at all."

Imani shook her head. "Neema, if she were going to forget it, I think she'd have done it by now. Maybe she needs to talk about it or maybe not. But I don't think bullying will help." Neema widened her eyes and turned her mouth down in a pout. Imani continued. "I think you should consider having her move out here to Bagamoyo with me. That way she can have people around and perhaps learn to trust again. The girl's been deeply traumatized."

Neema looked sideways and gave an indifferent shrug. "Well, fine, if you think it might help. It'll actually be a relief for me." Imani's eyes narrowed again. Neema was tired of feeling judged. She got up and left the room.

At dinner that evening, Neema brought up the idea of moving.

"Esther, *Bibi* Imani and I were thinking that maybe you'd like to move out here to Bagamoyo," said Neema as she offered a plate with beef ribs to Esther. The girl took one but didn't respond to Neema. Neema looked over at Imani and raised her eyebrows before biting into her own ribs. Surely her mother could see the problem.

"Esther, do you like it here?" asked Imani gently. Esther raised her eyes to look at Imani without raising her head. Imani continued, slowly and softly. "I'd love to have you live here with me, Esther. Would you like to come?" Esther still didn't raise her head, but she tilted it slightly to the side as though considering the question. Then she moved her shoulders almost imperceptibly and gave a small nod.

"Alright, Esther," said Imani with a smile. "You can stay

here tomorrow when Neema goes back to Dar. She can bring the rest of your things next time she comes. I'm so glad you'll be here."

Neema was in her office one afternoon when someone cleared his throat at her open door.

"Well, hello, Neema," boomed Mark Tibaijuka. "So good to see you again. How're you keeping?"

Neema's fists tightened at the sight of the man. She assumed the most impassive stare she could manage. She watched, seated and motionless, as he entered her office and sat down in a chair across from her without any invitation. She let a silence grow, deliberately avoiding greeting him.

"I wondered when I'd see you again," she said.

Mr. Tibaijuka blustered right past her blatant rudeness. "Well. And here I am. What do you say we go out for lunch, Neema?" He looked around pointedly. "That is, unless you'd rather talk here in your office?"

A fine sweat broke out on Neema's forehead. She'd been expecting to see Tibaijuka again and she had some questions for him, but she also dreaded the conversation. She reached into a bottom drawer of her desk, pulled out a small package, and put it into her handbag. She stood up. "Okay. Let's go to lunch."

Mr. Tibaijuka drove them, while Neema planned what she was going to say to the man. Neither of them made an attempt at conversation as they wove through the traffic.

She expected they'd go back to the same place they went the first time, but instead he pulled up at a run-down chicken-and-chips restaurant right on the side of the road. They had to step around a few piles of rubbish to enter the place. Once they were seated, in straight-backed wooden chairs, he leaned towards her across the fly-specked plastic tablecloth.

"So, you've been enjoying the little bonus you got?" he asked with a smirk. "Nice sum you made off our deal."

Distaste rose in Neema. Taking a deep breath, she stiffened her back and challenged him directly. "You told me the manufacturer was reliable — a Chinese businessman you'd dealt with before."

"Well, he was," Tibaijuka protested, maintaining a half-smile. "What was wrong with the deal?"

Neema kept her voice low and controlled. "What was wrong is that I've recently seen some boxes of ACT, manufactured in China, that are almost surely counterfeit. I know at least one child died as a result, and of course there must be others." She pulled the package out of her handbag, took out the green-labeled box, and handed it to Tibaijuka. "Is this the drug we bought for the Ministry?"

Tibaijuka examined the box for a few seconds. "Sure, this is the product." He looked up at her. "What's the problem?"

"What do you really know about this supplier?"

"Like I told you, Neema," said Tibaijuka, looking bored. "We've used him in the past. He's supplied us with various antibiotics and antihypertensive drugs. We've never had any problems."

"But you've never bought ACT from him before?"

"No. But I've bought other drugs. What's your worry?" Tibaijuka said, drumming his fingers.

"Take a look at the package insert."

Tibaijuka opened the box, unfolded the paper inside, and scanned it quickly. "So?"

"Notice the misspelling?" Neema said, leaning over and pointing it out.

"Well . . ." faltered Tibaijuka. "Okay. But what does that prove?"

"It suggests," said Neema icily, "that the manufacturer wasn't too careful and that quality control measures were lax. It may not prove anything by itself, but I saw the drug fail completely. I saw a child die when this drug didn't work."

Tibaijuka leaned back and crossed his arms over his large belly. He picked up a toothpick, put it into his mouth, and rolled it around with his tongue and lips. "Neema, I'm surprised at you. Are you actually suggesting that we investigate this? Send it to one of the Kenyan centers that check drug integrity?" He paused, examined the toothpick for debris, and put it back in his mouth. "I don't think you want to go down that path, do you?" He smiled at her around the toothpick, then spat it out and reached for a piece of the greasy chicken on his plate.

Neema watched with revulsion as he chewed the meat. A memory popped into her head. When she'd first met him, his name seemed familiar. Now it came to her.

"Tibaijuka is an unusual name. Are you related to a health worker who used to be out at the Matei Health Center some years back?"

He looked at her for a long moment. "Well, I wondered if you might remember that eventually," he said. "Funny thing when I saw you'd been assigned to this unit a few years ago." He nodded slowly and looked at her through narrowed eyes. "Sure. I had a sister there. But a self-righteous young doctor made a fuss about some minor thing my sister was doing and she had to run. She was just trying to make enough to feed her family." He shook his head sorrowfully. "I tried to tell her that no one was going to come after her for such a small thing, but she was afraid. After she left her job with the Ministry she tried to make a living farming, but she really struggled. Her last-born didn't even get to finish primary school. What a shame that was."

Neema couldn't resist defending herself. "But she was cheating the health system. She thought she'd get away with it."

"Uh-huh." Tibaijuka nodded, looking up at the ceiling and

then slowly back at Neema. "Now. Back to the issue of the ACT. Do you really want to follow up on testing it? Start talk about the quality?" He raised one eyebrow. "We both know who signed the purchase and payment orders, and those records wouldn't be hard to find." He smiled at her. "I thought we might talk about another opportunity."

Neema had already worked out how she'd deal with this possibility, but she needed to be careful. How far would Tibaijuka go to expose her role with the ACT if she angered him? She was ready with a reply.

"Mark, we're not going to be able to do this again. Dr. Shilio's changed procedures in the unit. I only sign for purchases now, and even that requires two signatures. Payments are signed for by two different people."

"Hmm," he said, looking hard at her.

Was he doubting her word? Unbelievable that she'd ended up in this position with a cheap — not to mention crooked — salesman. She held her breath, waiting to see how he'd react to her explanation.

He smiled at her, but his eyes remained cold. After several seconds he spoke. "Okay, Neema. You just remember who signed the orders — I know I will."

He got up to signal the end of the meeting and walked to the counter to pay the bill. He started walking out the front door without a glance back at Neema. She rose and followed him out of the restaurant.

29

IMANI AND NEEMA, 2007

"Esther, why don't we go out to the beach this afternoon," suggested Imani. Since Esther had moved to Bagamoyo, Imani spent several hours with her each day, often walking along the seashore in front of the house. Sometimes they walked early in the morning and watched the sun come up over the horizon of the Indian Ocean. Other times they went out in the late afternoon. Esther's first view of the ocean from the miles of white sand beach left her open-mouthed with wonder. She never seemed to tire of watching the waves rolling in and breaking.

The first time she volunteered a sentence on her own was several weeks after she moved to Bagamoyo. "I wish my mama could see this," she whispered, walking down the beach.

"Well, perhaps she can sometime," said Imani with a smile. Then she grabbed Esther's hand and pulled her out across the sand after the latest receding wave. "Let me show you a game I loved to play with the waves as a child. Come on now! Who dares to stay out the longest without getting drenched?" she called over the noise. Then she shrieked, because it was already too late. The water covered their feet and legs as they turned and ran together back to dry sand. It was the first time Imani saw Esther laugh since before that terrible day in the village when she'd learned what happened to the girl.

Soon they were competing every time they went to the beach. They collected shells and rocks and pocketed them or threw them back. "Oh, look at this one." Imani grew used to hearing as Esther picked up first one and then another. Sometimes Esther took one and hurled it with all her strength out into the surf. When she did this, Imani would look at her with a solemn smile.

"You're a strong girl, Esther."

With increasing frequency, Esther was smiling and talking. Imani felt the first stirrings of confidence that Esther was healing. She was coming back to life.

As Esther gradually started to laugh and speak again, however, she didn't warm to Neema or resume the enthusiasm she'd shown her in the past in Ndungu. Neema sometimes brought her gifts, mostly clothing from shops in Dar, but, after a polite expression of thanks, Esther didn't have anything to say to her. And the spontaneous hugs of her young childhood were over. Neema started skipping some of her fortnightly weekend visits and, gradually, Imani expected to see her only about once a month.

"Mama, what is wrong with that girl?" Neema asked, scowling and slapping the air with the back of her hand. "I've done so much for her and she barely greets me when I come out here."

Imani sighed deeply. "Neema, sometimes I feel many regrets for the way you have become. Have you thought about Esther and what she's been through?" She ignored the look of surprise on Neema's face. "Is there any room in your heart for kindness?"

"Well, I've just tried to be strong so that I could help this country — make things right when they were wrong. Fixing wrongs. Isn't that what the fight for Independence was all about?"

"Not exactly. Fighting for what's right needs to be done with humility and love. And love, Neema, love is work. It grows when you push yourself to give even when you don't feel like it. Have you ever done that? Strong love doesn't grow in a beautiful garden. It grows when the weeds try to take over and you have to work to allow the blooms to emerge."

"But, Mama . . ." began Neema.

However, Imani didn't want to hear it. She shook her head. "I'm sorry, Neema, I'm very tired now."

Imani went to bed very early that night. She was deeply troubled by seeing the woman Neema had grown into. She loved her daughter, but she rarely asked herself if she *liked* her. Where had she learned to be so ungenerous, so controlling and self-centered? When did it start? Imani hadn't wanted her own disappointments to infect Neema, but maybe more honesty about those disappointments would have helped her daughter learn. How much had Neema heard that Imani was not aware of? Did she know how desperately Godfrey wished she were a son?

Unbidden, a memory filled Imani's head. When their two-day-old son died, Godfrey had gone out and screamed into the wind and rain that tore around the Bagamoyo house that night. Neema couldn't have heard or understood the cry Godfrey threw up to the sky that night, but Imani had never forgotten it. "Why couldn't it have been the girl?" he howled in the wind. She bent her head with the memory of the pain. It was true, what she'd heard once: a girl sees herself through her father's eyes.

That cry had opened the first crack in her marriage to Godfrey. How had she made such a mistake in judging him so many years ago? She'd believed that Godfrey married her because he respected her strength and her intellect. At some point she understood that he just liked the way these qualities reflected on him as her husband.

She was tired. Neema was well into middle age and she'd never be happy. Imani was going to try to help her, but hopes weren't high. Neema had a few more decades to live with the person she was.

Neema was tired too, but she couldn't fall asleep and the noise of the waves wasn't helping as it often did. Moonlight poured through the window and she lay on her back and stared at the gray ceiling. What had happened with Esther? How had she lost that girl's affection? It stung to see how Esther seemed to have transferred her love to Imani overnight. Neema hadn't meant to annoy the girl when she tried to encourage her to get registered for school in Dar. She was pushing her for her own good. No one seemed to appreciate how much she'd done for Esther.

She turned over on her side and plumped up the pillow, settling into what she hoped would be a better position for sleep. But the many other wrongs that had been done to her crowded into her thoughts. Mark Tibaijuka had used her to make money for himself, and now she was going to have to be careful how she dealt with him. She'd had to work with difficult people in every job she'd ever had and she didn't get the promotion she deserved. The list of injustices she'd had to deal with rolled on. Her father had never really supported her. Her barrenness was so unfair, and that thought allowed the biggest betrayal of all to rush into her mind — Junior. Not only had he left her, but he'd created another family with someone else. Maybe she should have told him about her possible fertility problems, but could she really be blamed for keeping it quiet? After all, she didn't know what was going to happen — there was always a chance she could have become pregnant.

But none of these rationalizations made her feel better. Junior was living another life and she had nothing to offer him. She sighed deeply and flopped back onto her other side. Then she thought of the deal with Tibaijuka again. No one knew what she'd done, so did it really matter? But she couldn't get rid of the vision of the little girl in Ndungu who died — the little girl and her mother.

For the first time in her fifty-some years, she knew what guilt felt like. It was self-hatred. Her deed was reflected everywhere — she couldn't go anywhere without seeing little children and she saw her wrongdoing in every one of their faces. The depth of the pain in that mother's eyes at the bedside of the dying child still terrified her. How many deaths might she be responsible for? She was a murderer, even though her hands were clean.

She sat up on the side of the bed and stared at the gray shapes in the room. The night was going to go on forever. She was empty. Desolate. The future stretched ahead with a night like this at the end of each of her days.

"Joy, I need to talk to you about something," Madam said one day at lunch. "Let's sit down together before I go back to work."

"Of course," Joy replied, telling herself not to worry while anxiety crept into her mind. When everything was cleared away from the table, Joy found Madam sitting in the living room in the same chair she'd been in when she hired her ten years ago. Joy took a seat and waited for Madam to speak.

"Joy, it's been a pleasure to have you working here," she began.

Joy swallowed and shifted in her chair.

"I know this is probably hard for you to hear," said Madam slowly, staring down at her hands, "but it's time for James and me to leave Tanzania." She gave a feeble smile. "We aren't going immediately, but our work here is over. We need to be at our next jobs in three months and we'll be moving to Zambia."

Joy slumped in her chair. "Oh, this is bad news for me," she said softly around the lump forming in her throat.

"Yes, I know. I'm sorry." Madam smiled faintly again. "You know, Zambia's not so far away."

Joy couldn't return the smile she thought Madam was hoping for. Zambia might as well be on the other side of the world as far as she was concerned. She made quick calculations. "So, you'll leave in June?" she asked. She tried to calm her voice as thoughts of school expenses and the monthly rent raced through her mind.

"Yes. I think we'd plan to go in mid-June."

"Do you know who will move into this house?" asked Joy, grasping at the first possibility that came to her mind.

Madam smiled sadly. She probably realized her comment about the nearness of Zambia was a pitiful way to cushion the blow. "I don't know, Joy," she said. "It could be anyone, or it could stay empty for months like it did before we moved in."

"Oh, Madam. This is not good."

"I know. We've had great years here and you've been such a help. We've loved having you work for us." Joy could see moisture in Madam's eyes. She was genuinely sad to give this news, but still, it was more terrible for Joy to be hearing it.

"Could you write me a letter that I can use to try to get another job?"

"Oh Joy, of course I will. And we'll pay the standard end-of-contract gratuity. Your housekeeping and cooking have been wonderful. We'll do whatever we can to help you." Madam reached out to put her hand on Joy's. "I'd love to see you find a position that . . . well, that uses your skills as much as possible. Really, you're such a good organizer, Joy. And you make good decisions. You're a smart woman and I hope you can find a job that takes advantage of those abilities."

This was all very nice to hear, but Madam didn't know what jobs were out there. Once again, Joy recalled her feelings on the day she'd had to quit school. She slumped under the reality of her situation.

≈

Nothing changed over the next month and Joy tried to push the future into the back of her mind, from where it emerged when she least wanted to think about it. Then one day, Madam started going through closets and pulling boxes out of the storage shed in the back garden. Joy had to face the fact that she'd soon be without a job.

Since she'd started working for Madam, Daniel had had a couple of positions, but none had lasted more than a year, and often months passed when he had nothing. Joy was the main wage earner — the family counted on her. She'd told Daniel that Madam was leaving the day she learned of it, but she hated to remind him. His lack of steady work ate away at his mind.

"I'll put things we can't use on the bed in Sam's old room and you can take anything you'd like," said Madam one Monday.

"Daniel, I'm afraid it's really going to happen," Joy said that night as she washed up the bowl after everyone had eaten. "Madam's starting to clean out the house. There's a lot we can take, and maybe we can sell some of it. Can you get a barrow to start carrying it away this Friday?" Daniel's brow creased in concern. A few tears slipped down Joy's face, but there was nothing else to say. It would be nice to get Madam's castoffs, but they would need to sell as much of it as they could. And, even though the neighbors might be impressed with the apparent windfall, none of it would make up for the loss of a steady job.

The house emptied out slowly, and shipping boxes began to pile up in one of the empty rooms. Much of the furniture belonged to the landlord; Mrs. Chatterjee came over one day to walk through the house so that everyone could agree on what belonged to her. Madam insisted that Joy be part of the tour. Although she and James would leave mid-June, one of their colleagues who was already at the house had asked to stay on for an additional week. Madam agreed, since the rent was paid through June anyway. Joy's employment would officially end the last day of that month.

"Joy will be in charge of the official hand-over at the end of the month," Madam informed Mrs. Chatterjee, who frowned, as the three women walked through the house. Joy smiled when Madam raised an eyebrow and added in a no-nonsense tone, "She'll use the list we're making right now. She's been working in this house for ten years and there's no reason she can't close it up for us."

No one could remember who had bought the small gas oven in the kitchen, which was installed just after Madam moved in. "Well, Joy, it looks like that can go to your house," said Madam with a smile after Mrs. Chatterjee left. But Mr. Chatterjee, who was in charge of the business, sent one of his workers over later with a receipt showing that he'd paid for the oven, so it should stay with the house. Madam shrugged in acceptance. "Sorry, Joy."

∾

The day that Madam and Mr. James left was a gray one, with rain pelting down and splatting off the gravel in the yard. Both Joy and Daniel had walked along the cold, muddy road to be at the house early to say good-bye. Joy had always celebrated rain, as it fed the crops, but today she understood why Madam found it dreary. Yussuf let them in the gate and they stood under the porch roof, waiting for Madam and Mr. James to come out. It wasn't long before the gate creaked again as Yussuf opened it to let Peter pull into the drive to start loading up the vehicle.

"Oh, Joy and Daniel, we're going to miss you. Thank you for coming to say good-bye," said Madam with a smile as she and Mr. James came out the door and onto the porch. Madam and Joy shared a hug, and Daniel shook hands with her and Mr. James. The American couple climbed in among the suitcases and boxes. Yussuf opened the gate solemnly once more, and the last picture Joy had of them was of Madam and Mr. James twisting around in their seats to wave good-bye.

Daniel left to walk home through the rain. As the gate clanged closed Joy walked into the house, wiping tears mixed with rain from her face. She started to collect breakfast dishes from the table and considered the work for the day, suddenly reduced to only a few chores for the remaining guest.

~

On the last day of June, another gray and rainy one, with the guest gone and the house cleaned and emptied of all but the furniture it had held ten years ago, Mrs. Chatterjee came by. She and Joy went through the house quickly, checking items off the list.

"Do you have someone else coming to live here?" Joy asked, hating to ask for anything from this woman.

"No, we don't. I suppose you're looking for another job?" Mrs. Chatterjee said, eyeing Joy through narrowed lids.

Joy nodded without a word.

"Well, I'll send the word around with Yussuf if someone new moves in." Mrs. Chatterjee sniffed. "This is an excellent house and I'm sure we'll let it again soon."

"Thank you," said Joy, standing tall. "I have a lot of experience."

With that, Joy was once again looking for work.

31

JOY, 2008–2009

In the ten years since Joy had last been forced to search for work, job possibilities hadn't changed much. Madam had suggested that she should look for something more challenging than being a cook, but given her limited formal education, what might that be?

The long rains had finished and it was hot and dusty again in September. She still hadn't found anything, in spite of knocking on many gates. She'd even gone to the church to ask about cleaning but there was nothing for her. New hotels had sprung up in town and she visited each of these, describing her previous hotel experience and years of running Madam's household, but no one was hiring. Emma and Elijah both needed new school uniforms. She hated telling the children they couldn't have light at night for their schoolwork, and she worried as she watched the family's meager supplies of staples dwindle. They'd sold most of the things Madam had given them and, for the moment, it was Daniel's small jobs that kept them going.

In late October the jacarandas were starting to bloom again when Joy finally had some luck. She heard about a

South African family who had moved in near Madam's old house. So, as soon as she dropped off Elijah and Emma at school, she hurried to the place, straightening her *kanga* and knotting her kerchief at the back of her neck as she walked.

The gate at the house was iron, huge and heavy. A concrete structure over two meters high with coils of razor wire along the top formed a wall around the compound. Still, the guard who peeked at her through a small opening in the gate responded courteously to her *shikamoo* and the explanation she gave for knocking. He apologized for asking her to wait outside on the road while he went to talk to the woman of the house. Ten minutes later, he came back and let her in through a small door cut into the large gate.

"Mrs. Ribeck will interview you, but you should go around to the back door and wait in the kitchen," he said. Joy bypassed the elegant front door and walked around to the back, where she was let into the kitchen by a young Tanzanian girl with a bald white baby tied to her back.

"Just wait here. Madam will let you know when she's ready," said the girl as she disappeared into a hallway. Joy waited for fifteen minutes before the girl reappeared, this time without the baby on her back. "Come with me," she said solemnly and led Joy into a small room where a heavy woman with long blond hair sat in an easy chair, sipping a cup of tea and reading a magazine. Joy stood for several minutes before the woman looked up.

"You can sit down," said the woman, gesturing at a small stool. "I'm Mrs. Ribeck, the lady of this house. I understand you want a job as a cook?"

"Yes, Madam," said Joy, giving a small nod with her head but looking the woman in the eyes.

"What is your previous experience?" demanded Mrs. Ribeck, before Joy could state her name.

"I was the cook and housekeeper for an American family for ten years," stated Joy confidently. "I can read and follow recipes. I was in charge of the weekly shopping and I kept track of the money used for that. I took care of the laundry for the family and I kept the house clean. I supervised the guards at the house and I also took care of many guests who visited." Mrs. Ribeck raised her eyebrows in a way that made Joy wonder if she doubted her words.

"Really? Well, that's impressive," she said with a dismissive wave. "However, I just want a cook. I have someone else to take care of the housekeeping and I have a nanny for my baby. And we don't have house guests. Do you have any references to show me?"

"Yes, I do," Joy said, drawing Madam's letter from her bag and handing it to Mrs. Ribeck.

"Hmm," she muttered as she read the recommendation. "She says you can follow recipes in English. I don't suppose you can read Afrikaans, can you? Oh . . . never mind. English will have to do." Joy sat silently, unsure what to say.

"Okay. I'll give you a one-week probationary period. You'll report to me and only me. I expect you to stay in the kitchen and dining room. There will be no reason to go into the rest of the house." She leaned back into her chair and sipped her tea, holding the thin china handle delicately. "I'll let you know every morning what you're to cook. If you see Mr. Ribeck, do not bother him with any questions or comments. He's a busy man. Your hours will be from nine a.m. until four thirty p.m. with thirty minutes off for lunch. You may make a cup of tea for yourself mid-morning and mid-afternoon. I'll show you which mugs you may use." She paused for a moment, then looked closely at Joy. "Is all this clear?"

"Yes, it is clear, Mrs. Ribeck."

The wage that Mrs. Ribeck offered Joy was slightly lower than what Madam had paid but still better than many other jobs did. She'd be paid every Saturday. Joy was in no position to be choosy, and she'd have worked for less money if that's what had been offered.

"Can you start on Monday?"

"Yes. I'll be here at nine."

"Good. Don't be late. And, one other thing: any stealing will be immediate grounds for dismissal. I don't care what Tanzanian law says about warnings. I won't put up with it and I know exactly what I have in my kitchen."

"Yes. I understand." Joy nodded and stood up to leave. Mrs. Ribeck looked down at her magazine and Joy decided that was her signal to leave. She went back out through the kitchen, where she noticed the nanny playing with the baby. She was out the gate and on her way home before she remembered that Mrs. Ribeck had never asked her name.

Walking home, Joy wished she could feel happier about the job she'd just managed to get. She decided to buy a small packet of sweet biscuits to have with her family that night as a celebration; then, with even more satisfaction, she bought a credit coupon for the electricity meter.

"Ah, Joy. What a relief this is," Daniel said that evening, smiling. She pushed the disquiet she had about the job to the back of her mind and smiled back at him.

In the first week at work, Joy found that this would be a lonely job, in spite of the fact that there were other workers in the house. She would mostly be alone in the kitchen. When she made her tea at mid-morning, she offered to make some for Jenny, the nanny, and for Martha, the housekeeper. "No, Joy. Mrs. Ribeck doesn't want us to take tea together, so we each make our own," explained Martha. "I'll fill a flask for the guard when I make mine and take it to him outside." She and Jenny were both nice enough but they weren't overly friendly. Joseph, the guard, continued to be pleasant too, but aside from his letting her through the gate as she came and went each day, she almost never caught sight of him. She put the kitchen rubbish outside the back door at the end of the day as she'd been instructed to do and it was gone in the morning.

Mrs. Ribeck gave her orders for making lunch and dinner each day and the ingredients she needed were always available. Joy offered to keep track of the stores so that she could make a shopping list, but the woman looked at her with narrowed eyes. "That won't be necessary," she said. But one day when the dessert required a tin of condensed milk and there wasn't any in the pantry, Mrs. Ribeck was annoyed. "Why didn't you let me know we needed this when you used the last tin?" she asked sharply.

"Well, I did offer . . ." started Joy, but she was talking to her employer's back.

Mrs. Ribeck gave luncheons for her friends several times a week, and it was Joy's job to serve these as well as to prepare them. The ladies who sat around the dining table took no notice of Joy and she usually slipped in and out, putting out dishes and removing them silently.

One day, as she bent to put a tureen of just-boiled beef soup in the middle of the table, one of the women at the table pushed her chair back unexpectedly, knocking Joy and the tureen into the wall. Hot soup hit the wall and splattered Joy's arms, and she very nearly dropped the tureen.

Without a glance at Joy, and before the woman in the chair could say a word, Mrs. Ribeck spat out her annoyance. "Oh, what a clumsy girl! Stupid! Myrna, are you alright?"

As Myrna began to apologize, she was overridden by Mrs.

Ribeck, speaking through clenched teeth to Joy. "Get this cleaned up!" Joy, with a hot face, disappeared into the kitchen and emerged a few minutes later with a cleaned and refilled tureen. Then, as surreptitiously as she could, she wiped off the floor and the wall. Myrna turned and offered an apology, to which Joy smiled slightly and nodded, but anger smoldered in her heart.

"I hate working in that house," she cried to Daniel later that night. He nodded his understanding. But the family was depending on the job, so he just listened. "I don't like being treated like I'm a thief or like I'm stupid. And I don't like being blamed for things that aren't my fault."

By December, Joy had been with the Ribecks for two months. The jacaranda blooms that covered the ground had always signaled to the children that Christmas was around the corner, but this year there was less excitement than usual.

"No, I don't have time to help you make your little car better," she snapped at Elijah after he'd collected a pile of old wires, painstakingly bent them into shape, and then watched them fall apart the first time he pushed the toy across the road. The look on his face wounded her, but she was out of energy. She was relieved to see Daniel helping him later, but she had to force herself to try to act more cheerful than she felt. The usual little pleasures around the holiday didn't raise her spirits.

Thoughts of Zahra, never far away, intruded constantly and she felt the pain almost as acutely as she had just after they'd lost her. She remembered things she didn't want to about the terrible ride to the hospital. She dreaded going to work even as she knew she had to, and sometimes at night she poured out her despair to Daniel.

"Daniel, I'm going to see if I can find another job," she finally said in February. He frowned.

"Joy, are you sure? It's so hard to find anything that pays well. I know you're unhappy and I hate how that work is making you feel, but . . ." Joy gave a deep sigh as he looked at her with concern. "You won't quit the Ribecks yet, will you?"

32

JOY, 2009

J oy hung on at the Ribecks, and in March she had a small surprise. As she was leaving the house one afternoon, a little girl from the neighborhood approached her.

"*Shikamoo,*" said the child, bending her dusty little legs into a curtsy.

"*Marahaba,*" responded Joy with a smile, thanking the little girl for her respect.

"You're Joy, the mother of Emma and Elijah, is that right?" Joy nodded and the child continued. "I was asked to find you and give you this note. It's from a *mzungu* lady who says she knows you."

"Where is she now?" asked Joy, intrigued by the thought of a small diversion.

"She's at the Uhuru Guesthouse. She said she knew you when you worked for Mr. James's family."

"Oh. *Asante sana,*" murmured Joy, to thank the child who stood waiting solemnly.

"She said to wait for a reply."

Joy nodded and opened the envelope to read the note.
Dear Joy,

I hope you are fine. You may remember me. I'm Julie, who met you several years ago when you worked for Mr. James' family. Frank and I met your father in the village. I'm visiting in Moshi now and I'd like to see you. Can you meet me at Uhuru Guesthouse on Sunday afternoon around 2 pm? My little friend can bring back your response.

"Oh," Joy said again, a smile spreading across her face. "Yes. Yes, please tell the lady that I'll be there on Sunday. I'm very glad to meet with her." She walked home thinking back on a happier time in her life and how good it would be to see Julie again.

Joy left the social gathering after church the following Sunday to hurry to the guesthouse. She had to look carefully to find Julie. She remembered her as another too-thin white woman with short brown hair and spectacles, which she often wore on a chain around her neck. She spotted several white women sitting in chairs, which made it difficult to judge their sizes; most had white or gray hair and several had spectacles on chains around their necks. She stood for a moment looking around and pondering. To her relief, one of the women stood up from a table under a shady mango tree and called her name. "Joy! Joy, is that you?" she called, waving a pair of sunglasses. Joy moved towards this woman with a smile and they came together in the sunlight for an embrace.

"Joy," cried Julie again. "It's so good to see you. Stand back and let me look." Joy laughed and took a step backward from where she could also look at Julie. Her hair color had definitely changed and she was heavier than Joy remembered, but the voice was the same.

"Do you prefer tea or a soft drink?" asked Julie as they sat down. "Oh, it's good to be back here. Just look at that mountain." They were meeting during one of those short afternoon breaks that occurred in the dry season when the clouds cleared and the majestic peak of Kilimanjaro rose into an intense blue sky. Julie ordered tea and biscuits for both of them and, as they waited for it, she reached over and put her hand on Joy's wrist. "Joy, I was so sorry to hear the news about Zahra."

Joy met her eyes and felt her own fill with tears; her voice trembled as she spoke. "Yes. Thank you for sending the card. It's been very hard." They held a gentle silence and, in the gaze they shared, Joy felt that this foreign woman from far away understood how deeply beloved Zahra had been. Some small piece of her heart was restored. Eventually, Joy put her other hand gently on top of Julie's, gave a small squeeze, and withdrew her arm.

"And where is Frank?" asked Joy, remembering Julie's husband.

"Ah, Joy. I lost him almost three years ago. About the same time you lost Zahra. I miss him, but Frank had a long and happy life. One of the things he made clear before he died was that he wanted part of our money to come back to Tanzania to support a women's group. I'm actually here now to look into this."

"Oh, I'm sorry about Frank. Madam didn't tell me about that."

"Well, I expect she didn't want to add additional sorrows to your life at that time. But thank you." A waiter in a brightly patterned shirt delivered a plate of sweet biscuits and tea in a pot. Julie poured the hot black liquid out in cups and offered the milk and sugar. Joy enjoyed the feeling of being served.

"Now, tell me what you've been doing," said Julie after she took a sip of tea, then puckered her lips and added some sugar. "What job do you have now? And tell me about the children."

Joy spoke first about Emma and Elijah. "Emma got a first last week in maths," she said with a broad smile. "And Elijah is reading all the time. The school has a little library and he spends all his spare time there now."

"Fantastic," said Julie. "Tell me more." So Joy talked about the children's personalities, how they were different and how they were alike. They finished the tea and Julie ordered another pot.

"And what about your work, Joy? What are you doing? What job did you find?"

"Oh, well, it's okay. I have a job as a cook for a South African woman." But Julie knew the Tanzanian culture and she wasn't quick to accept that all was well just because Joy didn't offer a complaint. Complaining put a burden on the listener. Julie cocked her head.

"But do you like the position? I thought you enjoyed your previous work. Isn't this similar?" And thus encouraged, Joy gradually told Julie what it was like to work for Mrs. Ribeck.

"I just couldn't find anything else," she eventually admitted. "I'd be willing to work for less money to get away from that house. But I can't afford to quit without another job."

Julie nodded her understanding and bit her lower lip. "No, of course not," she said sympathetically. She and Joy talked for a few more minutes before Joy said she needed to go.

"I'll be in Moshi for two weeks," said Julie. "Is there a way I can reach you?"

"Sure," Joy said, pulling a worn cell phone from her bag. Julie looked surprised and Joy laughed.

"Everyone has one of these phones now and it's not hard to find old ones for sale. Most people don't bother trying to get a landline anymore. Remember Yussuf, the guard at Madam's house? Well, he has a phone too. He probably has no credit on it, but at least he can receive calls. Did you know that in Kenya they can transfer money using their phones?"

Julie laughed as she handed Joy a scrap of paper and a

pen from her purse. "Well, I have one too, so give me your number, please." This made Joy smile.

"Why don't you just tell me your number and we'll do a missed call so I can show you how to save my number into your address list."

"Ah, Joy," chuckled Julie with delight. "I'll admit I don't use this phone much at home. I certainly didn't expect to be learning how to use it in Tanzania." Joy showed Julie how to save her number into the contacts list.

"Thank you, Joy! I'll call you in a few days."

As they got up to walk to the garden entrance, Joy had the final word: "Oh no, Julie, you should learn to text. It's much cheaper."

~

The week after she met with Julie, Joy had a text message from her:

Can we met at guesthoud 5 clock Frday? Sory textnig harder than it loks!

Joy laughed and tapped back an "ok."

On Friday she left the Ribecks' house at four thirty and hurried to the Uhuru Guesthouse. After exchanging greetings with Julie, Joy explained that she didn't have much time today as she needed to get home to the children. "But tell me about what you've been doing in Moshi the past few days."

"Well, I talked to a few organizations that help women, trying to find the right one to support. Some of them are doing very good work. They're all run by strong Tanzanian women and Frank would have approved of them." Joy smiled at this.

"One of the groups I talked to this week I especially liked and I think it'll be expanding. It's a fairly small nongovernmental organization. They provide training to rural women in how to manage money and even start small businesses."

Joy widened her eyes in interest at the idea of such an organization. An idea sparked in her head. "Did you say it's getting bigger? Are they hiring more people to work there?"

"Well, I don't know. Maybe they are. Actually, now that you mention it, the woman I talked to did say they needed an assistant to help keep the office clean and set up rooms when they have trainings."

"Where is the place?" asked Joy. "I wonder if I could apply."

"Well, no harm in trying," said Julie. She rummaged through her straw bag and pulled out a small colorful brochure, which she handed to Joy. There were pictures of Tanzanian women, working singly or in groups, beading or sewing. Some looked intent at their work and others were smiling and laughing. There was an address at the bottom.

"I'm going to go see them," said Joy. "I'm going to see if they have any jobs." She stood and they said their good-byes, promising to be in touch again before Julie had to leave. Then she hurried home thinking of the pictures in the brochure. She smiled at the thought of talking to someone at the place.

Mrs. Ribeck was not happy when Joy asked on Monday if she could come to work an hour later Tuesday morning, for personal reasons.

"If you're sick you shouldn't come in the house at all — even today," she said sharply.

"I'm not sick," said Joy, but she offered no other explanation as she continued to stand there, looking directly at Mrs. Ribeck.

"Alright then," the woman relented, with a roll of her eyes. "But you'll need to stay until five thirty to make up the time. And we won't make a habit of this."

"Yes, Mrs. Ribeck. I'll stay late," said Joy with relief.

Thus, Tuesday morning at nine, Joy, in a clean dress and with her hair smoothed into a bun, entered the front room of a small house that had been converted into an office. The wooden sign over the door, neatly painted with red letters on a blue background, said *Wanawake Husaidia Wanawake (WHW)* and underneath, in small yellow letters, *Women Helping Women*. A young woman working at a computer on a desk looked up, nodded, and smiled as Joy entered. "*Habari ya asubuhi,*" she greeted Joy in a soft pleasant voice.

"*Nzuri sana,*" replied Joy, suddenly realizing that she truly *was* feeling very well this morning. There was something about this place she liked. Her ritual "*Habari yako?*" in return was delivered with a genuine smile. "I understand that you're looking for an assistant. My friend Julie Wilson was here last week and she told me about the organization."

"Ah, yes," said the girl as her face lit up. "Mama Julie met with the director last week. She's a nice woman. It's not often a *mzungu* has such excellent Swahili. How do you know her?"

"She used to visit the house sometimes where I worked for ten years as cook and housekeeper. We often talked."

"I see." The girl nodded. "So she told you about our work?"

"Yes." Joy pulled the brochure from her bag. "She gave me this information about the organization."

The girl looked a bit surprised. "You read this? You do understand that we're looking for a cleaner for the office?"

"Yes, I do. I can do that job."

"Well, you'd need to talk to our director. She was planning to interview applicants tomorrow at ten. Can you come back then?"

Joy's face fell in dismay. "Oh. Oh, I'm afraid the woman I cook for now won't give me any time off tomorrow. She's already unhappy that I'm coming in late today."

"Hmm, I see," said the girl, wrinkling her brow. "Well, wait just a minute, please." She opened the door into an adjoining room and disappeared, while Joy twisted her hands. The girl emerged a few minutes later and closed the door with a smile. "Okay, I explained the problem to the director and she'll see you this morning. It will have to be brief. Please take a seat."

After five minutes the door opened again and a tall, big-boned woman called from the doorway, "Joy? Can you please come into my office?" Joy, who'd expected someone in a business suit, wondered for a minute if this woman, in a brightly colored dress made from local fabric with a matching wide band holding back her short, neat picked-out hair, was actually the director. She offered Joy a broad smile that showed a small, even space between her front teeth. Her quick movements caused the light to glint off her round, red-framed spectacles and her large, colorful dangling earrings. Joy recognized the earrings immediately from a picture she'd seen in the brochure where women were working together to make them. The woman ushered Joy in and offered her a chair. Even though their time was limited, the two women went through the standard greetings. Then the director quickly got down to business.

"Joy, I'm sorry to rush things, but I understand you have a job now as a cook. A lot of the work you'd need to do here would be cleaning. The salary we can offer is probably less than you make now. Wouldn't this be a step down for you?"

Joy had expected this and she'd been thinking about it. Talking to Daniel over the years had helped her understand and put words to her feelings about work. "I've always done my work well, but I've had some jobs that helped me get better. I've learned that I like the chance to make decisions. I want to work somewhere where I'm trusted and where I like the people I work with. My current job doesn't give me that chance at all, even if the pay is good." The director nodded slowly as she listened to this. Joy continued. "I read the brochure for your organization. I like what you're doing. I grew up in a little village and I know the women you're trying to help. I want to work here."

The director smiled. "Yes, I think I see. We'd like to make a decision this week and get someone to start next Monday. Would you be able to do that if we selected you?" Joy nodded, thinking, but not caring, what Mrs. Ribeck might say about an abrupt departure. The director continued. "As you know, I'll be interviewing others tomorrow. I expect to make a decision immediately after those interviews. Leave a contact number with the secretary, please, and we'll let you know one way or the other tomorrow."

Both women rose at the same time. "Thank you for seeing me today," said Joy with a smile as she turned to leave.

A few minutes later, Joy was hurrying to Mrs. Ribeck's. She slipped into the kitchen just as the hallway clock chimed ten and Mrs. Ribeck entered to look for her.

Joy told Daniel later that night about the interview. He was positive, although he looked disappointed at the mention of a salary cut. Still, he didn't try to discourage her. "I can see what working for the Ribecks does to you. Money isn't everything, even for poor people."

Joy's phone beeped the next day just after lunch and she felt her heart jump. For once she was glad to be alone in the kitchen so she could answer in private. "Joy? This is Fatima, the secretary you met yesterday at WHW. I'm so happy to tell you we'd like to have you come work for us. Can you come in next Monday at nine to start and meet everyone?"

"Oh yes, I surely can. Thank you so much. I'll be there on Monday at nine." With a big smile, she put her phone back in her bag.

She read over the new recipe she'd been given that morning. As she cut up the chicken and put it in the skillet to brown, she considered what she'd say to Mrs. Ribeck.

It was nearing four o'clock when Mrs. Ribeck came into the kitchen to check that the dinner preparations were satisfactory. "Hmm," she said, opening the lid of the cooking pot and stirring the chicken. "Not enough tomato. Didn't you follow the recipe I gave you?"

"Yes, I did exactly as it said. Three tomatoes."

Mrs. Ribeck glanced at the basket of tomatoes on the counter. "Well, you should use more common sense. Those tomatoes are small ones." Joy continued to clean the countertop she'd been working on. She bit back the desire to point out that she'd never made this dish before so didn't know what it was supposed to be like. And Mrs. Ribeck knew the size of the tomatoes in the basket when she gave Joy the recipe.

Suddenly it seemed like the right moment to tell her employer that she was leaving. Folding the dish cloth neatly, she faced the woman.

"Mrs. Ribeck, this will be my last week here. I'm leaving."

"What?" Mrs. Ribeck said, flinging her hands out in annoyance. "Haven't you ever heard of a two-week notice? I'll not be responsible for your final week's pay under these circumstances. And don't expect a referral letter from me either."

Joy wasn't surprised by the woman's reaction and she already knew what she'd do. "Alright, Mrs. Ribeck," she said, taking off her apron, folding it neatly, and placing it on the countertop. "Then this will be my last day." She picked up her bag from the corner, smiled at Mrs. Ribeck, and left the astonished woman with her spoon in the pot and the flame roaring under the chicken. "Don't add more tomatoes now or it'll make the chicken tough."

33

JOY, 2009

On Monday morning, Joy was the first to arrive at WHW. The director was close behind her.

"Good morning, Madam," said Joy cheerfully as the director climbed the few steps to the veranda.

"Well, I like your enthusiasm to get to work. And please call me Ciku," laughed the director. "It's short for Wanjiku, the name my Kenyan father insisted on." They entered the office together and by the time Ciku showed her where to put her bag, Fatima and several other staff members had arrived.

"Okay. First thing, let's introduce you to everyone." Fatima smiled, taking her arm and starting down a hallway.

"Foshi, this is Joy, our new assistant. She'll be taking care of our office. It's going to make a big difference to have her here. I know there'll be lots of things you and others want her to do. But she'll be reporting to me, so let me know when you need her and I'll be able to help her schedule so there aren't conflicting demands on her time."

"Kichaka, Joy's our new assistant. She'll help with setting up the room for the trainings you run. Let me know at least a day in advance and I'll be sure she's free for however much time you think you need." Fatima turned to Joy with a laugh.

"We're going to love having you for this. Sometimes it's been crazy the hour before we start when we've realized no one's got the room ready and we all have to pitch in."

Around the office they went with introductions, and Joy began to get an idea of what she'd be doing. She was grateful to know that she'd be taking orders from one person and not everyone in the office. And she liked the way the women welcomed her. Fatima gave her a list of cleaning duties that she needed to do daily as well as weekly and explained that there would be many other small jobs she'd need to do, but these would vary from day to day, so they'd discuss them each morning.

On Friday morning, Fatima stopped Joy as she was on her way to fetch a mop and pail to clean the floors. "Just do a quick cleaning job this morning. We'll be having an office staff meeting at eleven and we'd like you to make tea for that. Oh, and you'll need to run out and get biscuits. You'll find the things you need to do tea in the little kitchen and I'll give you money for the biscuits."

Joy had everything set up a few minutes before eleven. Once everyone was seated she started to leave the room. "Wait, Joy. You should join this meeting," called Ciku. So Joy sat down and listened while the staff discussed how their various projects had gone that week and then talked about new ideas some of them had.

At home, Joy described the work to Daniel. "Oh, they've got so many projects going! They make beads — look at these on my earrings — from old paper! And they're the ones who make those natural cleaning products Madam used to have me buy at Deepak's. Salma is the one who helps them find places to sell things they make. Some of the staff help women set up projects raising goats. And Kichaka teaches the women about simple accounting and business. For lots of the women they work with, it's the first time they've ever had money of their own. One of them told me the other day she can now pay school fees without having to ask her drunken husband for money. Another told me she's able to buy more food for her family. Oh, Daniel, I love going to work there every day!"

"Whoa! Slow down, Joy," Daniel protested. But he smiled. "I can see the job agrees with you. I love seeing you so happy at home and the children do too." He planted a kiss on her forehead.

One day, Joy spotted the little girl of one of the women in a bead-making group drinking a Fanta as she waited for her mother to finish. She didn't want to embarrass the woman, but at the same time she felt like she should say or do something. Maybe the woman just didn't know any better than to give the child sugary drinks. She mentioned it to Fatima the next day while they were having a cup of tea.

"Yes, it *is* a worry," agreed Fatima, stirring milk into her tea. "But some of the women are thrilled to have a little money for the first time and they want to buy something for their children." She furrowed her brow as she sipped the tea. "I just don't think they know how bad those drinks are. Seems like everyone was healthier when they lived out in the village without all this stuff."

"Well," said Joy, filling the kettle to boil for another round of tea, "maybe we could offer a little program about it. You know, when the women are here making beads or other projects, we've got a great opportunity to teach them about other things — like good diets."

Fatima set down her teacup with a clatter. "Joy, that's a great idea. I think Ciku will love it." Then she smiled broadly.

"In fact, why don't you present it at the next staff meeting? It's your idea."

So, at the next meeting Joy, with trembling hands, stood up and described her idea. There was a brief silence, then several of the women began to talk.

"It'd be better with some training materials. Like we've had for other projects."

"And we ought to have a teacher who's had some education in nutrition."

"We could do some demonstrations on healthy cooking."

Ciku smiled. "These are all good ideas. Let me think about this. Thank you, Joy."

Joy smiled at everyone. "And I have one other idea. You know the project to set women up with chickens to produce eggs for sale?" The women all nodded and waited for her to continue. "Can you advertise those as 'happy chicken' eggs?" she asked. The women looked puzzled, so Joy explained. "If these chickens are roaming around the yard rather than sitting in cages like they do at the big egg production plants, then the yellows will be dark. The American woman I used to work for called these 'happy chicken' eggs. And she was willing to pay more for them."

Ciku laughed. "Joy, I had no idea what I was getting when I hired you. It's time to end the meeting now, but let's all think about these ideas." The women rose and walked out of the room still chattering excitedly. Joy stayed behind to clean up, smiling the entire time.

Two months later, Ciku called Joy into her office.

"Joy, last week I had a visit with someone who works for a local organization that helps women. They focus on health and especially on nutrition. They'd like to work with us in some way. I told them about your idea of providing basic nutrition education while the women are here working on other projects, and they liked it."

"Oh good," said Joy with a proud smile.

"Actually, they suggested that they could send someone here to do the training, but I had a better idea." Joy raised her eyebrows in interest and Ciku continued. "I suggested that they train one of our staff to provide the education." Joy's eyes widened involuntarily. She stood up straight and looked right in the eyes of Ciku, who laughed and nodded. "Yes, Joy, I think you could do this. Would you like to?"

Joy breathed out slowly. "Oh yes. Yes, I'd like it very much."

"I was pretty sure you would," said Ciku with another laugh.

"But there's one thing," said Joy with a small frown. "Do they know I only finished standard four?"

"It doesn't matter, Joy. You're smart and you work hard. And you have better ideas than many people with more years of school than you have. School isn't the only place one can get educated. Now," she said briskly, "training would start next month and run for two weeks. Meanwhile, I need to find someone who can fill in to take care of your duties while you're away. It seems like we really need you here." Joy's smile grew to crease her face from ear to ear and she could hardly keep from dancing out of the room.

On the day Joy was scheduled to give her first presentation to the women's bead-making group, she had a surprise. Fatima hurried down the hall to find her checking the setup in the training room. "Joy, you have visitors. I asked them to wait in the tearoom," she said mysteriously and then hurried away before Joy could ask any questions. Joy started towards the tearoom to see who was there, glancing at the clock on her way. She was relieved to find she still had a half hour before she had to start. In the tearoom, she was astonished to find not only Daniel but her father sitting there.

"Oh Daniel, are the children alright?" she cried, as the fears of a parent swamped her.

"Yes, Joy. Relax. Everything is fine," said Daniel with a grin. She noted then that her father was also smiling. "We wanted to be here for your big day," said Daniel. "I checked to be sure it would be okay and then decided to ask your father to come too."

"Oh, I'm so glad you're here. Let me make tea," she said in relief.

As she poured cups for everyone, her father cleared his throat. "Joy, there's something I want to say to you," he started, then hesitated.

"Okay, *Baba*, what is it?" said Joy, taking a seat and lifting her cup to sip the hot liquid.

"Well, Joy, I know you always felt shame about my lack of education."

Joy put her cup down and started to shake her head, but her father stopped her with a raised hand. "No, Joy, I've felt it too — the shame. I've wished it were different my whole life, but it's something that cannot be changed now. Still, it helps to see how far you've come. I'm so proud of how well you read and write."

"No, *Baba*. You're wrong about this." She put her cup down and made a dismissive gesture with her hand as she shook her head. "It's true that when I was a child I thought that schooling was everything. I thought it was the only way to earn respect from others and even to respect myself." She looked up at her father. "But I've learned it's not like that. What I learned from you was worth more than any schooling would have taught me. I'm sorry it took me so long to realize that."

Joy's *baba*'s eyes filled with tears and he bowed his head.

After a pause he spoke again. "Thank you, Joy. I'm so happy to hear you say that. And I must tell you something else. I regret making the decision to send your brother to school instead of you. It was not a good decision. So I guess we've both learned lessons." He smiled at Joy. "Daniel and I want to come watch you today. Can we do that?"

"Oh, of course you can, *Baba*. To have you and Daniel there will be wonderful." She laughed and wiped her eyes. "You know, I'm a little bit afraid."

"No need," said her *baba* gravely.

The room was small but well organized. The single light bulb hanging from the ceiling wasn't needed, as afternoon sun flooded through the windows along with the smell of a recent short rain on dry earth. Through those same windows, framed by boughs of jacaranda just coming into flower, it was possible to make out the top of Kilimanjaro, visible mid-afternoon above its collar of clouds. Twenty women were seated in a semicircle on wooden benches and stools. They wore colorful *kangas*, although some were so faded from washing and drying in the sun that they'd become pastel prints, ghosts of their former vibrant selves. Many of the women had babies snugly tied to their backs with the well-worn cloths. Two men were also in the room, not easy to miss even though they sat silently at the back.

The chatter died away as Joy entered the room and took her place at the head of the semicircle. There was an aura of efficiency and earnestness about her, but her smile was generous and kind. There were so many things she wanted to talk to these women about, to help them understand. She started to speak, and her voice was clear and confident. "*Habari yako*? I'm Joy and I'll be your teacher."

GLOSSARY OF SWAHILI

- *baba* father
- *bibi* grandmother
- *bwana kubwa* big man, big boss
- *dalla dalla* minivans that provide local transportation
- *duka* small shop
- *duka la dawa* medicine shop, pharmacy
- *habari* the news
- *habari ya asubuhi?* What's the news of the morning? How are you this morning?
- *habari ya jioni?* What's the news of the evening? How are you this evening?
- *habari yako?* What's your news? How are you?
- *hajui* s/he doesn't know
- *hodi* polite greeting called out when approaching someone's home
- *kanga* patterned cotton wrap 1.5 meters x 1meter, worn by women. Similar to sarong or pareo.
- *marahaba* polite response when a young person greets an elder with *shikamoo*
- *mwalimu* teacher
- *mzee* respectful term for older man

- *naomba* I ask (beg) you.
- *shamba* small farm or field
- *shikamoo* respectful greeting for an elder
- *shilingi* Tanzanian shilling, unit of currency
- *shuka* plaid blanket / cloth worn by Maasai
- *tafadhali* please
- *nzuri* fine, good
- *nzuri sana* very fine, very good
- *ugali* a thick, dough-like staple food cooked from maize meal
- *ujamaa* extended family, brotherhood, socialism
- *wazungu/mzungu* (pl. / sing.) term for white people from abroad

QUESTIONS FOR DISCUSSION

1. The author wanted to write a story that counters common stereotypes about Africa. How did this book change your view of Tanzania - the country or the people?

2. What cultural differences between each of the women's lives and your own most impressed you? What were the points in each woman's life at which you most identified with her? Did the life of either woman seem very "foreign" to you and if so in what ways?

3. What do you think of Neema's decision not to tell Junior about her potential fertility problems? How do you think her marriage would have been different if she'd been able to have a child?

4. At what points in the story did you see Joy take steps towards increased self-respect? Which of these were the biggest leaps?

5. What did you think of the relationship between Joy and Madam? What were the episodes that demonstrated cultural

and social distances between the two women? If you were Madam, in which incidences would you have acted differently than she did?

6. Joy is surprised when Madam touches her arm in sympathy when she is caught crying over her third pregnancy. Why might Joy have been surprised?

7. Did you feel any sympathy for Neema? How much do you think the dysfunctional health system she worked in contributed to her actions? Have you ever known someone like her? How do you characterize someone with a personality like hers?

8. Joy's father tells her that having hope means you believe what you do matters. What do you think of this definition? What do you think Neema would have thought? What role did poverty play in Joy's ability to hope?

9. What do you imagine happened to Neema after her story ends?

10. How do you think Imani could have helped Neema become a more caring individual?

11. Americans are often surprised to learn that they are usually classed as "Europeans" in Africa. Can you put yourself in the shoes of Africans and imagine why this is so? Is this any different from Americans imaging that all Africans are alike?

12. Some prominent African women have defended the decision to send a boy to school rather than a girl if there is not enough money for both. The defense is purely practical: an educated boy is more likely to get a good paying job than an

educated girl. What aspects of a culture and society must change in order for women to be viewed as deserving education?

13. Compare the husbands of the two women (Junior and Daniel). How do you think Daniel would have reacted if Joy had not been able to bear children? In what ways did Neema's inability to have children contribute to her personality?

14. How does what you learn about Joy and Neema in the beginning of the book help you predict their characters, attitudes and actions throughout the book?

15. One of the themes is systemic corruption in post independence Tanzania. Joy's father says: "Corruption and evil have always existed. We can waste our lives trying to get rid of them from the top. What we have to do is build the best families and villages we can, in spite of it." How are his comments relevant to corruption in Western countries?

16. What is Neema's greatest character flaw? How did this flaw impact the story?

ACKNOWLEDGMENTS

So many people helped me to complete this book. A short writing course offered by Candace Conradi got me started in sketching out a few scenes. Showing someone the first draft feels like running out onto a stage naked, and I was lucky that my sunny niece, Brynn Lewallen, offered to look at my first effort. Her encouragement helped me go on. Dear, language-loving friend Nancy Smith read it next; she fixed things, asked good questions, and discussed character motivation with me for hours. Maryn Lewallen, an avid reader, provided useful comments. By the time I got the manuscript to my mother, it was more or less all together and she swears she stayed up late reading it. I took this with a grain of salt since she's my mother, but it was still gratifying. My son, Tom Courtright, felt no compunction to be as kind as my mother, but he wasn't brutal, and he surely saved me from making some comments I'd have regretted. ("It's not about you, Mom.")

Irene Donelan, a volunteer from my mother's book club, was the first stranger to read it. She thought I had "the bones of a good book" and her honesty forced me to think hard, rewrite, and expand many sections. Teri Powell kindly read and offered comments on what needed to be clarified. Many thanks to Helen Bokea, who read it to look for accuracy — it took an East African to remind me that cattle shouldn't be described as skeletal at the end of the long rains. Jan Lewallen went through the next version with a fine-toothed comb, uncovering errors and posing questions — and she did it fast! Ron Pickett and his writing group at the Rancho Bernardo library provided useful comments. Lilita Hardes was my faithful writing partner, meeting with me once a week over many months to comment on chapters. We shared many laughs as we struggled together over how hard it can be to describe facial expressions — and we struck out a lot of repetitious "lip pursing."

Ryszard Kapuściński, an extraordinary journalist, wrote about the delightful concept (in *The Shadow of the Sun*) that the time to start a village meeting in Africa is when all the people get there. Young Kimaro wrote passionately for a local newspaper about a girl like Esther, and her local NGO work inspired me to write some of the conversation on the veranda in Bagamoyo.

Thanks to every one of the people I knew and worked with in Tanzania, who shared their lives. Edson Mwaipopo Eliah answered many questions about Swahili and Tanzania. Working in Terrie Taylor's renowned malaria research project in Malawi, I learned about — and learned to fear and respect — severe malaria.

I want to thank the staff of the Kilimanjaro Centre for Community Ophthalmology (www.kcco.net). Their patience and humor gave me a unique opportunity to learn about another culture.

Cornelia Feye from Konstellation Press gave me excellent advice on many structural points. Her gentle insistence on several changes improved the story. Lisa Wolff provided final polishing, and pointed out several subtle errors.

And finally, anyone who knows me will suspect that Paul

has to have been involved. Of course he was. As we hiked, walked to the grocery store, shared our meals, or worked at our desks, he endured hours of my musings over the plot, always ready to listen and offer his good ideas. He read everything before anyone else ever saw it.

ABOUT THE AUTHOR

During the twenty years Susan Lewallen lived in eastern and southern Africa she worked in medicine in over a dozen countries while raising two sons. She developed a curiosity for what makes people and cultures alike and different. As a doctor, she also faced challenges with the health systems she worked in; her experiences motivated her to write the novel, *Crossing Paths.*

THANK YOU FOR READING THIS BOOK

Thank you for selecting this book. To follow the author and progress on future books, please subscribe to blog updates on her website, https://www.susanlewallen.com and like her facebook page: Susan Lewallen Author. Finally, if you enjoyed this book please leave a review with your favorite retailer and encourage your local bookstore to stock it.

CPSIA information can be obtained
at www.ICGtesting.com
Printed in the USA
LVHW111256151019
634258LV00001B/133/P